Cirsova®

P. ALEXANDER, Ed.
Mark Thompson, Copy Ed.
Xavier L., Copy Ed.

Exciting Novels of Swordsmen and Other Worlds

A Dramatic Novelette of Interstellar Travel

Five Thrilling Short Stories

Poetry & Reviews

Summer Issue   **Vol.2, No 11**
2022   **$15.00 per copy**

Vran, the Chaos-Warped (Book 1)

By D.M. RITZLIN

Vran the Chaos-Warped has sworn that the wizard Foad Misjak must die for his debaucheries! Vran's strange nature due to a sorcerous accident, however, twists with unpredictable results all magic around him... and strands both on another world!

Chapter I
Dark Avenger

A pair of half-moons gleamed ominously in the night sky. From behind silvery clouds, the heavenly bodies Uzz and Gluzz peered down upon the village of Otoro like the eyes of a salacious voyeur. Had the moons in reality been the eyes of some individual inclined to derive pleasure from spying upon the unwary, they would have witnessed many a wanton act performed in Otoro of late. But on this night, certain events would transpire inside the manse of the wizard Foad Misjak—events so unprecedented that not even the most jaded, world-weary personage could claim to have beheld with their own eyes anything remotely similar.

The manse was not a vast towering structure such as one would expect a wizard to dwell in, instead being low to the ground. Traditionally, the manse was reserved for the burgomaster of Otoro, but Foad Misjak claimed the residence for himself after he supplanted the lawfully-elected official by foul means. While Misjak had not modified its architecture, a sinister alteration was noticeable—not to the eye, but to the psyche. Even the citizens of Otoro, befuddled into subservience by the wizard's magic, were aware of a new aura around the building.

Shadows were now gathering before the manse—not an unusual manifestation for a sorcerer's abode. From the mass of shadows emerged the shape of a large man. Slowly, menacingly, the figure drew closer to the perimeter of the wizard's grounds.

Clouds parted, and a thin beam of moonlight fell on the figure's face. This was no nether-spirit or ghostly apparition, but a living man, albeit one whose eyes held a strange glow like a pair of emeralds that had been... corrupted, somehow. Vran was his name, but after a sorcerous experiment resulted in unforeseen consequences, men knew him as "The Chaos-Warped."

Apart from his eerie green eyes, Vran blended well with the gloom of the night. His beard was black, his waist-length hair was black, and black was the color of the leather coat he wore which covered his broad shoulders and hung to his knees. His only garment of a lighter shade was his white silken shirt, an item of very fine quality. At his hip swung a basket-hilted sword, his favored tool for extracting the price that those who crossed him must pay.

While many of Foad Misjak's enemies wished him dead, Vran the Chaos-Warped had not been employed by any of them to assassinate the wizard. Rather, he had appointed himself to the task. Although Misjak had never caused Vran any direct harm, he knew the deed must be done. Witnessing the customs Misjak had encouraged among Otoroans during his reign was more than enough to convince him.

Shortly after arriving in Otoro, it became clear to Vran that it was a town populated by madmen. In all his travels throughout Nilztiria, he had never heard of, let alone set foot in, a land where pederasty was normalized and encouraged. Old men dallied with young boys while the womenfolk were scorned. Such appalling habitudes horrified Vran. He controlled his disgust long enough to converse with some of the Otoroans, and learned that these customs were not long-held traditions but only recently introduced. The adoption of such conventions that any sane individual would reject as depraved coincided with the instatement of Foad Misjak as burgomaster. None Vran spoke to expressed any dissatisfaction with Misjak or his pedophilic policies. It seemed as if their own wills had been held in abeyance and overtaken by Misjak. Once Vran learned that the new burgomaster practiced the art of sorcery, he had no doubts that this must be so.

Vran immediately vowed to execute this despicable abuser of children. He had made similar vows before (and fulfilled them

quite successfully), but the previous subjects of his ire had all personally wronged him in some way. Though he had never met this Foad Misjak, Vran found his deeds so reprehensible, so foul, that he felt an overwhelming compulsion to deal the wizard death.

Of course, assassinating a wizard was no simple task, and certain aspects of Vran's nature additionally complicated the matter. Earlier in life, he had dabbled in sorcery, which resulted in irreversible alterations to his constitution. The hue of his eyes had changed from pale blue to their present unnatural green. Less noticeably, and more significantly, the characteristics of his blood were modified in such a way that any magical spells cast in his vicinity would create unintended and unpredictable effects. They could be harmless or they could be fatal; it was impossible to guess beforehand. Therefore, Vran's strategy was to take the wizard by surprise and murder him before he could vocalize even one arcane word of power. He had not set an easy task for himself.

Vran stroked his beard as he studied the manse, searching for a suitable point of entry. The main portal in the building's façade was unguarded—or so it seemed. This aroused Vran's suspicions, so he avoided it and investigated the rest of the building's outer walls. This took little time—the rectangular manse was not large, for Otoro was a village of middling size and little means, and could not afford a grandiose home for its chief dignitary. Vran saw no lamps glowing in any of the windows. All was as silent as an unpilfered tomb.

Vran crept closer to the western wall and

peered into one of the windows. He saw naught but blackness beyond the glass. The next window likewise revealed nothing. Growing impatient, he attempted to raise a window and discovered it had been left unlocked. *This is fortunate,* he thought as he clambered over the sill, but then he quickly realized that might not be the case. He stiffened and stood silently, all senses alert. No threat presented itself.

He wondered why Misjak seemed so lax in his measures of security. Perhaps his hold over the people of Otoro was so powerful he did not fear reprisal. Or perhaps he had deadly sorcerous wards elsewhere in the manse. Vran hoped his first guess was correct.

Taking steps slowly and cautiously, Vran moved across the chamber. Due to his powerful frame, he was ill-suited to missions requiring stealth. Still, he succeeded in reaching the opposite wall without stumbling over any objects which might be concealed by the darkness. He groped blindly until his hand fell upon a doorknob. Looking down, he noted that a trickle of wan light seeped from beneath the bottom of the door.

He turned the knob and pulled inward, again acting with deliberate slowness. The door had only opened a crack before the hinges emitted a muted creak. Vran immediately paused. He brought his face to the opening and peered with a green eye into the chamber beyond. Inside the room, two men conversed below an eerily-glowing lantern that hung from the ceiling.

The men were of approximately equal height, but one was thin and frail while the other was corpulent. The facial features of the pair were similar. Both possessed sharply pointed chins, pinkish, almost feminine, lips, and small, shifty eyes of dark brown. Had they both been of a comparable frame, one could have easily been mistaken for the other. Their garb—dark robes with hems that barely reached their knees, headbands emblazoned with mystic runes, and high-strapped sandals worn in the Jalpian fashion—matched as well.

Vran had never seen his enemy Foad Misjak, but had been told he was slender. Could the thin man before him be the one he sought? "Frail" or "emaciated" would describe this man more accurately than "slender," but the populace of Otoro would not apply such unflattering terms to their beloved tyrant. Adding credence to Vran's theory, the thin man was issuing orders to the other in a domineering tone.

"Fyad, in an hour, go to the seraglio and wake a boy—no, two. Then bring them to my chambers below. I will be ready for a diversion from my studies at that time."

"As you wish, brother," said the heavyset man in a shrill voice.

The two men turned and parted ways. The one called Fyad marched down a hallway to the right from Vran's perspective, and the other descended a staircase of stone on the far side of the chamber.

Vran quickly came to a decision. When they were both out of sight, he paced down the hall, stalking Fyad. He planned to first pry information from the obese one. Afterward, he would dispense ultimate justice to him for his complicity in Foad Misjak's crimes.

Fyad waddled his way down the hall, his only concern being how to amuse himself for the next hour. Perhaps he would peruse his brother's vast library of erotic literature and vicariously experience the joys that had been denied to him. His thoughts were interrupted by the sound of a heavy footstep behind him. He turned and found the point of a sword a hair's breadth away from his throat.

"Cry out and you die instantly," said Vran. Fyad nodded, indicating he understood.

Vran cocked his head toward a door on his left. "Is that room empty?"

"Yes," whispered Fyad. "It's a storeroom."

Vran opened the door and forced Fyad inside. "Light a lamp," he ordered, and Fyad did so. The luminance revealed shelves and tables crowded with an assortment of supplies, most of which were of a mundane nature and could be found in any Otoroan household, but some, such as alembics and censers, were clearly intended for arcane usage. Vran commanded his captive to sit upon a creaky stool.

"Who are you?" asked Fyad.

"I would ask the same of you," said Vran, still wielding his sword threateningly.

"My name is Fyad Misjak."

"Then the man you spoke to a few moments ago is Foad Misjak?"

"Aye. He is my brother."

"Does anyone else reside in this manse?" Fyad shook his head.

"I heard him speak of a... seraglio."

Fyad began to sweat. "Oh, well, yes, the boys..."

"Then you lied to me." Vran pressed the tip of his blade close enough to Fyad's throat to draw a trickle of blood. "Never do that again."

"Please, sir," whimpered Fyad, intimidated as much by Vran's menacing stare as by his sword. "My brother is a powerful magician. If you harm me, he will send you debilitating curses. But if you leave now and do not return, I swear I will say no word of your intrusion to him."

Vran scoffed. "Tell me, how were you able to pervert the folk of Otoro so easily?"

Fyad stared at him blankly. "I don't know what you mean."

"Your disgusting, degenerate ways!" snarled Vran. "How did you convince the Otoroans to accept them?"

It suddenly dawned on Fyad what his captor referred to. "Sir, pederasty is neither disgusting nor degenerate, but perfectly natural," he said. "The unenlightened look down on love between men and children because the idea is new to them, and they fear what they do not understand. Since the unwashed yokels of Otoro were unpersuaded by my brother's stirring oratory, it was necessary to introduce an alchemical mixture into the town's water supply..."

Vran, growling like an angry bear, clutched Fyad's throat with his free hand. "You vermin! Not only do you abuse children, but you do so without guilt or shame!"

"No, no, you misunderstand!" squeaked Fyad, coughing and sputtering. "I do not take pleasure with the children."

"You don't?" asked Vran, relaxing his grip on Fyad's throat slightly.

"No... You see, I guard the seraglio, and it would be improper to take liberties with Foad's boys. Therefore, to ensure no unbecoming conduct took place, I became... a eunuch."

Vran found this revelation perplexing and nauseating in equal measures. "He castrated you?"

"It was necessary," replied Fyad matter-of-factly.

"I believe it is necessary to remove another part of your body," said Vran, and raised his sword.

The cellar of the Otoroan burgomaster's manse had been converted into a chamber of sorcery. A large pentagram embellished with runes was inscribed in chalk on the floor. Shelves along the walls sagged beneath the weight of tomes of arcane lore. Sitting at a desk, engrossed in one of these tomes, was the new burgomaster himself, the wizard Foad Misjak.

The volume he studied was *The Second Treatise on Magick and Power* by Xaarxool the Necromancer. As he had been unable to procure a copy of the previous work, he found it difficult to follow at times. Foad had hoped to learn some technique to strengthen the efficacy of his mind-dominating magic, but had discovered nothing of the sort in Xaarxool's grimoire so far.

A sudden clamor of something tumbling down the staircase startled the cadaverous wizard. "Brother, is that you?" said Foad Misjak. "It is not yet the appointed hour for amorousness." He rose from his desk and moved toward the stair. In the dusky lanternlight, he noticed an object lying at the base of the stairs and squatted to examine it. A cry of disbelief and anguish sprang from his throat, for the object he beheld was the severed head of his brother.

No sooner did he utter this ululation than a massive weight fell upon him. Vran, perched at the head of the stairs, had launched himself upon the distraught wizard. The two men collapsed in a heap. While Foad got the worst of it, the landing did not go well for Vran either, whose right elbow struck hard against the floor. He used his unscathed arm to grapple with the wizard, attempting to clutch his throat so as to prevent him from invoking a spell. Foad struggled feistily but was no match for the larger man's brawn. However, he managed to block Vran's stranglehold by keeping his chin close to his chest. Vran tried to clasp his hand over Foad's mouth, but the wizard sank his sharp teeth into his fingers. Vran withdrew his injured hand, and Foad seized the opportunity to enunciate words of power.

"Yladerb-ylaned endib!"

Immediately Vran's vision dimmed and his muscles contorted, just as Foad had intended. Although Vran's sight was diminished, he could sense an unnatural and dangerous event occurring.

Contrary to the wizard's expectations, however, a swirling azure effulgence began to seep through the walls of the chamber. Foad stared in awe as the mystical luminance twisted itself around him and his assailant, enveloping them like a radiant whirlwind. He wriggled free from Vran's grasp and endeavored to flee the chamber, but before he could do so, a thunderous crack paralyzed him. The azure light vanished from the room, the two enemies with it.

Chapter II
Land of Ice

First, stygian blackness. Then, swirling, pulsing light. Vran felt like he was staring into a bright sapphire sun. He wanted to shut his eyes to block out the blinding brilliance, but they were already closed…

Vran sat up. His sight had returned. The overwhelmingly strong radiance was no more, but apparently Foad's magic had created a vast illusion. If what he visually perceived could be trusted, he was outdoors, in a wide plain blanketed by snow. The sun hung just above the horizon, obscured by pale grey clouds. Whether the hour was closer to dusk or dawn, he could not guess. Flakes of frost fell gently from above. He brushed them from his beard and hair and stood upright.

Vran began to suspect that unless Foad's spell affected more than his eyesight, this strange landscape was not illusory after all. The chillness of the winds, a peculiar and unfamiliar odor, the crunch of snow as he trod upon it: all these directed him to the conclusion that he had been transported to some far-off land. But where?

Most likely, he was in the northernmost region of Nilztiria. His knowledge of the geography of that area was hazy at best, for his travels had led him to the border of the barbaric land of Cythera, but not much further. His stay was not long, and little else of the north had he learned. For all he knew, there might be nothing beyond Cythera but wilderness and wastes.

This was an unprecedented experience. His chaos-warped blood had created a bewildering array of effects before, but nothing of this magnitude. He must have travelled hundreds of leagues instantaneously. This would certainly make his quest of dealing death to Foad Misjak more difficult—unless the wizard were teleported along with him.

Vran turned, looking in all directions. He was alone. Not even a hare or fox scampered across the wintry countryside. Apart from a few withered trees bereft of leaves, he saw naught but a snow-covered expanse.

With no immediate danger threatening him, Vran made it a point to look for shelter. In the distance, a pair of hills rose from the ground. Surely they would make a good vantage point to survey the land. He marched forward.

As Vran drew nearer to the hills, their shape reminded him of a woman's bosom. He chuckled at this thought. To meet a lady of such ample proportions would be quite exciting—but hopefully she would not be nearly as cold!

The snows ceased falling by the time Vran reached his destination. The boreal winds rose in intensity as he crested one of the hills. He drew his leather coat tighter about him, grateful that it had not been left behind in Foad's darksome chamber.

From this height, Vran could see that the world beyond the hills was not nearly so featureless as the plains he had crossed. A league or two off was a range of mountains, appearing like the jagged teeth of a monstrous beast's lower mandible. Straight ahead, close to the mountains, was a wooded area. Its trees were leafless but looked in better health than those of the plain. To the right of the woods stretched a valley, which, to Vran's eyes, did not appear especially deep. Snow covered all.

Squinting, Vran believed he detected a few clouds of smoke rising above the valley. Smoke indicated fire, which indicated inhabitants. Hopefully, the people of the valley would amiably offer to feed and shelter him. If they were hostile (which Vran anticipated, due to his unsettling green eyes), well, he carried a sword to defend himself with.

He trekked across the snowy field. A predatory avian, a hawk or the like, soared overhead. This heartened Vran, for another sign of life lessened the bleakness of his new environs.

When the swordsman had covered more than half the distance to the valley, he noticed a commotion of some sort occurring in the woods. A group of men, wielding spears or javelins, burst from the tree line while shouting inarticulately. The source of their consternation presently became clear: a giant rampaging lynx, which dwarfed even the largest stallion he had ever seen, pounced upon the men. If they had been hunting the beast, the roles were now reversed.

Vran unsheathed his sword and increased his pace. It was slow going through the icy terrain. He hoped he would arrive in time to aid the hunters. As he drew nearer, he could see their apparel was primitive, being nothing more than the hides and furs of beasts. Their hair and beards were long, unkempt, and tawny. Vran counted eight of these savage men still standing.

One hunter poised his spear to hurl it at the grey-furred lynx, but the beast struck him down and pinned him with a claw as easily as an ordinary cat would overpower a mouse. It lowered its head, desiring to gnaw on the screaming man, but his companions thrust their weapons into its flanks. Enraged, it batted the spears aside and leapt upon two more men and trampled them, the gracefulness of its movements incongruent to its violence.

By the time Vran reached the battle, another victim of the lynx lay motionless, his lifeblood staining the snow crimson. The heads of man and beast alike turned to Vran upon his arrival. The savage huntsmen gaped in awe at the steel he brandished. With a ferocious snarl, the enormous feline lunged at the newcomer.

Vran dove to his left, thereby avoiding the brunt of a vicious sweep of a claw. The lynx's slash left a small rent in his coat, but the thick leather prevented it from puncturing his flesh. Now it was his opportunity to strike, and his sword left a long, bloody mark on the big cat's hide. The beast howled shrilly like a banshee.

The hunters found encouragement in Vran's success. Their spirits now lifted, they lifted their spears as well and struck hard with renewed vigor. Soon the lynx was bleeding from myriad wounds.

With the appearance of the sword-wielding newcomer, what had begun as a game for the lynx was no longer to its liking. It decided it had had its fill of blood-sport and bounded over the head of a savage, intending to flee into the forest. The savage, his morale bolstered a bit too much, grasped the lynx's tail with both hands. His thews strained from the effort to prevent the beast from retreating. Unfortunately, his rash actions, while impressively heroic, were shortsighted, and the lynx ripped out his guts with its rear claws.

The valiant savage might have made the ultimate sacrifice, but it was not in vain. The remaining fighting men were able to surround the lynx while it was detained. Flint-tipped spears pierced the vital organs of its body. Vran delivered the finishing blow, shearing its head from its neck.

With the battle over, the hunters took stock of their deliverer. Plainly they had never seen a man of Vran's like before, for they were awestruck. One stepped forward and clapped his palm against his chest. Vran assumed this gesture was intended as a salutation. "I am Oo-Rahg," he said in a gruff voice. "You?"

"My name is Vran."

"You are not from the valley."

"No, I'm from far off… I don't know how I came here."

"What is your shiny weapon?"

"That is my sword."

Oo-Rahg and some of the other savages drew closer to inspect the unfamiliar weapon. Their eyes opened wide with amazement.

"You will have much to tell us later," said Oo-Rahg. "Our chief, Urg-Thal, will have many questions. But other things come first."

The savages examined the bodies of their fallen. Amazingly, many still survived, but others would never rise again. Oo-Rahg ordered his men to strip the dead of their furs and spears. He used those furs to bind the bleeding wounds of those who still lived.

They collected the corpses and laid them side by side. Once this was done, they began to bury the dead beneath the snows. Vran could see it would be a long, tedious process, as they had no shovels, so he assisted them.

"Is this the best way to bury them?" asked Vran. "Won't they be exposed once the snows melt?"

Oo-Rahg looked at Vran as if he had spontaneously grown another head. "The snows do not melt," he said simply.

Some of the savages began to mutter amongst themselves. While grateful for Vran's battle-prowess against the lynx, his alienness was disconcerting.

After the dead men were inhumed, the savages turned their attention toward the lynx. Several of them lifted the bloody remains of the beast on their shoulders and marched off toward the valley. Oo-Rahg took the cat's severed head and impaled it on a spear. He handed the trophy to Vran.

"You slew the beast. The honor is yours," he said.

Vran had no desire to carry such a grisly object, but nevertheless he accepted it and spoke words of gratitude.

"Come back to the valley with us," said Oo-Rahg. "Tonight, there will be a great feast, thanks to you."

The journey to the valley where the savages made their abode was a silent one. Oo-Rahg desired to learn more of the mysterious stranger, and likewise Vran longed for enlightenment regarding this strange land and its people, but it was agreed that such discussions must not be held without the chief.

During the trek, the sun descended behind the mountains and night spread its black wings. A light flurry of snow began to fall. Ghostly moonlight, reflecting off the snowy terrain, brought about a sense of tranquility tinged with eeriness. Vran looked up to the sky and was astonished by what he saw.

"One moon!" he gasped. "Where is the other?"

"What other?" said Oo-Rahg, perplexed. "There is only one."

Now Vran realized that Foad Misjak's magic had carried him much farther than he could have imagined.

Chapter III
Back in the Village

The people of the valley rejoiced at the sight of the hunters' triumphant return. The lynx meat would make for a bountiful feast this eve. The valley-dwellers hailed and praised Oo-Rahg and his party, but viewed the stranger accompanying them with suspicion.

"This is Vran," announced Oo-Rahg. "He is a great warrior. He is the one who took the lynx's head. Hold it high, Vran, so all can see!"

Vran raised the spear on which the head of the lynx was impaled. The villagers were suitably impressed, vocalizing their awe wordlessly. A few even knelt.

As Vran basked in the villagers' admiration, he looked them over. They were just as primitive as the members of the hunting party. All were clothed in skins of beasts like the lynx. Some wore bits of bone as jewelry, either as necklaces or entwined in their hair. Their fair skin and coarse blond hair lacked of cleanliness. In spite of this, the womenfolk were all reasonably attractive to Vran's eyes. They reminded him, slightly, of the women of Cythera.

One man stepped forth, an elder whose hair and beard showed streaks of grey. "Oo-

Rahg, where did you find this man?" he asked. "He is not like us."

Oo-Rahg bowed reverently to the elder. "Hail, chief. Vran appeared as we fought the lynx. He says he comes from far away. This must be true, for he says many strange things."

The chief approached Vran, looking him up and down. "I am Urg-Thal, chief of the valley people," he said. "Vran, you are welcome to feast with us tonight. Afterwards, you must come to my cave and tell me your tale."

Vran nodded. "Aye."

"Good." Turning to his people, Urg-Thal said, "Now, skin that beast and light a fire! We eat well tonight!"

The villagers eagerly obeyed their chief and set themselves to work. They went to their caves and returned with wood, which was collected in a central gathering area. Some of the villagers reached into the folds of their furs and brought forth snake-like creatures with red scales. Long tongues shot out from the creatures' mouths and licked the wood. Immediately the wood began to smoke and sizzle. Such creatures were unheard of to Vran, and Urg-Thal laughed at the look of bewilderment on his face.

"Haven't you ever seen a tezbou, Vran?" The chief laughed again and spread his voluminous beard with his fingers. A small serpentine head popped out. "They are harmless. We have trained them only to open their mouths when tapped on the head, like so." He pressed his thumb against the top of the creature's head, and a black tongue shot out, then quickly retracted. In the brief moment the tezbou's jaws were open, Vran could feel the heat emanating from it.

"Fascinating," said Vran.

"Here, take a closer look." Urg-Thal placed the tezbou on Vran's arm. Now he could see that the flame-tongued beast had four short legs, like a salamander. It scurried up and down Vran's arm, then enwrapped itself around his wrist.

"Ah, it's taken a liking to you," chuckled the chief.

Vran was not sure how to feel about that. He held the tezbou closer to his face. Its jaws contorted, seeming to smile at him.

Now that the kindling was ablaze, the villagers placed the giant lynx's carcass on a spit. They began to salivate at the scent of the roasting flesh. Soon pieces of meat were carved from the carcass and distributed among the villagers. Although lynx-meat was not Vran's preferred cuisine, he was quite hungry and wolfed down his portion.

During the feast, the mood of the villagers was mostly joyous and convivial but at times inexplicably became somber for brief intervals, like a dark cloud momentarily passing before the sun. Most of the villagers kept a respectful distance from Vran, although they looked upon him with admiration and curiosity. Vran noticed one particular girl, a maiden of superlative beauty, occasionally glancing in his direction, but whenever he tried to meet her gaze, she turned away. After a few such instances, he decided to pay her no heed and turned his attention toward the strange reptile he had somehow befriended. He held a morsel of meat before the tezbou's face. It snatched it from his hand, almost too quick for the eye to see. He felt a tingling sensation where

the tezbou's tongue had brushed against his fingers, as if he had briefly touched a hot stove.

As the revelry was dying down, Urg-Thal took Vran aside. "Let us talk now, Vran. Join me in my caves."

Before they left the feast, Urg-Thal signaled to the beautiful young lady that had caught Vran's eye. She was conversing with Oo-Rahg. "Come, Olo," Urg-Thal said to the girl. "I can't leave my daughter at the feast unsupervised." The girl obediently broke off her conversation and followed her father, to Oo-Rahg's chagrin. She walked side by side with Vran. Up close, her beauty was even more striking. She was as physically appealing as any minx one might encounter in the fleshpots of Desazu, but unlike the coquettish city girls Vran was familiar with, she possessed a charming innocence.

The chieftain led Vran and Olo to an oblong formation of rock jutting out approximately fifteen feet from the valley wall. A row of cave-mouths, each barely of sufficient size to accommodate a man of Vran's height, was contained within this formation. The roof of these caves formed a broad shelf.

"This is where the chieftain rests," Urg-Thal informed Vran.

"Here?" asked Vran, pointing to one of the caves.

"No. The one above."

Urg-Thal and Olo began to climb up the formation. Vran followed, but not without difficulty, for the rocks were slick with ice. Vran was impressed the elder could make the ascent, and remarked upon it.

"If I could not, I would be unfit to lead

my people," said Urg-Thal.

At the end of the rock shelf, a hide curtain hung from the valley wall. Urg-Thal parted it, revealing a cave-mouth, one much larger than those below. Vran and Olo stepped past him into a spacious chamber. Urg-Thal followed them, letting the curtain fall, then produced another tezbou from his furs which he used to light a pile of kindling in the center of the cave. Once ablaze, the illumination revealed more of the red-scaled reptiles, either lounging about or skittering across the floor, like strings of ruby necklaces moving of their own volition. The three seated themselves around the fire.

Urg-Thal turned to his daughter. "Olo, you need not trouble yourself with this. You may go to your chamber and sleep."

Olo shook her head. "By your leave, I would stay and hear of this warrior."

"So be it," said the chief. "Vran, you say you came from far away. How far?"

Vran hesitated before replying. "I don't know, but it is an incredible distance. The land I hail from is called Nilztiria. Have you heard of it?"

"No. Do all men of Nilztiria have hair dark as a moonless night, and eyes like a devil's?"

"Some have dark hair, others light. But no one has eyes like mine."

Urg-Thal nodded. "I was told you carry a weapon of incredible power. May I see it?"

Vran slowly drew his sword from its sheath and handed it hilt-first to Urg-Thal. "Be very careful with my sword. The blade is sharp."

Urg-Thal gingerly grasped the weapon by the hilt and examined it intently. He was engrossed, spellbound even, by the firelight reflecting off the blade. At length he asked, "What is its name?"

"Its name?"

"Yes. It is a magic weapon. It must have a name."

"Its name is…" Vran paused. "…Ruinator."

Urg-Thal laughed, a short bark. "Ruinator! A fine name indeed. Hopefully it will bring ruin to our enemies!"

"It always has so far," said Vran.

"Good, good," said Urg-Thal, returning the sword. "Now, Vran, how is it you came to our valley? What led you to leave your land and travel such a great distance?"

Vran took his time formulating a reply, as he did not know how the primitive cave-dwellers would react to the truth. Even though Urg-Thal seemed wiser than most of his kin, Vran decided a simple answer would be best. "It was through the work of a wizard."

Olo shuddered at that word, and Urg-Thal grimaced.

"We have our own troubles with wizards," said the chief. "But go on."

"In short, this particular wizard had committed reprehensible deeds which I could not abide, and I swore to slay him. I entered his home and attempted to make good on my promise. In the ensuing struggle, he cast a spell, and I went blind. When my senses returned, I found myself here."

Urg-Thal stroked his beard. "Strange… very strange…" For a moment, the chief, his daughter, and Vran sat in silence. Naught could be heard but the crackling of the fire. Finally, Urg-Thal said, "So you have no liking for wizards, then?"

Vran shook his head. "I usually prefer to keep as much distance between them and myself as possible."

The chief grinned. "Who does not! But we have little choice in the matter these days…"

"What do you mean?"

"Several moons ago, a wizard appeared before us," said Urg-Thal. "Where he came from, he did not say, but it must be far, for we have never seen one like him before. He does not look like you, either, Vran. I would say he looks more like a skeleton than a man.

"The wizard came accompanied by dwarfs who live in the mountains. They serve him now. He demanded we pay him tribute of food, furs, and a virgin maiden. I balked at this, of course, and told him if he wanted a maiden to look for one among the dwarfs. I regret doing so, for he was greatly offended. He made a display of his magical powers… I do not like to remember that day. I had no choice but to obey him.

"I thought that by providing him such wealth, I was purchasing our safety, and we would be done with him, but no. A few days later, he returned, making the same demands. Once again, I protested, but, fearing his wrath, I had to give in. It was for the good of my people, I told myself. Better for one maiden to be carried off screaming than to have the entire village suffer. But time and again he returns, always demanding a virgin maiden. This cannot continue. Before long, he will take my lovely daughter Olo. She is all the family I have left, for my wife died birthing her, and our sons were trampled while hunting a mastodon."

Vran pondered the chief's words before replying. "You must have a reason for telling me this tale, and I believe I can guess it."

Urg-Thal nodded. "I need a brave warrior to defend my people. Will you aid us?"

"I might. But answer me this: did this wizard ever reveal his name?"

"Yes, many times. He is quite arrogant. He calls himself Foad Misjak."

"Misjak!" exclaimed Vran. "That's the bastard I swore to kill!"

"Ho ho!" cried Urg-Thal. "Then you'll fight for us?"

"Aye. I guarantee that vile creature will never lay a hand on your daughter." Vran turned to Olo, who timidly returned his smile.

Urg-Thal clapped Vran on the back. "Misjak will be in for a surprise the next time he visits us. I cannot wait to see you tear him apart with your magic weapon. Oh, that will be a glorious day!"

Vran found Urg-Thal's jovial mood and optimism infectious. At this moment, he had no doubts as to the outcome of his confrontation with the wizard. Foad possesses powers, yes, but of what consequence are they compared to a sword of steel and mighty thews to wield it?

"When will Foad come next?" asked Vran.

Urg-Thal shrugged. "I don't know. But soon. It has been several days since we last saw him. Perhaps he will come tomorrow."

"I hope he does!" said Vran.

Urg-Thal nodded in agreement. "You should rest, then. Olo, show Vran where he may sleep. Give him our finest furs, for a great hero deserves no less."

Olo rose and pulled a burning branch from the fire to use as a torch. She led Vran deeper into the cavern to a fissure in the wall, beyond which was a small enclosure. Furs of a variety of beasts, varying in hue and pattern, lay spread across the floor.

"Most of these furs were prizes captured by my brothers," Olo said wistfully. "It has been lonely and quiet here without them. I feel safer with you here, Vran."

Vran thanked her and bid her good night. After she departed, he divested himself of his boots and coat. He lay down and draped the furs over his body. His sword he left within arm's reach. Although he doubted an intruder would appear while he slept, he gained nothing from incaution.

Weariness overcame Vran, yet sleep eluded him. He could not divert his thoughts from the forthcoming battle with Foad Misjak. Slaying a wizard was no easy task, and he could not afford to be reckless. At least Foad was unaware he had followed him to this world of ice. Or was he? The extent of Foad's capabilities was not fully known to Vran. He could have a spell of clairvoyance in his repertoire. It would be best not to underestimate his opponent.

Another thought occurred to him: after he killed Foad, what then? How could he return to Nilztiria? Would he have no choice but to remain in this primitive world?

After an hour of restlessness, Vran felt himself dozing off but still could not quite reach the desired slumberous state. He pulled the furs tighter around his body to ward off the chill of the stone floor.

Vran thought he heard a faint noise. Yes, he was sure now, it was the sound of soft footsteps—and they were drawing nearer. Slowly he moved his hand toward the hilt of his sword. He paused. Someone was whispering his name.

"Who's there?" he said.

"Olo," was the reply. "Are you awake?"

"Yes. I couldn't sleep."

"Neither could I," said Olo. "May I join you?"

"Of course," said Vran. This was unexpected but not unwelcome.

The girl lay down beside Vran. "You must be cold," he said. "Come closer, there are enough furs for you, too."

After a moment's hesitation the girl slipped under the furs.

"Why couldn't you sleep?" asked Vran.

"I'm worried about Foad Misjak. I've seen the tears of the girls he takes for his brides. I can't bear the thought of that happening to me."

Vran, knowing Foad's tastes, believed he was taking the girls for a more nefarious purpose than wedlock. He decided mentioning this to Olo would only upset her, so instead he said, "You have nothing to fear. I swear he will die by my hand before he can ever come near you."

"Thank you, Vran. You make me feel safe."

The girl placed a small hand on Vran's chest. He put an arm around her, brought her closer to him, and crushed his lips against hers. She did not pull away. Instead, she reciprocated, inexpertly but eagerly. He ran his hands over Olo's body, from her slim waist to her soft, ample breasts. His passions rising, Vran stripped the girl of her garments. As he unbuttoned his shirt, Olo's hand brushed against his groin.

"Your spear is so hard!" she exclaimed.

"It grows harder still," he said as he hastily doffed his trousers.

In the ensuing hours, Olo partook in the pleasures of carnality for the first time, then a second and a third. The experience was a thoroughly enjoyable one. Afterwards, she cradled herself in Vran's arms, and the two lovers serenely drifted off to sleep.

Chapter IV
The Psychology of Demons

The battle between the villagers and the great lynx did not go unobserved. A short, dark figure lurked in the woods, spectating. As the victorious party carried their prize back to the valley, the figure stealthily dropped from a tree branch. This was a member of the race referred to by the valley people as "dwarfs." Though they were indeed short of stature, they were not a branch of humanity whose growth had been stunted. With their slate-grey skin, sharp, cat-like teeth, and bony claws, a native of Nilztiria would recognize them as goblins. But not until recently did a Nilztirian set eyes upon them...

The goblin, Twar by name, rarely ventured forth from the mountain caves where he dwelled. But even a goblin can grow weary of his own abode and desire the clean air and the solitude of the open plains. At certain times such a mood would strike Twar, usually in the hours of twilight, and he would steal away without a word to any of his fellows. Such jaunts were usually uneventful, so the arrival of a stranger wielding a mysterious glimmering weapon was remarkable. It required further investigation.

Once the villagers were a safe distance away, Twar moved across the snows toward the bloodstained battleground. He progressed slowly, for with each step through the snow he sank to his knees. By the time he reached the site of the battle, the moon had already risen. The goblin examined the hastily-packed mounds of snow that served as graves for the fallen villagers. He sniffed. With a furious celerity, he dug through the mound and disentombed a villager's arm. Twar bit off a chunk of meat from the limb. Disappointment set in, for the body was already too cold. Twar contemplated spitting it out but thought better of it and swallowed. No sense in wasting a piece of meat already in his mouth. But he did not care for more, so he replaced the arm and reburied it. After a few moments' toil, he believed (incorrectly) that should any villagers return, they would be unable to guess that the grave had been disturbed. Satisfied with his work, he turned his attention toward the blood-soaked area where the lynx was slain. He dropped to all fours, and from his mouth a forked tongue darted out. The ensanguined snows were also too frigid, but at least had a pleasing taste. He scooped up the flavorful snows with his claws, threw his head back, and dropped them into his mouth. A large portion of the stuff spilled down his chest, leaving crimson streaks on the shift of wolf's hide he wore.

Suddenly it dawned on Twar that his master would wish to be informed of the events that had transpired. Yes, the master must be told. Perhaps, Twar thought, if he acted swiftly enough, the master would reward him. The goblin rose to his feet and hurried back to the mountain caves.

Deep in the mountains of this frost-covered world, numerous tunnels twisted and serpentined, creating a natural labyrinth. But was it natural? Did some unguessable force carve these pathways in a distant age? None could say. Those who currently inhabited it did not even contemplate the matter.

Life in the goblin caves was tedious and brutish. There were few pastimes to be enjoyed other than feeding, fornicating, and physically abusing one another. Occasionally an especially impetuous goblin would lie in wait and harass people of the valley by throwing rocks at them. Most found this state of affairs satisfactory, or at least tolerable. Goblin society had remained unchanged for hundreds of years, perhaps thousands. Then came the portentous day when a human wizard arrived unheralded.

After the spell Foad Misjak had cast to defend himself from a mysterious assailant had gone awry, he had materialized in the bowels of the goblins' mountain. At first, they acted with hostility toward Foad, considering him an interloper, but were quickly awed by his demonstrations of magical might. They swore fealty to him—an oath borne from fear.

This primitive world Foad found himself trapped in disgusted him. He was accustomed to a more sophisticated lifestyle, one where he could enjoy any manner of sybaritic pleasure he desired. With such amenities denied to him, he grew surly. The goblins learned to avoid him when he was in a wrathful mood, which occurred frequently.

Without access to his grimoires, his repertoire of spells was limited. However, one particular ritual he had enacted a multitude of times, and now that it was indelibly pressed in his memory, he could perform it by rote. This was the invocation that would allow communication with his demonic patron, Andortiuxpyl. The ritual required numerous items for maximal efficacy; for example, a particular chalk used for the inscription of runes and pentagrams. Foad managed to improvise with the crude resources available to him, but no substitute was acceptable for the most important component—the soul of a virgin maiden.

"Master! Master!" cried Twar as he burst into the cave Foad Misjak had apportioned as his private sanctum. "I have news!"

"Gah!" shouted the wizard, who was sitting cross-legged with his face to the wall. "You dare interrupt my meditations?"

"It is… I think… it is important," stammered the goblin.

"Then out with it, fool, before I crack your skull with a rock," sneered Foad, turning toward Twar.

"I have seen a strange man, one who looks like no other. He is not of the valley people, but he fought beside them against a great lynx."

"Describe this man."

"His hair is long, but not bright like the sun, instead black as our caves. He had a weapon that was not a spear and not an ax. It was more like a knife, but very long, and it must be very sharp, because he chopped the lynx's head off with it. It… sparkled."

"What color were this man's eyes?"

"I don't know. I was too far away to see."

Foad grumbled under his breath, cursing the goblin's lack of courage and intelligence. "Where is he now?"

"I saw him go with the others to their valley. He must still be there."

"Perhaps... perhaps not," mused Foad. After a moment, he said, "Twar, I must summon the demon tonight. Bring the maiden from the holding pen to the sacrificial chamber."

Twar shivered, for he feared the demon even more than his master. He hesitated before answering, trying to find words that would not infuriate the wizard.

Foad, noting his reluctance, gnarred, *"Obey me!"* Twar turned and ran, his footsteps echoing throughout the caverns.

Foad found Twar's information distressing. Was this dark-haired warrior the one who had attempted to assassinate him? This required drastic action, for it was imperative that he know.

The wizard had not intended to invoke Andortiuxpyl so soon. His plan was to wait until a night when the moon was full and the stars in proper conjunction, for he thought that this might give him greater control over the demon. The results of his previous attempts to contact Andortiuxpyl from this plane were less than desirable, for the demon was able to terminate their audience whenever the whim struck him. Foad hoped that the demon would deign at least to provide the identity of the stranger before nullifying the spell.

A large pile of kindling blazed against the far wall of the makeshift summoning chamber. As Foad Misjak drew a circle around it with a piece of charcoal, he cursed his lack of arcane appurtenances. Carefully he inscribed runes of binding around the magic circle, but with such primitive materials he had little hope for their effectiveness.

A commotion came from the passage leading to the chamber. Twar marched in, pulling along a sobbing girl who had been captured from the valley. A leash of leather encircled her throat, the end of which Twar clutched in one grimy hand. Four more goblins followed, each armed with a spear, to ensure the girl could not escape.

"Put the wench on the altar," ordered Foad.

The altar he referred to was nothing more than a shelf of rock jutting out from the wall of the cave. The goblins stripped off the girl's furs and forced her down on the block of stone. Four of the goblins grabbed the girl's limbs and held them in place while Twar ogled her nude form, salivating. She screamed, driven mad with terror.

"Silence her," said Foad. Twar slapped the girl once, which was enough to halt her fearful cries.

Foad was now ready to begin the incantation. He cleared his mind, breathed in deeply, and spoke the arcane words of the spell.

"O benign maleficent daemon,
You who hold dominion over men of more worlds than are calculable,
I beseech you, grant me a boon
And delight in my gift of a pure soul, yet to be tormented by one of your kind."

The smoke from the fire suddenly took

on a purplish tinge. It swirled capriciously, as if mischievous unseen spirits danced through it. By degrees, the smoke sculpted itself into a horrible face. Sinister beady eyes like smoldering coals stared from an ashen, ghastly countenance. From beneath the eyes the stub of a nose lurked. A chaotic multitude of fangs and tusks burst from a mouth in an elongated jaw. The scalp was hairless, but a single curved horn, like that of an ibex but much larger, protruded from the center of the forehead.

"Hail, Andortiuxpyl!" shouted Foad Misjak, making the gesture indicating subservience as the ritual prescribed.

Andortiuxpyl laughed, a sinister rumble. "Foad Misjak… I see you still reside in the primitive world of ice. You must enjoy it here, else you would have returned to Nilztiria by now."

Foad sneered. "Must you mock me? You know well I lack the power to return to my own dimension. That is why I continue to call on you."

The demon laughed again, this time raucously. "Before we speak further, I require a gift."

Foad, a knife of flint in his hand, approached the altar of sacrifice. The girl begged for reprieval, to no avail. With merciless force, the wizard plunged his knife between the girl's quivering breasts. The girl, now silent, lay still as her blood stained the stone altar and dribbled onto the floor.

A ghostly essence fluttered from the dead girl's body. Slowly it floated toward the infernal face above the flames. Andortiuxpyl inhaled, sucking the girl's soul in through his nostrils. He laughed again, a sound so unsettling the goblins were forced to turn their heads away.

"Are you satisfied?" asked Misjak.

"Indeed," said the demon. "Innocent souls are the most gratifying to torment. You have done well, Foad Misjak. Now you may question me."

"First, I would know of this dark-haired stranger my lackey Twar saw with the people of the valley. Is this the same man who invaded my home, slew my brother, and assaulted me?"

"It is."

Misjak paused, expecting his demonic patron to expound further on the topic. When no such explanation came, he asked, "Who is he?"

"His name is Vran, or as he is sometimes called, Vran the Chaos-Warped."

"Chaos-Warped? How did he earn that appellation? Is he a madman?"

"No… not quite," said Andortiuxpyl. "His body, not his mind, was mutated by wild sorcery. That is why his eyes are a splendid shade of green you humans find so unsettling. But more pertinent to your query, his blood became altered, corrupted. Now whenever a spell is cast in his vicinity, the results are… unpredictable."

"So that is why I was transported to another dimension."

"You are very clever," said the demon in a condescending tone. "I should be the one imploring you to share your wisdom."

Misjak scowled. A scathing rejoinder sprang to his mind, but he thought better of delivering it. Instead he asked, "Why does this man wish me harm?"

"Does it matter? He has sworn to kill you. The reason why is immaterial. My recommendation is to prevent him from doing so by killing him first."

"Thank you. I am fortunate to be so well-advised," said Misjak, the sarcasm in his tone so strong it was nearly palpable. "But how am I to accomplish that? He can turn my magic against me."

Andortiuxpyl shut his beady eyes for a moment. "There is a way."

"Tell me."

"I can devise a spell which will temporarily abrogate the power of Vran's warped blood. Instead, it will incapacitate him."

"Will you bestow this spell upon me?"

"For a price."

"Of course. What do you wish?"

"You must deliver to me *five* virgin maidens tomorrow night," said the demon, grinning.

"Agreed," replied Misjak without hesitation. This was a greater number than the demon usually asked for, but the wizard had no bargaining power. Besides, such maidens could easily be acquired from the village. "Then, will you return me to Nilztiria?"

Andortiuxpyl chuckled again, a sound the goblins found so horrible they were forced to cover their ears. "One thing at a time. Kneel before me, Foad Misjak."

The wizard obeyed. The ghostly face hovering above the fire contorted. For a moment, Misjak feared the demon would depart without granting him the spell to overcome his sworn enemy, but then the demon's visage returned to its normal state. A violet tongue extended from the horrid wreck of a mouth. The appendage proved to be prehensile, for it wrapped itself around the wizard's cranium. Despite appearances, the tongue felt solid. Misjak

shrank from its clammy touch, but it slightly retracted and he was pulled to his feet. Pulses of xanthous lightning slid down the tongue to Misjak's head. The goblins cowered, shielding their eyes from the awful sight. The only thing keeping them from flight was the fear that if they did so, they would earn a punishment more terrible than death.

With each pulse of lightning that touched Misjak, his body convulsed like a marionette manipulated by an incompetent puppeteer. He felt no pain in his limbs or bones, but the torment to his psyche was excruciating. Was Andortiuxpyl truly endowing him with power, or was this nothing more than a jest that the demon took sick pleasure in?

When Misjak felt he could bear no more, the tongue released him from its grasp. The wizard crumpled. He lay on the freezing stone floor, panting, while his infernal patron laughed and laughed. Gradually he recovered his strength and stood upright.

"You now possess the power to overcome Vran," said Andortiuxpyl. "Can you feel it?"

Misjak nodded, his mouth too dry to speak.

"Good. Now you owe me five maidens. Bring them to me tomorrow at midnight as you reckon time. Remember, they must be virgins. If you renege, I will be most displeased." Without warning, the flames flared up, obscuring the demonic visage. The great column of fire died down just as suddenly as it arose, and no trace of Andortiuxpyl remained.

The goblins stood awestruck, awaiting direction from their master. "You have my leave to go," Misjak told them. Four wasted no time in hurrying away, but one remained behind.

"Master," said Twar timidly, "can I have the body?" He gestured to the corpse of the sacrificed maiden.

"You may," said Misjak. "Remove it from the altar and use it to sate your appetites."

Twar grabbed two fistfuls of the girl's long hair and began to drag her away. "I'm not going to eat her," he said.

"I know what you meant," snarled Misjak. "Now go!"

Twar quickened his pace. With fear as a motivator, the corpse was no burden.

Now alone in the chamber, Misjak paced its length, muttering to himself. "Vran the Chaos-Warped... this, the man who wants me dead. But why? What have I done to deserve such hatred? Well, Vran, whoever you may be, soon you shall know the folly of attempting to destroy me. Remorse you shall know as well, but it will come too late. None can cross Foad Misjak with impunity! Great will be your suffering!"

Chapter V
A Dangerous Meeting

When Vran awoke, panic set in. He had slept with Urg-Thal's daughter in his own domicile. How would the chieftain react to such an affair? Most likely, he would consider it a violation of his trust and hospitality. Such thoughts had not occurred to Vran last night while he was gripped by passion.

Olo stirred. "Good morning," she said, and kissed Vran on the cheek. Sensing something was wrong, she asked, "What troubles you?"

"Your father," said Vran. "I fear he will be upset with me."

"Why?"

"Men usually do not take kindly to those who sleep with their daughters."

Olo laughed melodiously. "Don't worry. I'll explain to him. He will be pleased."

"He will?"

"Yes. He will be proud and honored that such a great warrior would choose to take his daughter as a wife."

Wife? Inwardly, Vran was alarmed, but he refused to show any sign of consternation. Instead, he calmly replied, "You are my wife now? The marriage rites of your people are... different from most I am familiar with."

Olo laughed again. "No, we are not wed yet, but it is our custom that when a man and woman bond this way, they are betrothed."

"I see..." Vran spoke in a tone that indicated he was not overjoyed.

"Are you still worried about my father?"

"Huh? Oh, yes."

"I will speak to him now." She rose from the pile of furs and pulled her snow-leopard skin garment over her head. As she exited the chamber, Vran decided it would be best to clothe himself as well. If an angry Urg-Thal suddenly burst in, it would not be well to face him in the nude. He groped in the darkness for his leather trousers and shirt and struggled into them.

Vran sat down, his back to a wall. He was not as optimistic as Olo that Urg-Thal would react well to the news. A skittering sound interrupted his broodings. Although his eyes had become somewhat accustomed to the dark, he saw naught. Suddenly a spark of light flared up, and he realized its source. It was one of the flame-tongued beasts, opening its jaws.

Vran held out a hand toward the tezbou, and it scampered up his arm. "Hello there, little fellow," he said. "Are you the friend I met at the feast last night?" The tezbou coiled itself around his thick wrist. Amused by the reptile's antics, Vran's concerns over Urg-Thal drifted away.

When Olo returned, she said, "My father wishes to speak to you." Vran nodded and followed her back to the main chamber, where Urg-Thal awaited. Vran could not read the expression on his face.

"Come closer," said the chieftain, and Vran did so. Urg-Thal looked the warrior up and down. Abruptly he stepped toward Vran and embraced him with affection. "My son!" he cried. Vran returned the gesture, clapping Urg-Thal on the back.

"I began to fear I would die before finding a worthy mate for my precious Olo," said Urg-Thal. "But the gods have blessed me! Not only have they sent a wizard-slayer, but one who will continue my lineage and lead the people of the valley in years to come!"

"I… have no words," said Vran, smiling to disguise his inner thoughts. *So Urg-Thal has the rest of my life planned out for me. A wife, a family, a people to lead… Have I no say in the matter?*

"At noon, I will make the announcement," said the chieftain. "There will be much rejoicing."

"Indeed," said Vran. "But I am not in the mood for celebration yet. Not while Foad Misjak still lives."

"Well, that will not be long, ho ho!"

Vran laughed. "Still, I must prepare. If I neglect my training regimen, Misjak could gain some small advantage over me."

"You have my leave to go," said the chieftain.

"But not mine!" said Olo. "I want to stay by your side."

Vran placed his hands on the cave-girl's shoulders. "Matters of war are of great importance. There will be plenty of time for the two of us once the threat has been dealt with."

"I understand," Olo said dejectedly.

Vran bade Olo and Urg-Thal farewell and exited the cave. He stepped into the bright morning sunlight, raising a hand to shield his eyes. As he made his way through the valley, he attracted a great deal of attention. Some found his foreign appearance suspicious, while others were naively curious. A few approached him with questions he felt uncomfortable to answer, such as where he came from and why his eyes were so strange. The replies he offered were vague, and the villagers found them unsatisfactory. He removed himself from the crowd that was beginning to gather by using the same excuse he gave Urg-Thal. The villagers no longer detained him, for their greatest wish was to see Foad Misjak's head on a stake.

Vran found a secluded area of the valley which suited his need for solitude. He drew his sword and practiced feints and parries against an imaginary foe. Truly he did not need to drill himself, for his form was excellent. He simply hoped the physical activity would divert his thoughts from his current predicament. The effort was in vain, though. After nearly slipping on a patch of ice, he knew it was of no use. He seated himself on the cold ground, found a rock that made an acceptable whetstone, and began to sharpen his blade while he dove deep into the pool of his troubled mind.

So he was to be wed to Olo, was he? Not only was he expected to father many children with her, but to inherit the chieftainship when the time of Urg-Thal's passing came. None of this was accordant with his own plans, nebulous as they were. After slaying Misjak, he intended to return to Nilztiria... somehow. But how? He had no sorcerous powers.

Perhaps he had no choice but to remain here. Life in the caves might not be so dreadful. He would have a position of power and a beautiful wife who adored him. Vran wondered what his children would look like, whether their eyes would be similar to his.

A distraction caused Vran to cease sharpening his sword. The tezbou, still clinging to his arm, was stirring. He had become so accustomed to its presence that he was unaware it had crawled up the sleeve of his coat. It turned around and popped out its vermilion head. Vran smiled at the small reptile until an ill thought suddenly soured his mood. This creature, which was strange to him, was a normal part of this world. *He* was the aberrant one.

How could he lead the people of the valley? He was an outsider, an alien. Their customs were completely unfamiliar to him. His appearance was drastically different from theirs. Would they accept him as chieftain, even with Urg-Thal's blessing? Even if they did, how could he live among

them? Their lifestyle was so primitive, not to mention their intellect...

Vran looked up. He could tell by the position of the sun in the sky that noon was fast approaching. Had he been lost in thought so long? Urg-Thal would make the announcement soon, and Vran was certain his presence was expected. He stood up, sheathed his sword, and marched back to the center of the valley.

A crowd had gathered before Urg-Thal's cave. Tawny heads turned as Vran made his way through the villagers. The chieftain emerged from his cave, followed by Olo. Urg-Thal easily spotted Vran and hailed him. Vran scrambled up the stone elevation and stood by Urg-Thal's side.

The chieftain raised his voice to address his people. "My friends, I have called you here to share with you news of great import. As you know, the deaths of my sons threw our future into uncertainty. But I have found a worthy successor! He is the mighty hero from afar, Vran!"

The reaction of the villagers was mostly positive, but not to the degree Urg-Thal and Vran had hoped for. Many cheered, but some bore skeptical looks on their faces. A few villagers, young men who hoped to win Olo's hand, were upset and clearly struggled to contain their anger. Oo-Rahg was included in this number.

Urg-Thal joined hands with Olo and Vran. "It heartens me that my daughter has found love. No better son could I ask for. They will be wed in three days' time."

"No!" shouted Oo-Rahg.

"What is this?" said Urg-Thal. "You dare protest?"

"Yes, I dare!" said Oo-Rahg, his face en-

23

crimsoned with fury. "How can you give Olo to this man? He is not one of us! He is a stranger!" Several others voiced their assent.

"Silence!" ordered the chieftain. "Vran has proved himself in battle against the lynx. Leadership requires strength, and Vran possesses strength in abundance. And soon he will slay the wizard Foad Misjak. Can anyone say a man who can accomplish that task is unfit to lead?"

"Vran has not slain the wizard yet," countered Oo-Rahg.

"He most certainly has not." The voice of a stranger, dripping with disdain, came from behind the chieftain. Urg-Thal and Vran turned to discover Misjak himself, accompanied by Twar and a cadre of spear-wielding goblins, smugly staring at them.

Vran whipped his sword from its sheath. Before he could strike down his adversary, Misjak invoked the power granted to him by his demonic patron Andortiuxpyl. As soon as the wizard discharged the unholy spell, Vran succumbed to its dreadful effects. He felt a wave of searing cold engulf him, leaving him in a state of total paralysis. Even blinking his eyes became impossible. While his body was immobilized, his mind was not, and it raced with thoughts of how to overcome this disastrous turn of events. No solutions came to him, and Vran realized his doom was close at hand.

As Andortiuxpyl had not divulged the exact nature of how the spell would affect Vran, Misjak was wary that it might not have induced complete incapacitation. Once satisfied that Vran was impotent, he studied the man who had sworn to kill him, for during their previous encounter he had

been unable to look at him closely. The wizard's gaze met Vran's eerie green orbs. Finding them too unsettling to bear for long, he turned away and began to mock Urg-Thal.

"So this is your hero, eh? The one you expected to slay the great wizard Foad Misjak? The one who was your only hope of doing away with me? Look at him! He's helpless! Not even he can withstand my magic. You were foolish to think otherwise. And now you have angered me."

Urg-Thal stuttered, unable to speak coherently. He expected the wizard to deal him death, or possibly a worse fate, at any moment. Terror immobilized Olo as strongly as Misjak's magic did Vran.

"Such a heinous act of defiance cannot be disregarded. You must go to great lengths to appease your master."

"H-how?" stammered Urg-Thal.

"The tribute must be increased. No less than five virgin maidens will suffice."

"Five?" The chieftain was astonished. "But—"

"And included among that five must be—her!" declared Misjak, pointing at Olo. The girl shrieked.

"My daughter! Please, no!"

"If you refuse, I will speak a spell to tear your heart from your chest and your bones from your limbs! Then I will do the same to all the men of your village and take as many of your women as I please!"

As exorbitant as the wizard's demands were, Urg-Thal could see he had no choice. "I agree," he said, his head drooping from the weight of shame.

Misjak ordered Twar to pick four girls from the crowd to join Olo. None of the menfolk dared raise a hand against them. While the chieftain's daughter wept openly, she had enough self-control not to wail and tear her hair like the other doomed maidens. Once the selection was made, Misjak grabbed a spear from one of his goblin henchmen.

With careful deliberation, the wizard placed the point of the spear at Vran's throat. Misjak stared into his enemy's eyes, smiled wickedly, and delivered a forceful thrust. To the surprise of all, the point broke off against Vran's flesh.

"By the horns of Iljer..." Misjak muttered, staring at the broken spear in disbelief. He clutched Vran's throat with his bare hand. It was like gripping a block of ice, not only due to its frigidity, but its hardness as well.

"He's frozen solid," the wizard said under his breath. Turning to the throng, he proclaimed, "I have decided not to slay Vran. That would be too merciful. Instead, I will leave him in a permanently frozen state of living death. He will remain here as a reminder to you all. The next time you think of crossing Foad Misjak, look to your would-be savior and remember—you have no hope. None!"

Misjak commanded his goblins to herd the captive maidens into Urg-Thal's cave, then followed. Olo hesitated and turned her face toward Vran in supplication, as if by pleading with him he could somehow overcome the paralyzing bewitchment. Twar poked her harshly in the ribs with the butt of his spear, forcing her to follow the others. This was the last sight Vran saw before his vision faded and his consciousness diminished. His fall into torpor was complete.

The people of the valley looked to their chieftain for guidance, but he had no wisdom to offer on this occasion. He retreated to his cave, curious of what the wizard might be doing there, but found it empty.

Chapter VI
Fall From Grace

Vran's senses returned gradually, beginning with his sight. Shadows were falling, indicating a great deal of time had passed since his altercation with Misjak. A repetitive thudding sound nearby indicated he was recovering his auditory powers as well. Soon thereafter he felt his limbs losing their numbness. He began to believe that soon he would once again be a man of flesh and blood instead of one of ice and frost. Suddenly he felt a sharp pain in the side of his head. He cried out.

"So you're alive!" exclaimed Urg-Thal. The swordsman turned his aching head and saw the chieftain squatting before him, holding a heavy rock in his hand. Vran noticed several rocks of similar size at his feet.

"What are you doing?" asked Vran. Although the paralyzing effects of Misjak's spell had dissipated, he was left in a state of confusion.

"Grieving," gnarred Urg-Thal. "Grieving for my lost daughter." He raised his hand as if to throw the rock, but decided otherwise. He let it fall to the ground.

Vran touched his fingers to the temple which had been struck by Urg-Thal's missile. It felt bruised, but there was no blood. The pain stung, yet was inconsequential in comparison to the pangs of failure.

The ordeal of being sorcerously victimized left Vran woozy and uncomprehending. He sat beside the chieftain, but Urg-Thal backed away. Vran looked at him questioningly.

"Begone," said Urg-Thal.

"What?"

"Begone, I say. You have betrayed my trust."

"What do you mean?"

"How is it you do not understand?" exploded Urg-Thal, suddenly filled with rage. "You promised you would stop the wizard from robbing us of our women. Instead, he takes more than ever before! I promised you my daughter's hand, thinking you would protect her, but now she is in his clutches, and I will never see her again!" Urg-Thal wailed like a wolf.

"Calm down," said Vran. "I will hunt down Misjak in his lair—"

"Silence, betrayer! Tell me no more empty promises—tell me no more lies! Begone, now!"

"Hold your tongue, Urg-Thal!" Vran's anger was rising. "You name me betrayer, liar? Who else has the courage to stand before the wizard? Who else can you turn to for help?"

"No one," said Urg-Thal coldly. "Our only hope for survival is to appease Foad Misjak." He turned his head to gaze somberly upon the sunset. "I should have known your evil eyes were an ill omen. Vran, leave the valley and never return. I am chieftain, and this is my will."

Vran knew further argument would be useless. Urg-Thal, overcome by emotion, was not in a state conducive to clear thinking. "Very well then," he said, and departed without another word, or even a backward glance.

The Nilztirian swordsman made his way to the head of the valley. The villagers kept their distance from him, their faces twisted into expressions of shock and dismay. None spoke or attempted to halt him, but their disdain was clear. Plainly they held the same opinion as Urg-Thal of his character.

When Oo-Rahg caught sight of Vran, anger welled up within the strapping youth. Clutching his spear so tightly his knuckles turned pale, he kept his eyes on Vran until the disgraced warrior passed beyond the limit of his vision. Conflicting thoughts and emotions warred inside Oo-Rahg. He sprinted toward Urg-Thal's cave. There were important matters he needed to discuss with his chieftain immediately.

A multitude of stars gleamed brightly this night; jewels in the vault of heaven. The celestial light reflected entrancingly off the frost-covered earth Vran trod upon. The beauty of nature impressed him, for he had not experienced it to such a degree in Nilztiria. Even the weather was agreeable, as there was no snowfall, and the temperature, while not exactly pleasant, had risen to an endurable level. Or perhaps Vran's body had become accustomed to this far-flung frigid dimension. Whatever the reason, Vran thought it a perfect night for a walk—even though the journey would end at the lair of a malicious wizard.

But where, precisely, was that lair? He had been told that Misjak holed up in the mountains, but other than that bit of information he had no directions, no clues. Exploration would be required, and there was a good chance Foad or his henchmen would discover him first. The odds looked grim for Vran, but what else could he do? Turn back? Impossible. The people of the valley had cast him out. He knew of no other tribes or clans in this realm, and if he did, they would likely treat him no better. No, the only path open to him led to Misjak. Besides, he had never left an oath unfulfilled before and had no intention of doing so now.

Vran began to wonder about the spell of imprisonment Misjak had used to ensorcell him. His memory of the ordeal was foggy. He did not recall any surges of turbulent forces which were the usual consequence of his chaos-warped blood. What were the effects the wizard intended? Had he somehow devised a method to negate Vran's unique physiology? If so, a confrontation could be disastrous.

On the other hand, if the spell had been designed to permanently incapacitate Vran, it had failed. If Misjak knew it was of finite duration, wouldn't he have set a guard around him or ordered the goblins to drag his body back to the mountains? Too many questions, too few answers.

Vran thought back to his brief apprenticeship as a sorcerer. He had learned little before his instructor Zyx Zoxos perished in the calamitous experiment which altered him forever. Vran tried to remember any laws of sorcery which might pertain to today's events, but none came to him. Besides, no sorcerous "law" was immutable. Sorcery is not science, as Zyx Zoxos frequently reminded him. The law Vran understood best was the law of the blade. Perhaps he was born to be a swordsman. It was highly unusual for a fighting man to express interest at all in learning the arts of

magic, but Vran had never been ordinary.

The stillness of the night was disrupted by the distant sound of crunching snow. Vran turned in time to see a spear arching toward him. He stepped back, and the missile struck the ground where he had stood a moment before. As he drew his sword, he called out, "Show yourself!"

A man far off advanced without replying. It appeared to be one of the villagers, although Vran could not discern any of his features at this distance. Whoever he was, he brandished an axe and clearly intended to work Vran harm with it.

Vran stood in a defensive stance, ready to do battle with the stranger. As the aggressor drew nearer, Vran could see it was no stranger at all, but Oo-Rahg. The swordsman hailed him, but again received no answer. Perplexed by Oo-Rahg's hostility, he said, "I have no wish to fight you. Come no closer."

Oo-Rahg ignored the warning and charged. He swung his flint axe mightily at Vran's neck. Only quick reflexes saved Vran's head from being shorn from his body. The swordsman paced backward, shouting, "Oo-Rahg! I said I don't want to fight! Don't force me!"

The caveman, maddened by war-lust, paid no heed to Vran's words and made another wild swing. By now, Vran was fed up with Oo-Rahg's foolishness, and ferociously parried the blow. His blade cleaved through the wooden haft, sending the axe head hurtling to the ground. Oo-Rahg stared at his broken weapon in disbelief.

"Now do you see the senselessness of your actions?" asked Vran. Oo-Rahg did not move or reply, seemingly dumbstruck.

For a moment, Vran let his guard down, which was the opening Oo-Rahg needed. The caveman suddenly flung the broken haft at the knuckles of Vran's right hand. Startled by the pain, Vran lost his grip on his sword.

Oo-Rahg lunged at his enemy. Together they toppled to the snow-covered ground. Now they waged war not with man-made weapons, but the strength nature had gifted them with. It was a fighting style which suited the primitive caveman well, yet Vran, who had done his share of reckless brawling before, would not be dispatched so easily.

The two combatants rolled over the snows, fighting tooth and nail, but neither could claim dominance over the other. They were fairly matched in size and strength. His face inches away from Vran's, Oo-Rahg finally spoke. "Olo… gone… your fault!" he panted while trading blows.

Oo-Rahg's advantage lay in his brute force approach, Vran realized. If he were to overcome his foe, he must exert his superior intellect. Vran grabbed a handful of Oo-Rahg's beard with his left hand and jerked it to the side. With the caveman's temple exposed, Vran dealt a terrific blow to his head, staggering him. Vran pushed him aside and stood up.

Oo-Rahg began crawling away on all fours. Suddenly he leapt to his feet. Vran expected him to charge, but instead the caveman turned and ran. His goal, apparently, was a wooded area not far off. Vran recognized it as the woods where they had fought the giant lynx the previous day. "Hey! Come back!" he shouted. He picked up his sword and ran after Oo-Rahg.

By the time Vran reached the tree line, Oo-Rahg was nowhere to be seen. "Oo-Rahg!" called Vran. "There could be another lynx in these woods! You're going to get yourself killed!"

While Vran debated whether to follow Oo-Rahg into the woods, a clump of snow fell on his shoulder. A startling screech rang out from overhead. Vran looked up and saw Oo-Rahg perched on a thick branch. Presumably, he had intended to leap upon Vran, but now he was entangled with some hostile forest denizen. The caveman slipped and crashed to the earth, right at Vran's feet.

The creature swooped down upon Oo-Rahg. Without the concealment of branches, Vran could clearly see it was an enormous black-plumed hawk. Its wingspan was even greater than Vran's own height. Evidently it was nesting in the trees, and the intrusion of Oo-Rahg enraged it.

Oo-Rahg had landed on his back. The hawk stood on his chest and thrust its beak into his face, seeking to rip out his eyes. The caveman threw up his arms in an attempt to bat away the great bird, but it would not relent. It sank its talons into his chest, piercing through the hides he wore and drawing blood.

In a matter of seconds Vran calculated the risk of joining the battle that was unfolding before him. He must strike with the utmost precision in order to avoid harming Oo-Rahg. Taking careful aim, he plunged the point of his blade into the hawk's breast. The bird flapped its wings rapidly and released a deafening death cry. Vran held the blade at arm's length so as not to be struck by the hawk's beak or talons

Vran took careful aim to strike the hawk.

during its wild death throes. Once its thrashing ceased, Vran used his foot to push it off his bloody blade.

Vran knelt by the caveman, checking him for broken bones. "Oo-Rahg, are you hurt?" he asked.

"No…" replied Oo-Rahg groggily. "Only dazed." His face was marked by minor contusions, but the hawk had not succeeded in rending him with its beak.

The two men remained silent for a moment. Then Oo-Rahg sat up and asked, "Why did you save me?"

"I wondered that myself," answered Vran. "I'm usually not so forgiving of people who try to kill me. Maybe you're more useful to me alive."

"I can't forgive you for what happened to Olo," said Oo-Rahg, wiping perspiration from his face.

"Is that why you attacked me?"

Oo-Rahg nodded.

"That wouldn't bring her back."

"But what can I do?" said Oo-Rahg, desperation in his voice.

"You can join me," said Vran. "I swore to slay Foad Misjak. I may have failed before, but I'll try again until I prevail. And two have a better chance of success than one."

"You would dare confront the wizard again?"

"Of course! I am no coward. And neither are you."

"That's true…" After a moment's deliberation, he extended his hand to Vran. "All right. For the sake of my people, I will help you kill the wizard."

Vran accepted Oo-Rahg's hand and helped him to his feet. "Very good. Now,

we should hurry. The longer we wait, the longer Olo must endure her captivity."

Oo-Rahg scowled. "Let's go."

The two men marched toward the cliffs looming inauspiciously on the horizon. Somewhere within these mountains, their mortal enemy made his abode. Oo-Rahg had recovered his spear, but left his broken axe where it lay.

A sudden wind arose, brushing a light dusting of snow against their shins. Vran looked up to the full moon, blazing overhead like a beacon of silver.

"It still is odd to me to see only one moon," he said.

"How many moons do they have in your land?" asked Oo-Rahg.

"Two."

"You must come from very far away. How far?"

Vran answered without thinking beforehand. "From another world."

"What?" exclaimed Oo-Rahg. "How can there be other worlds?"

"I don't know. I am no cosmographer."

Oo-Rahg looked at Vran as if he were daft. "You speak nonsense. This is the only world the gods made."

"And what gods are those?"

"The gods, of course!" said Oo-Rahg, as if that were self-evident. "They live in the earth, the wind, the sky."

"What are their names?"

"They have no names. They are gods."

Vran decided to direct the conversation to more practical matters. "Do you know which of the mountains Foad Misjak hides in?"

"No, but it should be easy enough to

learn. He and the dwarfs will leave plenty of tracks in the snow to follow."

"Where I come from, we call dwarfs 'goblins'," said Vran.

"Gob-lins... The word sounds strange to me. Why not call them dwarfs?"

Vran knew any attempt at explanation would be fruitless, so he simply replied, "I don't know."

"They're crafty little devils. They're too weak to fight face to face, so they use coward's tactics. A group of them will come at you from behind, or they'll use some other trick. Don't let your guard down around them."

"I won't."

For a while, neither fighting man spoke. Only the sound of the whispering wind and their footsteps crunching the snow filled the silence. Abruptly Vran felt something stirring around his left arm. For a brief moment he was startled before realizing it must be the tezbou. His assumption was proven correct as the flame-tongued beast squirmed past the cuff of his sleeve. He surmised that the creature had lain dormant under the effects of Misjak's spell until now. Vran was heartened that the tezbou remained with him, for he felt a greater affection for the animal than for most people he had known.

Something suddenly dawned on Oo-Rahg. "Vran, what will happen afterwards?"

"What do you mean?"

"After we kill the wizard... and rescue Olo."

"You want the girl for yourself, don't you?"

Oo-Rahg stopped walking and stared at Vran sternly. "Yes."

"She chose me," said Vran, returning Oo-Rahg's stare without flinching.

"But *I* chose *her*. Before you came. You aren't one of us, Vran. The people of the valley need one of their own to lead them."

"The point may be moot if we stand here arguing all night. Let's keep moving while there's still a chance to save her." Not waiting for a reply, Vran continued on toward the cliffs.

Oo-Rahg caught up with Vran. "Perhaps one of us will fall tonight. If that should happen, it means it was not the will of the gods that Olo should be his wife."

Vran nodded. "There is sense in what you say. But if we both survive, what is the gods' will then?"

"We must settle the matter ourselves."

"With fair combat?"

"Yes."

"Agreed. But let us speak no more of this now. We have a dangerous task at hand."

With no more left to discuss, Vran and Oo-Rahg remained silent during the rest of the journey. In less than an hour, they reached the foot of the mountains. As Oo-Rahg had said, there were scores of small footprints in the snow to follow. The trail led to a narrow fissure in one of the cliffs. Before the two men entered, a grey cloud drifted in front of the moon, darkening the night sky. Both men thought this an ominous portent, but did not remark upon it.

Chapter VII
Death Comes Ripping

A pair of goblin guardsmen, armed with spears longer than their bodies, stood slouching before a cavern opening. They saw Twar approaching and immediately straightened their backs. In unison they hailed Twar.

"How are the prisoners?" Twar asked. "Causing trouble?"

"No, they just annoy us with their crying," replied a guard.

"It won't be long before that comes to an end," said Twar with a laugh. "Let me pass."

The guards stepped aside. Twar moved between them and entered the portion of the cave used as a rudimentary penitentiary. Five young red-eyed maidens sat in a circle. They turned their heads to him and began their wailing anew, a sound which did not evoke the least bit of sympathy from the goblin. He examined each girl in turn, poking and prodding them with his clawed hands. At last he came to Olo.

"Ah yes, this is a pretty one," he said impishly. "I'll ask the master to give me your body once he's done with you." Twar grabbed a handful of her tawny hair and yanked. Olo gasped and spat in the goblin's face.

"Let me go!" she shouted.

Twar struck her across the mouth with a clenched fist. Olo collapsed but did not cry out. Instead, she stared hatefully at the wicked goblin. A drop of blood from her lips splashed upon the floor. The four other girls backed away to the walls of the cave.

"A little less pretty now," mocked Twar. "But still good enough for me." He clapped his hands twice, and the guards entered. "Take them to the master's chamber," he ordered. "They will be needed very soon."

Vran and Oo-Rahg wended their way through the fissure. It led upwards for a considerable distance, terminating near the lip of a gorge. To the right, the path ascended, and the footprints continued in this direction. Vran spotted a group of five shadowy figures lurking further up the incline. He mentioned this to Oo-Rahg, whose reaction was to charge toward them, nearly slipping in the snow in his haste. Vran, irked that their chance for surprise had been wasted, advanced slightly less recklessly.

By the time Vran was able to join the battle, one goblin had already expired on the point of Oo-Rahg's spear. Not bothering to withdraw it, the wild caveman thrust his weapon at another enemy. In a matter of seconds, another goblin corpse hung limply from it. The remaining goblins stood open-jawed and awestruck at this display of untrammeled violence. Vran cut them down while Oo-Rahg shook his spear, dislodging from it the bodies he had skewered.

"Like I said, dwarfs are weak," said Oo-Rahg. "Easy work for us."

Glancing down, Vran counted four lifeless bodies lying before a wide gap in the rocky wall. "Oo-Rahg, how many did you kill?" he asked.

"Two."

"As did I. But I saw five. Where is the fifth?"

Oo-Rahg shrugged. "What does it matter? It's just another dwarf. We'll find more to kill."

"Yes, but—"

Heedless of what Vran was about to say, Oo-Rahg marched through the cave entrance. He paid for his lack of awareness, as a stone struck him between the eyes. As he wiped blood from his brow, he heard taunting laughter and scurrying footsteps. He began to run blindly into the darksome cave, but Vran held him back.

"Wait! We have no light. How can you catch what you can't see?"

Vran reached into his sleeve and brought forth the tezbou. "I have an idea," he said. He tapped the tezbou on the head, and it opened its jaws wide. Its superheated tongue shot out, glowing red against the blackness of the cave mouth. "It may not be as bright as I would like, but any help is better than none." *The same statement could apply to Oo-Rahg,* Vran thought.

With the aid of Vran's reptilian torch, the pair proceeded into the cave. The meager illumination provided by the tezbou revealed a straight path slanting upwards. They saw no goblins or other obstacles to bar their way, but did any await beyond the edge of visibility?

Vran and Oo-Rahg strode forth. Many tunnels branched off from the main path. Oo-Rahg poked his head into one opening, but Vran pulled him back. "Let's not stray too far," he said quietly. "We could easily become lost."

The passage continued to ascend for some distance, then flattened out. Vran and Oo-Rahg examined their surroundings, but little could be seen in the dim light emanating from the tezbou's mouth. One look at Oo-Rahg was all he needed to see the caveman was growing impatient.

"Where are they?" Oo-Rahg said. "I came to fight!"

As if in response to his boast, a mass of burning cinders dropped upon him. Oo-Rahg howled with fury and jabbed at the darkness above him with his spear. Failing to impale any goblins, he dropped the weapon and attempted to scale the wall nearest him. He was unable to gain any footholds that would bear his weight. "Show yourselves, you weaklings!" he shouted. "Vran, lift me up!"

Before Vran could take a step forward, another flaming pile fell from the roof of the cave. Oo-Rahg's anger surged to unprecedented levels, and he pounded against the wall with his fists. The men heard a mischievous cackling from somewhere above them, which then receded.

Vran spotted a branch among the pile of burning detritus. He reached for it and handed it to Oo-Rahg. "This is long enough to make a suitable torch. Now, allow me to lift you up." Vran locked his hands together to form a stirrup. Oo-Rahg placed his foot in them, and Vran raised him.

"What do you see up there?" asked Vran.

"A tunnel near the roof. It's empty and too small for us to fit through. Damn those dwarfs!"

"They can't hide from us forever," said Vran, lowering Oo-Rahg.

The two fighting men continued their exploration of the caverns. The path twisted and forked many times, all the while the inclination increasing in barely perceptible gradations. Before long the two became lost, although Oo-Rahg was much less perturbed by this development than Vran. He would worry about finding his way back after breaking goblin bones and spilling wizard's blood.

The pathway narrowed, forcing the men to walk single file. Vran took the lead.

Shortly thereafter, he stumbled over a solid obstruction that had been placed on the path. Before he could rise, stones flung from further down the passage pelted him. Oo-Rahg hurled his spear into the blackness, his anger empowering his thews. A high voice shrieked in pain, and the next sound they heard was that of a body collapsing.

Vran and Oo-Rahg moved over the obstacle to investigate. A dead goblin lay sprawled on the cavern floor, the spear protruding from its chest. In one hand it clutched a sling.

"Luck was on our side for once," said Vran.

Oo-Rahg said nothing as he removed his spear from the goblin's body.

And on they went. They continued through the cavernous labyrinth, ever wary of goblins lying in wait. Even with their increased caution, they could not avoid every ambush, but such encounters were much less successful for the goblins. The two men left a trail of diminutive corpses in their wake. Yet the tactics of the goblins took their toll, for Vran and Oo-Rahg suffered from a number of cuts and contusions.

Further and further they wandered, higher and higher they climbed. The two men lost all sight of anything but their war against the goblins and Misjak. With single-minded mania, they sought out and destroyed every denizen of the mountains they could find.

Many hours after the hunt had begun, Vran and Oo-Rahg discovered one of the goblins' dens. And then there was a slaughtering the likes of which had not been seen before!

Dozens, if not hundreds, of goblins swarmed against the invaders. Vran's sharp sword of steel tore through body after body, severing limbs and necks, releasing showers of blood. Oo-Rahg felt his spear was too cumbersome to use against such a mass of opponents and fought barehanded. With savage ferocity, he pummeled his foes. A skull cracked or a neck snapped every time he swung one of his great fists.

The goblins fought boldly in defense of their lair. They clung to Oo-Rahg's arms and legs in a vain attempt to pull him down, but in his maddened state he easily overpowered them. Some goblins threw hard stones at the two men, but in the chaotic whirlwind of battle, few hit their targets. Those that did, Vran and Oo-Rahg simply shrugged off. After hours of frustration, now that they could finally unstopper their rage, their soreness and hurts ceased to impede them.

Oo-Rahg clutched one goblin by its throat and hurled it into a mass of its fellows, knocking them prone. Some did not rise. But still countless ones remained, and the battle continued unabated.

One particularly nasty goblin dug its claws into the caveman's crotch. Oo-Rahg uttered a bestial ululation and drove his thumbs into the goblin's beady eyes. It squealed horrendously but would not release its grip until the life left its body.

A moment of clarity came to Vran as he struck down another enemy. Vaguely he had wondered why the goblins would not retreat, but now he realized that flight was not possible for them. This cave only had one exit, and two powerful fighting men stood before it. This knowledge renewed his passion for combat, and many more goblins perished on his blade.

As was inevitable, before long few goblins remained standing on that cavern floor which was now carpeted with corpses. As Vran's sword pierced the throat of his last opponent, his berserk bloodlust began to pass from him. He looked around and saw only two goblins were engaged with Oo-Rahg. The caveman picked up one and dashed its brains against the cavern wall. He grabbed the other, intending to do the same, but Vran stayed his hand.

"What—? What—?" said Oo-Rahg barely articulately.

"That's the last one alive. Don't kill it!" said Vran.

"Why not?"

"We need it—to lead us to Foad Misjak."

Chapter VIII
Blood Runs From the Altar

Midnight drew near. Foad Misjak paced the chamber of sacrifice, anxious for Twar to arrive with the maidens whose souls were to be delivered to Andortiuxpyl. A bonfire raged at the far end of the cave. Around it, Misjak had drawn the requisite arcane markings as best he could manage. Everything was in perfect readiness for the ritual to begin—with the exception of the maidens themselves.

The wizard's patience began to erode rapidly. He was about to seek out his henchman Twar and demand an explanation for his tardiness when five village girls entered the cavern, escorted by Twar and his troop of goblin guardsmen. Misjak exhaled in relief.

"You were nearly late, Twar," scolded Misjak. "Any later and Andortiuxpyl would have demanded your soul as recompense." Twar attempted a lengthy apology, but Misjak silenced him with a wave of his hand. "Be quiet. I must begin the ritual."

Foad Misjak closed his eyes for a moment, preparing his mind for what was to come. After sufficiently girding himself, he uttered the ancient invocation to summon the demon from his horrible realm on the distant moon Uzz. As he spoke the words, the smoke from the fire arose and contorted into a ghastly configuration. A pale face emerged—first, the elongated jaw appeared, then the misshapen fang-filled mouth. The miniscule nose, the beady eyes, and finally the singular ibex horn completed the abominable countenance of Misjak's patron demon.

The maidens, looking upon the visage of Andortiuxpyl for the first time, were overawed by its grotesqueness. Some turned away, intending to flee, but a quick prodding from the goblins' spears put an end to that plan. Resigned to their awful destiny, all the cave girls but Olo wailed hopelessly. As a chieftain's daughter, she believed it was required of her to maintain her composure even in circumstances so dire.

The disturbing laughter of Andortiuxpyl reverberated throughout the cave. "Foad Misjak, I see five maidens before me. You have done well."

"Thank you, my lord," said Misjak.

"They are all virgins, are they not? I specified virgins."

"They are."

"Good, good. The souls of innocent maidens are most delectable. They respond to torture in a way that satisfies me like nothing else. Begin the sacrificial rites."

The goblins pulled one young maiden toward the stone altar. The spirit of resistance arose within her, and she struggled against her captors.

"This will not do," said Andortiuxpyl. "Girl, look upon me."

The girl, her own will held in abeyance by the demon's command, turned her head toward him. Andortiuxpyl's eyes began to alter, first turning bright orange, then blue like tundra ice. In rhythmic pulses, the demon's eyes alternated between these two colors. Hopelessly mesmerized, the girl no longer fought against the goblins. She allowed them to strip her of her furs and place her upon the altar. The expression on her face was as lifeless and cold as the stone on which she lay.

Misjak approached the altar. His knife punctured the soft, delicate flesh between the girl's breasts. He withdrew the blade slowly, not wanting to get any of the sticky crimson substance on his robes, for he felt a phobic revulsion for the bodily fluids of women. A ghostly silver light began to emanate from the girl's entire body, then vanished in a flash. From the oozing wound in the girl's chest arose a silver radiance of mercurial shape. This radiance whirled around the head of the demon, its manner almost playful, before Andortiuxpyl sucked it in through his nostrils. The demon's eyes rolled back in ecstasy.

"Yes, yes…" Andortiuxpyl moaned. "This is good. I would have another."

The four remaining girls were still under the hypnotic spell of the demon. Twar grabbed the hand of one and led her to the altar. She moved sluggishly, like a som-

nambulist. Twar forced her to lay down next to the corpse of the previous victim. The girl demonstrated no sign of sentience, no will of her own.

Once more Misjak's knife swept down. Once more it rose, dripping with the blood of a virgin. And once more an innocent girl's soul was torn from her, to become a plaything of a sadistic Uzzic demon.

Andortiuxpyl was delighted, but not yet satisfied. His eyes aglow, he called for another sacrifice. The corpses on the altar were cast aside to make room for more victims.

Twar approached the maidens, debating which one should be the next to die. He considered Olo, but then said to her, "I will save you for last, my lovely." If the goblin's statement produced any emotion within her, she did not show it.

A third victim was slain upon the altar, then a fourth. They died quietly, too stupefied by the demon's magic to be cognizant of their fate. Misjak felt a twinge of annoyance because of this. A ritual sacrifice lacking the terrified screaming of victims made for a less enjoyable experience.

Two more souls departed their bodies of flesh and were consumed by the demon. The disordered fangs and tusks of Andortiuxpyl's horrid mouth twisted into something resembling a grin.

"Are you pleased, my lord?" asked Foad Misjak.

"I am, I am… but you promised me five virginal souls. Give to me the final one I am owed."

"Twar, do as our lord commands," said Misjak.

Twar cleared away the dead bodies from

the altar as if they were ordinary litter. He then took Olo by the hand, brought her to the altar, and bade her lie down upon it. After tearing away her fur garments, the goblin stared at her nude form lasciviously. He began to grope her breasts. Olo, still mesmerized, offered no resistance to any of this.

"Twar!" shouted Misjak. The wizard slapped his lackey across the face with the back of his hand. "Stop that! I told you that you could have her *after* the ritual!"

Twar turned away in shame, wiping drool from his mouth. "I'm sorry," he said guiltily. "I couldn't wait."

"I can't wait to be gone from this foul world and the incompetent buffoons which populate it!" said Misjak.

"Stop this bickering," bellowed Andortiuxpyl. "The maiden's soul—give it to me!"

"No—give her to me!" came a shout from outside the chamber of sacrifice.

All heads (except Olo's) turned to see Vran and Oo-Rahg, weapons drawn. The caveman also held a goblin under one arm, which he hefted and hurled at Misjak. The wizard dodged adroitly, and the goblin crashed against the wall. It fell to the floor in a heap, the bones in its neck shattered.

Misjak had not expected to see Vran again so soon. Thinking quickly, he rushed to the altar and placed the knife at Olo's throat. "You want the girl, eh, Vran?" he yelled. "Make no move, or she dies!"

At this commotion, Olo began to stir. "Vran...? Oo-Rahg...?"

"Release her!" said Vran as he entered the chamber. "Or we'll—what the—?" Vran halted, having taken notice of the infernal apparition hovering above the flames.

"The girl is mine," said Andortiuxpyl, laughing horribly. "She will die no matter what—as will you, if you attempt to interfere."

Oo-Rahg, bewildered and confused by the appearance of the demon, resorted to his usual tactics when confronted by a foe. He flung his spear at Andortiuxpyl, but the missile passed harmlessly through the demon's smoky visage.

The demon laughed his terrible laugh, like a tremor rumbling through the catacombs of Hell. Andortiuxpyl's prehensile tongue shot out from his disgusting mouth and imprisoned Oo-Rahg. He struggled to break free, but the demon's hold on him was stronger than chains of steel.

"I promised you interference would result in your death," said Andortiuxpyl with perfect articulation, in spite of the fact that his tongue encircled a large human being. "I will add you to my menagerie of sorrowing souls as well." An enervating feebleness came over Oo-Rahg, and he dropped to his knees. His eyes rolled back in his head, and his body went limp. Vran swung his sword at the tongue, hoping to sever it, but the blade passed through it just as Oo-Rahg's spear had. Thinking the demon had some sort of immunity to man-made weaponry, Vran tried to clutch the tongue with his hands in a bid to tear its coils away from the caveman, but this attempt was equally ineffective. The tongue was somehow immaterial to him while simultaneously tangible to its victim.

An argent effulgence appeared around Oo-Rahg, and began to sluggishly flow along the demon's tongue, up to the grotesque mouth. It moved slowly, as if it were resisting, but, as was inevitable, it reached Andortiuxpyl's cracked lips. He retracted his tongue and swallowed Oo-Rahg's soul. The caveman's lifeless body collapsed. Olo was still dazed from the demon's hypnotic magic, but was cognizant enough of what had transpired to weep tears of pity.

Vran stood transfixed during the ordeal, partly from awe, and partly because he was grimly aware that he could do nothing to prevent the terrible fate of his comrade-in-arms. He stared at Oo-Rahg's body. It had fallen with the head turned toward Vran. He felt as if the look on Oo-Rahg's face, twisted into a rictus, was one imploring him for help.

For a moment, all remained silent. Misjak's cackling broke the still. He and Twar stood beside the altar, the other goblins surrounding him. "See, fool?" he said shrilly. "See what befalls those who cross the great Foad Misjak?" He turned toward Andortiuxpyl. "Do away with him as you did the other, and then the ritual can proceed."

The demon snorted. "You give me orders now, Foad Misjak?"

"Er, no, but—" the wizard stammered.

"Perhaps I do not want to kill this man. He could serve me well."

"Serve you!" said Vran, astonished.

"Yes. You are quite resilient," said Andortiuxpyl. "The fact that you stand here before me is proof. A lesser man would not have been able to throw off the effects of the spell of paralysis. You could be useful to me."

"I swore an oath to destroy your creature Foad Misjak," said Vran defiantly. "I will not serve you and become ally to him."

"Misjak is not essential to me," said the demon. "I could be convinced to replace him."

"*What?*" squealed Misjak. "After all I've done for you? After all the souls I've provided? You would abandon me?"

"Silence, wizard," said Andortiuxpyl sternly. "Let Vran speak. Vran, I would cast aside Misjak, the object of your antipathy, if I could find one who can serve me better. If I withdrew my protection you could easily slaughter him, as you so greatly desire. But tell me, Vran, should I do this?"

Vran hesitated before answering. Never before had he bargained with a demon, and he had believed never would he do so. But Andortiuxpyl's offer was tempting. He had much to gain, and, he was forced to admit, little to lose. If he refused, he would die ignominiously as Oo-Rahg had. The alternative, being allowed to slay Misjak, was preferable. Then maybe the demon would transport him to Nilztiria, for he had no other way of returning.

"If I offered myself to you, would you let Olo go free?" asked Vran.

"The girl is dear to you? Hmm… I suppose."

"Very well. I accept," said Vran without pride.

"No!" shouted Misjak. "My lord, you cannot—"

"Be silent!" snarled Andortiuxpyl. "Vran, you misunderstand me. I must be *persuaded* to replace my loyal minion. Why should I? Think hard, for your life—and your soul—depends on it."

Now Vran was faced with a quandary. What argument could he put forth that would be convincing? In his heart, he had no desire to become thrall to a demon. But he must contrive something in order to save his own life—and hopefully Olo's as well. He searched his memory for some scrap of an idea that would be useful to him now. Recalling the speeches made by windy politicians and legislators he had heard in Desazu, he employed the time-honored tactic of slandering his opponent. But in this case, he would not need to stretch the truth much.

"Foad Misjak is a physical weakling unworthy of serving a great and terrible entity such as yourself. Why, he cannot even restrain helpless maidens on his own! He requires the assistance of goblins to subdue them. Furthermore, he is a degenerate sexual deviant, which makes him, like all of his kind, mentally unsound and untrustworthy. I have no such glaring flaws. In addition—"

"Enough!" cried Misjak. "I can take no more of these calumnies! Andortiuxpyl, I implore you, ignore the vile lies of this beast called Vran! Torture him instead!"

"I'll torture *you*, you disgusting—" Vran's threat was cut off by what sounded like an intense thunderclap, but was actually the roaring laughter of Andortiuxpyl echoing throughout the cave.

"Ho ho, this is rich entertainment!" said the demon. "But I must admit I was merely jesting with you both. I have no intention of replacing you, Misjak—at this time. Vran, to see you squirm and sweat, desperate to save your life—ah, what exquisite drollery! My genius in the art of comedy astounds even myself."

Vran became incensed. "Why don't you appear in the flesh, coward, and we'll see who laughs then! I'll tear that ridiculous horn from your head and shove it down your throat!"

"I think not. Vran, I grow weary of you. Momentarily I will extirpate you, but first, you can watch the girl die. Misjak, you may proceed with the sacrifice."

By this time Olo had completely regained her mental faculties. Misjak thrust his dagger at her heart, but she managed to clutch his wrist with both hands, the blade's point hovering mere inches above her chest. Vran charged, swinging his sword at the wizard's neck, but the goblins raised their spears to parry the blow. The steel glaive shivered the spears into a multitude of fragments. With the goblins impeding his way to Misjak, Vran had no alternative but to cut through them. His sword rose and fell, its cruel kiss taking a life or severing a limb with each swipe.

While Vran hacked the goblins apart, the struggle between Misjak and Olo continued. Twar came to his master's aid and dealt a forcible blow to the girl's face. Dazed, she lost her grip on Misjak's wrist. With maniacal fervor the wizard drove the knife between Olo's breasts. The girl gasped as her lifeblood spurted out from the gaping wound.

Upon witnessing the cave girl's death, Vran felt a surge of extreme anger, which quickly turned to paralyzing horror. Misty, silvery strands rushed forth from Olo's body like a cosmic river. Andortiuxpyl snorted, drank deep of the girl's essence. At first, his countenance bore a pleased expression, as it had while he consumed the souls of the four previous misfortunate ones, but suddenly grew sour.

"Faugh! Faugh! This girl is no virgin! Misjak, you *lied!* You lied *to me!*"

The accusation took Misjak by surprise. Knowing a refutation would be futile, the wizard elected to take a chance and attempt a spell that would banish the demon back to Uzz. He was aware the odds of success were not favorable, but he had no other means of evading Andortiuxpyl's wrath. He enounced the mystical words of the incantation, but in his haste to save his neck, forgot about his proximity to Vran.

Instantly the chamber surged with arcane energy. A pool of some murky, ink-like substance began to well around the ankles of those who still lived (which at this point numbered only Vran, Misjak, and Twar). With supreme suddenness, the level of the darksome liquid rose and gurged, submersing the men and the goblin. Just as abruptly as the churning waters appeared, they sank, as if through a large drain. When they had completely dispersed, nothing remained in the room apart from the horrible visage of Andortiuxpyl. The demon blinked twice, then chortled.

"Serves Misjak right for deceiving me," said Andortiuxpyl. "The next time he calls on me, begging forgiveness, I will be too occupied with my new playthings to answer." With that, the demon vanished back to his castle on Uzz.

Vran's adventure continues in the Fall issue of Cirsova!

D.M. Ritzlin is a Chicago-based author/publisher. He writes fantasy tales which mix action, horror, wonder, and gallows humor in varying degrees. His first collection of stories, Necromancy in Nilztiria, *was released in October 2020. Ritzlin also owns and operates DMR Books, the leading publisher specializing in sword-and-sorcery fiction.*

Orphan of the Shadowy Moons (Part 2)

By MICHAEL TIERNEY

The Black Assassins have slaughtered all the children of the Worldlord except Strazis, the strange golden child he adopted as his heir! Strazis's escape strands him on a mysterious isle as the Worldlord goes to war to secure the fragile empire!

Chapter Eighteen
Running With the Wavana

Strazis crept stealthily behind the bush, watching as a wavana stepped cautiously into sight on the other side of the glade where a tall, four-legged herbivore called a feera was obliviously grazing in the center of the glade. With long legs that testified to the power with which they could leap, the feera were considered to be a prize feast wherever they had not yet been hunted to extinction. On the unknown land Strazis had discovered, they still roamed in huge flocks.

The moment the feera caught a glimpse of the wavana, it instantly bolted in the opposite direction—where Strazis lay in wait.

Jumping from cover at the last instant, Strazis projected the creature's flight perfectly and whipped his hand past its neck, slashing it with his Assassin's blade. The creature bounded only a short distance away before its legs wobbled and it fell dead to the ground.

Strazis slung the body over his shoulder and carried it back to the grove of trees where the rest of the wavana pack would be waiting to feed.

Although they always avoided him whenever he made a fire and cooked his meat, the wavana were certainly willing to partake of the resulting feast. Their willingness to take him into their pack seemed completely uncanny and without reason to him. He had never read about such a thing happening before. For a time, he wondered if there might be some human master somewhere on the island, but none ever manifested.

Then he made a startling discovery.

He could communicate with the wavana.

It was not a language of words, but they seemed to understand his meaning from the emotion and tones with which he spoke. Soon, he too could recognize the wavanas' intent from the varied pitch of their growls and howls, finding himself baring his teeth and snarling right back at them. In this manner, he was able to coordinate their hunts.

Strazis soon found that he had no complaints about his new lifestyle. In fact, he had no thoughts of changing it, having

already accepted that he had no way to escape from the island. As he learned from the wavana how to live with nature, there was no more need for proud titles and well-trained armies. A strong body and quick wits were all he needed to satisfy his needs, and after his unpleasant experiences on Kalikantari, he no longer desired human companionship. He had found paradise.

Only one thing bothered him.

What had happened to the large wavana with white fur that he had seen on the beach? He had never seen that creature again.

Had the creature been a figment of his fevered imagination?

Chapter Nineteen
The Avenue of Trees

Before the main assault on Tyle could take place, another courier brought news that caused a pause as abrupt and unexpected as when the war had started.

A strange, unmanned craft had landed on Issandra, carrying baskets filled with the severed heads of the children of Eagal Ir Radin, as well as every other person on Kalikantari when it fell.

Since the slain were offspring from each of the Teluchi Islands, the leaders declared a truce in order to conduct a holy ritual and guide the departed into their next incarnation.

Masses of armies surrounded the waters of Issandra as their leaders gathered on an open plain outside the capital of Issandra, where graves had been dug in two straight rows, with mourners surrounding all but one. The wooden caskets that were lowered were pitifully small, making the ceremony feel more grotesque than honorable. Sapling trees were then planted into the dirt piled over each grave, creating an avenue of trees down which mourners could stroll and remember their sorrows over those who were lost.

Platitudes were respectfully offered by all except Told Maton of Tyle, who was conspicuously absent for his daughter's funeral.

The next day saw only two figures walking the short avenue under a hot, midday sun. The avenue was constructed as a dead end, with the end far from the city having been planted with a cluster of trees over where the caretakers' heads and the jaws of the terhali had been buried.

"The roots of these trees," Eagal Ir Radin said to Dextran Taa Constous, "will entwine with the remains of my children once the caskets have rotted away, and their spirits will fill the trees with their souls."

"I saw there were caskets for both Phaedra and Strazis," said Dextran. "His gravesite was the most obvious because there were no mourners standing over it. That was a wise secret to keep. Stop the rumor mongers before they start. Thank you. But their bodies weren't found on Issandra."

"Why would they have been kept prisoner?" asked the Worldlord.

"Neither was a treaty child of yours, so they were both most likely fed to the terhali."

Both men stopped walking and stood for a moment in somber silence.

"I hear that you've already promoted Eirlik to the command of a whole division of warriors," said the Worldlord. "Are you certain he's ready for that kind of responsibility?"

"He has to be. The Nameless Ones have marked our lands for conquest."

"But who are they? Where do they come from? All we know is that they're trying to break our alliance apart. We can't let that happen, no matter what." Eagal Ir Radin gripped the weathered hilt of his sword, with anger glinting in his eyes. "If we need to, we'll start the Worldquest all over again!"

Chapter Twenty
The City of Obsidian

Strazis relaxed on the high cliffs overlooking the emerald seas churning below. Without a care in the world, he dangled his legs over the edge and let the winds wash over him. How long he had lived this way, he had no idea. He had made no attempt to keep time, and that concept had lost all meaning to him.

His survival after swimming with the terhali had washed away all fear of death, leaving him with only a determination to embrace every day of life. He returned to the sea each day; the ocean waters still called to him as had the training cove where he learned to control a skier. Now he often swam with schools of fish in the tidal coves, spearing dinner with his knife tied to a stick. The sea became his second home, as familiar as the island woods where he ran with the wavana. He was truly in communion with nature, having observed and learned the ways of all the fishes and animals.

In his time that some might call isolation, his body had matured and blossomed. Constant contact with the sun had darkened his skin into a deeper, radiant bronze color, while living life in the raw had strengthened and toned every muscle in his body. His reflexes, always faster than anyone else, were now too fast for an eye to follow.

At night he slept in the grassy swards with his pack of wavana. Never had he felt so contented and happy. He thrilled to every day's new discovery of nature, and never missed human companionship... or so he thought. But on some days he experienced a feeling of melancholy that disturbed him. These were usually followed by nightmares about the fall of Kalikantari and the death of Tanith Woanan. On other days they followed dreams of Phaedra's enchanting beauty, from which he awakened to the certainty that she had perished on Kalikantari. These dreams spawned a cycle of emotions, usually filling his daydreams with fantasies of confronting Gaebel. No matter what he tried, he could not break free of this cycle that recurred ever more often.

Then one night an image from his dreams came with his first waking thought of realization. He had always been so distracted by his revenge against the Assassin who had killed his beloved Tanith Woanan, that Strazis had barely looked at Gaebel when he gave the death signal. For some reason, that image kept pushing itself ever more prominently into his thoughts, until he finally understood why. Around Gaebel's neck had been a golden chain that held a round object beneath his leather chest plate, the protrusion of which created an impression in the same shape as Strazis' own medallion.

He marked the name and face of Gaebel, which became emblazoned even more firmly into his consciousness.

Now he sat on the cliffs and regretted that he had never had the chance to thank Phaedra properly for coming to his rescue, and he wondered if he might ever have the chance to take revenge for her death.

Having thoroughly explored his current range of the island, Strazis began to grow bored and, with no challenges left to meet, turned his eyes inland.

When he had recently ventured deeper inland than ever before, he had glimpsed what he thought were the tops of spires similar to those Eagal Ir Radin had once showed him rising out of the ocean waters. Before he could investigate, the wavana had blocked his way, growing increasingly nervous and short-tempered. One had knocked him down while another dragged him away by his feet. This behavior had sparked his curiosity.

He set off inland along a high ridge that he knew the wavana never frequented. At this altitude only the grasses that carpeted the land and a few shrubberies could reach above the outstretched arms of the trees. The grass felt comfortable on his calloused feet, his scandals having long since been worn to discarded scraps of leather that were greedily gnawed by the wavana. His tunic had been shredded so many times that barely enough was left to wind as a loincloth around his private parts, while the golden locks he never bothered to trim flowed down past his shoulders.

Far away a wavana howled, but Strazis ignored it. They would not begin the hunt until dusk, when their bellies began to ache.

His absence would not be noticed until then.

He scampered up a rocky escarpment that led inland. It was a more dangerous route, but far quicker than following the sloping valley. Reaching the top, he looked down into the inner bowl of the island and knew the trip had been worth his time.

Below was a black city with basaltic outer walls and buildings with spires constructed from obsidian glass that rose high into the air.

Strazis ran with reckless abandon down the gravelly slope and leaped to scale the outer wall that circled the city, rather than take the time to look for an entrance. Standing atop it, he soon saw where several sections of the wall had fallen away.

It was the spires that commanded his attention. Here he found a new wonderland of mysteries to explore, and it filled him with excitement.

He hopped down onto an unusual basaltic causeway that ran straight to one of the spires. To his disappointment, he found nothing but more causeways leading to other spires. There were no artifacts or any other signs of habitation. He could see no ground anywhere—the spaces between the causeways and the spires were chasms with no apparent bottom. The whole city was totally alien to anything ever discussed in any book. Even the ancient watery towers that had been explored by island scholars were nothing like these. These were something unique. It was as though the island had raised the basaltic walls and causeways in protest to the spires that had sprouted from its center.

The rubble of decay was everywhere, and

several of the spires appeared ready to collapse, supported only by their crowded proximity with each other. Common sense steered him away from these, until he found one standing free at the center of the city, which looked fairly intact.

The exterior walls were covered with a profusion of undecipherable hieroglyphics. Strazis took a seat to study them, fully aware that they would be impossible to interpret. Then, when he was about to concede defeat, from somewhere deep inside the spire he heard a faint noise, like an echo trying to mask its own sound. He was at the same time tempted to investigate, and filled with an understanding about how a feera must feel when baited into a trap.

Strazis forced himself to rise and walk away.

Chapter Twenty-One
The Madness of Rymeso Coana

Strazis moved along the surface of the water like a fish basking in the sun, then inverted and used gravity to glide slowly into the depths of the tidal pool. He had mastered the watery realms so effectively, he could remain underwater for incredibly long periods of time, his youthful lungs already well-trained from years of practice. While he was certain that he could hold his breath longer than any other islander, such things no longer seemed important to him—most of his memories about Kalikantari were slowly fading away.

The depths of the water cooled his body until he decided to return to the surface, shooting up rapidly like a terhali about to strike its prey. Exploding onto the surface, he decided to float awhile, unable to stop

his mind from wandering back to the hieroglyphics he had seen in the obsidian city. He could recall what he had seen as if it were still before him. The hieroglyphs had utilized images contained one within another, rolling from one grouping to another with a flow that appeared to run from top to bottom, in lines from right to left. The only images that Strazis was certain about were arrangements he had once studied on stellar charts. But unlike in the books he had read, these stars did not circle the world, indicated by an image that had been used to represent the lands inhabited by every island culture. In the hieroglyphs, the world circled in a cluster like any other stellar object. This was a very controversial concept that had been the subject of many heated debates—especially from the worshippers of the Moon Gods, who considered it heretical thinking.

Strazis saw in those stellar alignments what he was certain to be the moon Strazis, prominent and repeating often throughout the hieroglyphics.

When the tide raised the tidal cove level to where a terhali might gain access, Strazis began kicking his way to the shore.

He then began to wonder if there might be a verbal cadence to reading the emblems covering the obsidian spires and decided to make another visit to the city.

As he passed through the wavana pack lounging in the shade along the shore, one looked up with disappointment to see that he carried no fresh fish, and then dropped back to sleep.

Soon, Strazis' calloused feet were back on the same causeway he had walked during his first visit to the obsidian city. But after one look at the exterior of the spire, it had lost all mystery to him, and he decided to explore deeper—to go inside this time.

The interior was lighted by openings higher up along the exterior, and he immediately saw things that should not be there. Scattered about the floor were the unidentifiable bones of dead animals, all of them having been cracked open for the marrow within. He noticed the many tracks of human feet in the dust on the floor.

Strazis never saw the net when it dropped over him. His arms were instantly entangled and his hands unable to reach for his blade. Strazis let out the call of a wavana in distress, realizing that it was futile.

Then a blunt object crashed over his head.

Falling to the floor, it was easy in his stunned state for Strazis to feign unconsciousness as powerful hands dragged him deeper into the spire. The interior room where he was taken was vast, with no apparent ceiling. A gnarled man rapidly closing on old age grunted and strained as he maneuvered Strazis up and onto a platform in the center of the room.

When he realized that Strazis was still conscious, the old man began gesturing methodically as he gibbered in an unfamiliar language. It was not the language of the Black Assassins, but something else, completely unfamiliar.

"I do not understand you," Strazis said in the common tongue of the island servants.

The old man drew back, looking around as if there might be someone else in the room.

This gave Strazis the opportunity to look around himself. Light came from openings in the roof far above and down a shaft that ran the entire height of the spire. But other than the raised area where he lay, Strazis saw nothing besides more hieroglyphs etched on every wall.

The old man gnashed his teeth and finally responded to Strazis.

"Why do you not speak in your own tongue?" he asked clumsily. "I know you know it. I saw you reading the writings outside."

"I read it," said Strazis, "but did not understand it. Why did you attack me? I mean you no harm. Who are you?"

"I am Rymeso Coana," the old man replied with a fist thumping his chest. "Who are you?"

"I am called Strazis."

The old man seemed momentarily startled. Then he stepped forward and poked at Strazis' skin.

"Strazis, the Moon?" he asked. "You are a Moon Child?"

"I don't know what a Moon Child is. Why not let me go, so we can talk better."

Rymeso hesitated, then laughed and turned, hastily walking out of the room. He returned with a rickety stool.

"We can talk now." Rymeso took a seat. "I know every language there is, and there's still enough time. Your namesake will be rising early today."

"Enough time? Time for what?"

"I've seen many people, but you are the strangest yet," said Rymeso. "You look like the spawn of the Moon Gods, although I've never seen one with such brightly colored skin. When the gods mate with a human, they're usually paler."

"What do you know about Moon Gods?"

"I thought I just answered that," Rymeso seemed momentarily confused. "My people are from another planet, and for a time after we were brought here, we were plentiful. Then the Moon Gods made war and went away, leaving this world in ruins. Now Arendahj rules what was once my home. They wanted me to play in their games. My brother and I escaped the slave-keepers. They caught us, of course, but they were impressed by our ingenuity. Made us into slave-keepers, like them. That's how I escaped sacrifice to Neth and Nean and found my way here."

"I don't understand what you're talking about."

"Oh, you will," said Rymeso. "You and every person on this world will soon feed Neth and Nean. So many different races have been brought here to feed their hunger. They just plant you and wait until it's time for harvest."

"Are you telling me that there are other people beyond the islands?" Strazis asked.

"They are all over this world, and many worlds beyond this one," Rymeso gestured in a circle. Then he pinched the skin on his own arm. "Look at my flesh. Have you ever seen anyone so dark?"

Strazis shook his head. Where his own skin was bronzed, the skin of Rymeso Coana was blackened, like he had been roasted on a fiery spit.

"There are no others left on this world like me," said Rymeso, "I'm the last of my kind." Then he noticed the medallion around Strazis' neck and grabbed it, instantly able to trigger it to open. "Ah... it's inert. Just a shell. That's why you can't read or understand the writing outside. If I hadn't found one of my own, I wouldn't have been able to, either."

"What do you know about my medallion? What do you mean about it being a shell?"

"You got to keep these things hidden, or someone will take it away. You don't see me wearing mine!"

"You really believe the Moon Gods are a real thing?"

"It was long ago, when they beat their drums and marched in streaming lines to glory. None could stand before them. Wherever the Moon Gods passed, no other living creature dared to walk. Not even their own spawn that they called Men. It's said that they are only known as the Moon Gods on this one particular world. On other worlds, they are known by different names."

"You talk a lot but don't make much sense." Strazis had been continually trying to untangle his wrists in hopes of reaching for his blade, but was having no luck.

"The Moon Gods first came from beyond our own universe, from another that was dying. That's something Neth and Nean share with them; they consumed their own universe and now hunger for ours. That is why the Moon Gods made men in their image, to help fight off Neth and Nean. Of course, the worshippers of the elder gods would say men were always intended as nothing more than food for Neth and Nean. It all depends on who you ask. One legend says that a Moon God will open the cleft to unleash Neth and Nean, and another says that a Moon God will block the way. Who knows which is true? We only know that

Neth and Nean watch and hunger. And, of course, there are many other ways in which a world can be destroyed, so Neth and Nean want to feast before that happens."

Rymeso paused, watching the course of the fading light above.

"But none of that has happened yet, and you're the first person I've seen in some time. Sorry about that. Necessity always comes before glory!"

"You've convinced me of one thing," said Strazis. "That you're insane."

"Thank you," Rymeso replied. "Now, look up—see the Shadowy Moon you're named after? Moons are what always inspire men to travel to other planets!"

Strazis was surprised to see the Shadowy Moon of Strazis had risen into the center.

"I've seen worlds without moons," said Rymeso, "where life is still and stagnant—and men there are stagnant, too. Take away the moonlight, and it turns their souls dark. Now Strazis, gaze upon Strazis. It will be the last thing you see."

Rymeso Coana then began running about the chamber, touching the symbols along the walls in patterns, pausing from time to time to hum to himself before deciding which one to touch, bouncing back and forth from foot to foot as though in time with the beat of music only he could hear.

The surface of the once-cool obsidian beneath Strazis began to feel uncomfortably warm, which was completely illogical considering the time of day, and how the moon above offered only reflected light.

"Forgive me for cooking you," said Rymeso, "but this entire building is one giant battery and generator combined, and Strazis above is its source of power. I've never bothered to find out what this place was really intended for, but it is a great way to cook without a fire! I'm flipping just enough switches to slow roast you. Don't want to burn you to a crisp."

Strazis once again released the howl of a wavana in distress, his voice echoing up the shaft. He was certain that his situation was hopeless—he called out for the pack in a faint hope that they might avenge his death but knew they were too far away to hear.

"Now, now," said Rymeso. "That's enough of that. Cannibalism is a long and respected tradition. It's always best to cook your dinner while it's still alive. That way the juices keep the meat moist. What the...!?"

Crackling forces of energy had begun searing through Strazis' body, as though the tiny fishes of the sea were biting him everywhere at the same time, when he heard the ferocious growl of wavana on the hunt. A white form flashed through the gloom and pounced on Rymeso Coana. A moment later, the wavana's blood-stained jaws were dragging Strazis out from beneath the light of Strazis, quickly chewing through the straps that restrained him.

Breathing a sign of relief, Strazis was finally able to pull his blade and finish freeing himself. That was when he realized he was no longer being helped by razor-sharp wavana teeth, but instead by the shapely hands of a woman.

Strazis watched in awe as the woman stepped away from him, turned without a word, and headed for the exit. Her perfect, naked figure was amply formed, and she walked with a regal elegance that enhanced her presence.

Having no idea where she might have come from, Strazis looked about for the white wavana that had saved him, but it was nowhere to be found.

The woman paused at the exit.

"I had to save you," she turned said. Her face reflected the golden glimmer of the moonlight—a glimmer that Strazis at best could only equal. "Meeting you gave me hope that my daughter might still be alive... even if you don't believe it."

Strazise hurried to catch up to her.

"You're speaking in a language that Rymeso tried to use a little while ago," Strazis said. "I couldn't understand it then. But now I understand you easily. Why? How?"

"You're curious." She reached a hand for his. "That's normally a good thing, but right now we don't have time. Activating the machine will attract attention, so you have to leave the Isle of View."

"Is that what this place is called? Who are you?"

She smiled demurely and let his hand drop.

"Don't you know? Look at yourself, and then at me, and tell me what you see."

Strazis was slightly embarrassed to look at the strength and elegance of her unashamed bearing and the pride in her eyes. Then he blinked and found himself alone.

Blinking again in confusion, Strazis held his breath, listening for any sound. After a moment, he faintly heard her voice from outside the building.

"Escape may already be too late. But, whatever it takes, find my daughter. It is through you that I'll find her. This world is doomed, so learn how to carry the things you have discovered to another world."

By the time Strazis reached the exit, her voice had already faded. In the moonlight, he saw the white wavana watching him from atop the basaltic outer wall. She gave a yelp and then loped away up the slope and vanished over the edge of the ridge.

Chapter Twenty-two
Introduction to Arendahj

Chasing after the white wavana, Strazis sprinted down the moonlit slope, desperately trying to catch her before she entered the woods. That was when he heard a wild clamor coming from the direction of the shore and the distinct cries of dying wavana.

In a sudden bolt of speed, the white wavana disappeared into the darkened woods. Strazis was soon running madly through the trees, catching only the occasional glimpse of the wavana that steadily put more distance between them.

Strazis had lost all sight of the white wavana by the time he reached the beach, where he discovered the still forms of three dead wavana sprawled in pools of blood around the shredded form of what had once been a man.

The dead man was like none Strazis had seen before—tall and lean, with a skin that was a deep brown color. Lying next to the man was a metal instrument that he recognized. It was a portable cannon often used on newer skiers to fire metal projectiles in place of the liquid fire spewed by those of ancient design.

Then he heard sounds and saw the light of torches coming from the deep shadows of the woods he had just left. He whirled, instinctively raising a hand to shield his head at the same moment an unidentified object struck and knocked him to the ground. He had learned from previous experience that attackers always went for the head, while the wavana went for the neck.

As he had done with Rymeso Coana, Strazis feigned being stunned while several men emerged from the woods and approached.

"Good throw!" one man shouted in the language of the Black Assassins, which Strazis was now somehow able to understand.

"Was it? What have we got?"

"We've caught a were-creature; a wavana-boy."

"Quit talking fantasy," the thrower said. "Philandreas told us to collect anyone found. Look, he's still moving."

Strazis propped himself up on one arm, noticing how his attackers were dressed differently than the Black Assassins. Then he heard the wails from other wavana fighting in the woods. Strazis had lost one family to strange men invading from the sea, and now he was about to lose another.

Rising defiantly to his feet, Strazis drew his blade and prepared for a battle to the death.

"Hit him again," the thrower shouted to a man who ran for a metal discus lying not far away, but he was nowhere near fast enough. Strazis made a quick leap and slashed at his neck when he stooped.

Clutching the blood geysering from his throat, the sailor dropped the discus and sagged to his knees, his mouth voicing silent pleas for mercy until his eyes rolled backwards and he collapsed.

More invaders carrying torches poured from the woods to surround Strazis in a semi-circle, aiming their portable cannons. One of them held a strange device in front of his face.

"Time to go!" he shouted. "Let's leave before any more creatures attack. Take that boy prisoner, and we'll have everything we came for. I've gotten the readings we were looking for. Now all we need to do is report them, and this place becomes someone else's problem."

With the wild snarl of a wavana, Strazis flung himself amidst the invaders before anyone could fire their cannon. His knife flashed at the soft spots between their armor, and blood filled the air until the hammering of gauntleted fists finally beat him back down into the sands. When he tried to rise, several boots stamped down on his chest, and a hand cannon was leveled at his face. Several others knocked his knife away while his hands were bound.

Once again, Strazis had a metal rod inserted into his mouth and secured behind his head with leather straps. This time his hands were bound as well. Dragged aboard a vessel of familiar design, Strazis was taken below and locked in a metal cage without enough room even to stand. Having lived so long with the wild abandonment of nature, the stink inside the cargo hold overwhelmed him.

When the ship began to move, he heard the mournful wail of a distant wavana.

Strazis curled himself into a fetal ball and tried to relax the racing of his blood as the long night slowly passed. The sun was high before he was finally removed from his cage and led to the upper decks, where his leather bindings were replaced by chains.

Because he had lain for so long in an uncomfortable position, his legs ached when he walked, causing him to limp. This in turn fired the imaginations of his captors, who whispered suspicions to one another that he was a shape-shifter.

Led to the forward deck, Strazis saw that they were approaching a mass of land far larger than any he had ever seen before—stretching from one edge of the horizon to the other.

"Welcome to Arendahj," a sailor said sarcastically, certain that Strazis had no idea what he was saying.

As the ship powered its way up the river delta, Strazis was spellbound by the sights of long sandbars, inhabited by all sorts of birds and creatures he had never seen before. Then a fantastic bridge passed directly over his head, and he turned to see the foreboding city that was their destination.

They soon passed an island in the center of the river, where a large rock had been engraved with the image of a door, while all around it, heavily scented fires burned.

Finding the oddly carved rock of little interest, Strazis looked instead at the spired buildings passing on both sides. The residents he saw there were few and looked gaunt, while naked slaves followed them through the paved streets. Then he saw what he determined by the refinement of their clothing to be the noble class, and snarled when he saw one of them abusing a naked woman chained to a post.

The man standing next to him smacked Strazis on the back of the head and ordered him to remain quiet.

Strazis gritted his teeth on the metal gag when the woman began being severely whipped.

The ship slowed to a stop next to a building with a cavernous mouth for an entrance right next to the dock. Though it was wide enough for a whole army to enter, only two men led Strazis off the ship and inside. There he was prodded, poked, strapped to a chair, and his face and head shaved. They burned what was left of his tunic and offered him nothing in return.

Guards then took a fresh grip on his gag-chain and led him down an underground tunnel and into a toilet-less room filled with other naked and bald men standing amidst their own filth.

Finally freeing Strazis of his gag and chains, the guards departed and locked the door behind them.

Standing defiantly alone, Strazis looked at the incurious men surrounding him. They were all different shades of white and brown, the lighter-skinner people being islanders, while others looked more like the Assassins who had captured him. Their eyes and expressions were all downtrodden.

After some time had passed, one man whose eyes still held a glimmer of hope approached Strazis.

"You were the last one," he said. "Any idea what they're going to do with us?"

Strazis shook his head.

"I guess we're finally about to find out," said the other man when one of the walls split down the middle and opened to reveal a dark hallway.

"Move it, slaves," barked a guard who appeared with several others. All the prisoners quickly stood and shuffled away. Behind them, they heard buckets of water being tossed to clean the room they had just left.

From the chattering of the prisoners as they were herded, Strazis learned how everyone else there had been captured in or around the city of Arendahj, and then stored in the holding cell until a certain quota was met. They were led into a brightly lit room where they would be tested to decide what duties they would serve.

With hands shielding their eyes from the brightness of the light, the men were led onto a central stage surrounded by elevated balconies filled with seated observers. The guards stepped away, leaving them alone on the stage where several attractive women had been gagged and chained naked to beds.

"Praise Neth and Nean!" one man declared. "We're being tested for the stud farms."

Strazis turned his head away from the savagery that ensued, finding the whole proceeding perverse. He folded his arms and refused to watch, staring instead at the ghouls who leered from the balconies.

The two closest and most gaudily dressed observers pointed directly at Strazis and talked rapidly back and forth with a sense of authority. His eyesight having sharpened after trading long hours of reading books for life in the wild, Strazis found that he could easily read their lips in the new language he had recently absorbed.

"I don't believe it, Philandreas," said one man. "Do you think he knows?"

"Calm yourself, Ameron," the other replied, "of course he knows. No man would pass on the banquet we laid out unless he knew."

"Look at his skin. So that's the golden wild boy they found on the Isle of View?"

"Exactly," Philandreas replied. "That's where they found those readings we've been chasing after for so long. But that boy is no wild child. There's definitely an intelligence about him."

Having concentrated on watching the conversation, Strazis heard it before he saw it. First came the light moans and stiff cries of surprise, followed by ever louder screams of agony. Turning, Strazis saw all of the other men locked in states of copulation from which they could not withdraw, and the beds where they lay were turning crimson.

Masked assassins, who had entered the room with mallets in their hands, were staving in the heads of each couple.

Only the woman Strazis had left untouched was spared.

Strazis turned back to the spectators.

"That should show him our power," said Philandreas.

"Do you think we should tell him that we never intended to allow him to participate?" Ameron asked.

"No," said Philandreas. "Let him wonder in horror at the mysteries of our ways."

Strazis clenched his fists.

Chapter Twenty-three
The Testing

The guards ushered Strazis away from the carnage done to his fellow prisoners, marched him out the side door and down another long hallway. Moving walls and doors were everywhere, and he had a sense of hidden eyes watching his every step. This land of slavers had a very effective puzzle box security system, and he wondered how he might ever find an avenue of escape.

He was taken to a smaller theater room, and his chains were fixed to his chair in the center of the stage. A guard stood on each side of him when Philandreas and Ameron made their leisurely arrival in an overlooking balcony. This time they were the only spectators.

As the two men lounged in even greater comfort than before, Strazis' eyes were focused past them and on the balcony doorway they had left open behind them. Through the doorway, he could make out a door-lined hallway, through which beautiful women adorned in fantastic garments strolled with a casual gait, accompanied by clean and evidently well-cared-for slaves.

"A pleasure to meet you, Moon God," Philandreas said in the common tongue. "I hope this language is not too primitive for you, since I'm told the language of the Gods is far too complex for a mortal to comprehend."

Strazis knew that he was being taunted and decided not to react.

"I understand you," he replied in a monotone, emotionless voice.

"Good," Philandreas replied. "That will make this easier. I'm told you were captured on the Isle of View, where my men recorded some very interesting readings coming from the island's center. Are you the keeper of this place? I know you're no were-wavana. Who are you?"

"I am a son of the Teluchi Islands," Strazis replied. "I was lost at sea and washed up on that shore. Then your men

came and took me prisoner. There's nothing more to tell."

"I recently heard a story that the Worldlord of the Teluchi Islands had a son with skin like yours, and that no one knew who the mother was. He too was lost at sea."

A guard slapped the back of Strazis' head.

"I'm the son of a simple fisherman," he replied.

Ameron leaned forward.

"He admits that he comes from those savage islands ruled by a man who claims to be Lord of the World," he said to Philandreas. "They are as ignorant as inbred slaves. Will you allow me to test him?"

"Let me think about it," Philandreas replied. "Moon God, tell me your name—or die now."

A guard placed his bare blade next to Strazis' throat.

"Strazis," he replied.

"Just Strazis? Just 'The Unknown?' Nothing more?"

"Nothing more," Strazis replied.

The two men began whispering, each holding a hand to his face so that his lips could not be read. Strazis wondered if they had realized that he had that skill, and if it was because of simple intuition that he still knew they were discussing his fate.

Ameron motioned for one of Strazis' guards to leave the room.

"That's all the proof I need." Ameron kept his mouth covered. "He says he is named after one of the Shadowy Moons—a home of the Moon Gods."

"That could be a coincidence," Philandreas replied. "Lots of people are named after places and things."

Strazis heard the guard return when Ameron next addressed him.

"Tell me, Strazis," said Ameron. "Can you read hieroglyphics?"

The guard stepped in front of Strazis, carrying a carved tablet adorned with writing similar to what he had seen in the obsidian city, only this time their meaning was as clear to him as any book he had ever read. It told a story of a great migration from one universe into another.

"No," he replied, wondering how he understood the concept of what a universe was. "It's just pictures, isn't it?"

"This is a waste of time," Ameron declared.

"I have a solution," said Philandreas. "I owe you a debt from the last games. What say I give you this strange child as a down payment. You train him any way you want, and then we'll have him fight one of my men in the style of combat that the Teluchi Islands are known for. Double or nothing?"

"I don't know if I'd want to take that kind of chance on a fisherman's whelp that washed up out of the sea," Ameron hedged.

"Then put a qualifier on the bet," said Philandreas. "Decide first if he is worth the gamble. Give him a destroyed skier. If he can reassemble it, that might prove he's smarter than he pretends to be."

"It would," Ameron weighed the wager. "It would be valuable to find someone besides Gaebel who fully knows how to use those ancient skiers. Perhaps this slave could be useful."

At the mention of Gaebel's name, Strazis had to fight the urge to react, forcing himself to remain stony-faced as the guards led him out of the theater.

Again he was taken through an endless procession of tunnels with so many turns, cross paths, and rising and falling walls that even with his recall, he doubted that he could find his way back. Ever lower the tunnels led, until he was once again ushered into a small room.

The place was filled with what looked like random junk. Piles of useless-looking machinery were strewn about the walls and work tables.

Ameron was quick to enter behind them, and he instructed the guards to remove the chains. His whole demeanor had changed from before; no longer bantering with casual confidence, he was now rigid and intense, as though he were afraid of what might happen next.

"You don't have much time," he addressed Strazis. "You are now a slave of Arendahj, from which the only escape is through the satisfaction of your master. That's me. You're an investment that I will spend as I deem fit. Serve me well, and you'll be rewarded. Disappointment me, and it won't happen a second time. And realize this, you're one of the lucky ones. Most slaves never get the kind of pampering that I'm about to afford you. Make certain that I consider this to be a good investment. Do you think you can do it?"

"Do what?" Strazis looked about in confusion.

"This," Ameron gestured at the piles of junk. "Prove to me that you're smarter than you act. You said that you're a child of the island people. They ride skiers like this one once was. It's said your people regularly build new ones from the scraps of the old. What you see here was once a fully-functioning skier from the ancient days, not one of the newer builds. It was damaged when I lost a previous bet with Philandreas. It's taken me a long time to get back on the positive side of the ledger with him, and I don't intend to start going backwards again."

"I still don't understand what you want me to do," said Strazis.

Ameron's expression was one of exasperation.

"I want you to rebuild this skier! Make it functional and ready to ride again."

Strazis took a fresh look at the twisted pile of metal and worried that he was being asked to do the impossible.

"Do this," said Ameron, "or die. Guards, we'll need a larger escort to show him to his quarters."

Two more guards were summoned, and together they led the still unbound Strazis ever deeper beneath Arendahj, down gloomy halls lined with doorless cubicles crammed to overflowing with slaves.

"These halls are lighted by a system of mirrors that reflect the sun," said Ameron, "and it's getting late in the day, so we don't have a lot of time. At night it gets pitch black down here. You can move about freely down here, but be sure you're back at the workshop in the morning. That's where you'll be fed, and we'll get you some fresh clothing. You'll work there until dusk and then return to your room. Remember that we're always watching."

They stopped when the hallway came to a dead end, and Strazis was pointed to a small cubicle with an emaciated man lying crumpled on one of two cots.

"This is where you live now. I'm sure it's a lot better than what you had on that island. Remember what I've told you. Serve me well, and you'll be rewarded. Disappoint me..."

Ameron never finished his sentence. He turned and left with the guards.

Entering the gloom of his cell, Strazis pulled the single sheet and thin mat off the vacant cot, shaking them futilely until he took a sniff and decided to lie on the supporting mesh of chains.

"My name is Haflit," said the other occupant without turning to look.

"Strazis," was his only reply.

As soon as the room was enveloped in total darkness, an argument erupted from the cell next door. It seemed that a man's wife had been raped by a group of the other prisoners. The couple each blamed the other for it having happened.

"You didn't have to enjoy it!" her husband screamed.

Her outrage at his admonishment carried far into the night, long past the point where her husband had given up the fight.

Strazis was not sure which of them he pitied more, trying to block the voices out while he mentally tried to retrace his steps back and out of this nightmarish hole.

Chapter Twenty-four
Ameron Chooses a Slave

Having realized that Ameron and Philandreas were not fully in league with the Black Assassin named Gaebel, Strazis threw himself into his work. While the task at first looked daunting, he found a certain allure to the challenge, having always wondered how these ancient skiers were constructed. He also had an ulterior motive.

After spending most of the night trying to devise an escape route, he had realized that his situation was hopeless. However, if he were to find an opportunity to get a working skier on open water, then the only thing blocking his way would be the iron gates on every tributary flowing into the main river. But before he could devise a way around them, he first had to build the skier.

To Strazis, the room of parts was a complicated puzzle, which he immediately organized into sections. Each piece seemed to rely on another, and within a few days the disparate piles of machinery began to form into the outline of a skier.

It was the times when he was not working that were the worst for him. After his initial silence, Haflit had started rambling on endlessly into the night, gossiping about the intrigues and affairs that were happening throughout the slave pens. Strazis would eventually doze off while Haflit droned on, always wishing that he had never been taken away from his island paradise and thrown into the pits of Arendahj.

During his trips to and from his workshop, Strazis could see how the slaves had been organized into sections, with fresher, healthier slaves housed on the upper levels, while the infirm and weak were steadily moved down to the lower levels. It seemed to him that this arrangement was part of a systematic plan to deal with the chronic overcrowding by starving the older, weaker slaves, and constantly replacing them with fresh stock.

The level where Strazis stayed was right on the border between the two.

There was also a band of rogue slaves, run by a man named Cerry, who were rumored to be the last survivors of a colony that had been exterminated after being stricken by disease. They terrorized those assigned to the lower levels, stealing their food and any comforts they might still have. Strazis wondered if this might be part of some plan devised by Ameron and Philandreas to hasten the demise of the slaves who had become less productive.

Then one day, Ameron appeared in Strazis' workshop in what was apparently intended to be a surprise inspection, but it was Ameron who was surprised.

"By Neth and Nean," he exclaimed with a smile, "you're actually doing it! I'm starting to think that you might be a Moon God, after all."

"I am Strazis from the Teluchi Islands," Strazis said as he continued to work. The skier was taking shape well, but he worried that the engine might be missing. He found no means of propelling the craft or of supplying the cannons.

"Keep doing what you're doing," said Ameron. "I promised you a reward, and you're about to find out that I'm a man of my word."

Strazis stopped and looked Ameron directly in the eye.

"There is one thing I would like," he said. "When I was captured, they took a medallion away from me. I'd like to have it back. It was a gift from my parents."

"Fair enough," said Ameron, "but that's not the prize I had in mind. You'll get your medallion back when this thing moves on water, and not before. But for what you've accomplished so far... come with me."

A pair of guards escorted Ameron and Strazis back to the upper levels, but into a different section where the fresh slave women were being processed. Strazis was shocked to see island women being systematically stripped, branded, and led away in tears.

Ameron saw the reaction on his face.

"Your island women are a special treat around here," he said. "Spicy, but not too fiery. When you lived on the islands, didn't you ever notice how so many of them disappear all the time?"

"You kidnapped them with your Black Assassins?"

Ameron chortled.

"There are no Black Assassins," he said. "That's what your people call Gaebel's men whenever they raid your shores. But trust me, that man is a problem for more than just your islands."

Strazis empathized with the pain he saw on the face of every woman, regardless of her skin or where she came from. He made a silent promise to find a way someday to stop the scourge of Arendahj.

"Here," Ameron stopped in front of a cell where a naked woman was sprawled face down and unconscious. "Guard, how many of you have been with this woman?"

"All of us," the guard replied in a matter-of-fact tone. "Some a couple of times."

"When did she arrive?" Ameron asked.

"This morning. She's a pretty one. We were hoping to keep her here for a while."

Ameron shook his head and started to lead the way to the next cell, when an island girl was dragged past them with a fresh brand still steaming on her shoulder.

"Hold," he commanded. "Is she a new arrival?"

"As fresh as they get," said the guard.

"Perfect," said Ameron. "Strazis, this is your new companion. You'll still be sharing your room with Haflit, but I'll send down a bigger cot that fits two."

"I don't want a slave of my own," Strazis argued.

"You don't want a woman?" Ameron scoffed. "What's wrong with you?"

Before Strazis could say another word, the young woman in the grip of the guards looked at him with pleading eyes.

"Please," she gasped, "save me?"

Strazis nodded.

"Good thing," said Ameron. "I was about to put you under the knife. What's her name?"

Strazis looked closer at the island girl. She was many full cycles of the sun older than him, and far shorter, with dirty brown hair and a complexion that was unusually tan for island girls, who typically kept to the shade. She was not unattractive, but when he found himself comparing her face to Phaedra's, he immediately realized it was an unfair comparison.

"Her name is Sanina," replied one of the guards.

Allowed to leave his workshop early that day, Strazis was given time to spend with Sanina after she was delivered.

She did not talk much, and her eyes seemed downtrodden when she declared her willingness to serve her master in any and every way, thanking him for saving her from molestation by the guards.

"When they finally fed me," Sanina undid the waistband of her tunic and produced several morsels, and handed them to him.

Like all the food in the slave pens, there was no way to tell what it was, but it certainly looked better than anything he had eaten since arriving.

"I saved the best for you."

"I can't take that," Strazis replied. "It's your food."

"And I'm giving it to you," she replied with her first smile, followed by a frown. "Please don't insult me by not accepting it."

"Then I thank you in return." Strazis returned the smile and marveled at the taste. It was the best thing he had eaten since his arrival.

Afterwards, Sanina's face and behavior became coquettish when she took a few steps around the room and made a slow spin with her arms raised above her head, displaying the shapeliness of her body.

"You've thanked me... enough." Strazis hesitated when she dropped her tunic to the floor and reached for his.

Still a virgin, Strazis was not sure how to react. He had passed on previous opportunities with the servant girls on Kalikantari because his head had been filled with the tales of romance in the library's books, which told how chastity was ultimately rewarded with true love. Now the slave girl Sanina stood before him, having been freshly bathed and appearing far more attractive than she had before. After his long isolation on the island, when she began touching him in ways he had never experienced before, he quickly abandoned all resistance. In the gloomy and smelly slave pits of Arendahj, he learned lessons in lovemaking that no book had prepared him for.

By the time Haflit returned from his daily duties, Strazis and Sanina were both well enamored with each other's company.

"What is this?" Haflit complained. "Some new torture by making me have to watch you two?"

Strazis ignored him, as he and Sanina continued the process of getting to know each other. Then Haflit heard Strazis explain what he was doing in the workshop.

"You're going to kill us all!" he exclaimed. "Don't you know what happened to the last idiot they made work on one of those things?"

Having never discussed his work with Haflit before, Strazis was perplexed by his reaction and shook his head in response.

"I don't know the details," Haflit said, "but I know the results. There was an explosion that collapsed the whole inland section of slave burrows. That's why we've been so overcrowded down here!"

For the first time since the night Strazis had arrived, Haflit did not have a lot more to say the rest of the night.

That changed the next night, when Haflit stopped Strazis before he reached their cell.

"You should know that Cerry noticed your new mattress today," he said.

"Don't call her that," Strazis retorted.

"Don't say I didn't warn you whenever Cerry and his friends come for her. They've got knives now."

Strazis immediately wondered if it had always been Ameron's intent to give him a reward and then have it taken away.

It was a sleepless night after the husband in the next cell began complaining about his weeping wife having been raped again that day by Cerry's crew.

Chapter Twenty-five
Cerry and his Crew

The next morning Sanina was still asleep when a bleary-eyed Strazis prepared to follow Haflit out the door. He hesitated, worried about leaving her alone. Having no duties other than to serve him, there was nowhere else for her to go, and he had already been informed that he should never take her with him to the workshop.

When he entered the hallway, Strazis immediately noticed how all the chatter that typically filled the air had stopped. At the end of the hallway, he saw Cerry and his crew standing beneath the curved mirror that illuminated this section of the pits. Their focus was on him.

When Strazis reached the main junction that connected with the main hall, Cerry and his group immediately moved to circle him.

"I'm Cerry," the largest man with a face pock-marked by disease said while scratching an irritation around his crotch caused no doubt by an assortment of venereal infections. His teeth were decayed and pitted, his breath foul, and his eyes cruel.

Cerry held a hand to Strazis chest to block him from passing, which he had no intention of doing with Sanina sleeping unguarded behind him.

"You don't have to introduce yourself," said Cerry. "I know your name is Strazis. People say you claim to be some sort of Moon God. I couldn't care less. What I want to know about is that new girl, Sanina. Tell me, does she know how to show a man a good time?"

"Stay away from her," Strazis said in a firm, low voice.

"So you're going to be stingy? That's no way to make friends. As soon as you walk away, we're going down to your room and get to know her better. What do you think of that, butter boy?"

Strazis had tried not to react, but the threats were too overt and too obvious. None of the gang saw him throw the punch, it happened so fast. They only saw Cerry stagger backwards and sprawl unconscious to the ground.

"I've heard and seen too much rape while I've been here." Strazis unintentionally growled like a wavana.

Cerry's gang all backed away, a couple of them stooping to drag his body with them.

"If I ever hear of that word connected with any of you again, then we'll continue this conversation." Strazis looked into each of their eyes in turn.

In the days that followed, Strazis saw no sign and heard no talk about Cerry and his crew.

Chapter Twenty-six
Battle in the Dark

Ameron continued to drop by the workshop to check on Strazis' progress in assembling the skier. The majority of it had been reconnected or hammered back into place, but he still had the problem of figuring out how to power it.

In Kalikantari, to ride an ancient skier, one simply hopped on and went. No one knew how or why they worked, but they operated with a silky smooth elegance when compared to the shivers, noise, and smelly fumes created by the modern imitations built by islander engineers.

Strazis knew where an engine would go in a modern, chemically fueled skier: the same area from which all the operating equipment on the ancient version seemed to flow. He finished the construction, keeping the fittings that would access that area loose. When he was done, there was only one item left in the room, an object with a shape that might actually fit in the place that remained and connect to the power train: a box with a single glass lens.

He looked into the lens but saw only darkness inside. Shining the light from a welding torch, he thought he could see a pair of looping tubing. Nothing about it made sense to him.

Another mystery was that he had found no fuel tank or reservoir to supply the box. He rattled it and heard the tiniest drop of liquid hitting the sides. The concept of a fuel source that could also be an engine was something he had never read about in the Institute's library.

Much to Ameron's consternation, Strazis tore the skier back down to what he thought should be the engine compartment, and after a long reexamination, finally conceded that he had not interchanged any wrong parts. Connecting the box with the optic lens, with the lens aimed at the power train, he abandoned any hope of arming the cannons. He could see no place and no way to load the collection of stones he had been gathering for projectiles.

Stumped, Strazis knew the only other thing he could do was to test it on the water, and sent word to Ameron.

That night he hurried back to his cell before Haflit might arrive. As she had done every night since she arrived, Sanina had once again saved the best of her daily meal for him.

"There are some things that I need to tell you," he said, taking Sanina's hands in his. "One of two things might happen tomorrow. Either Ameron will have me killed, or, if I get the chance, I'll try to escape."

"You'll die if you try," she said. "No one has ever heard of anyone escaping from Arendahj. It can't be done. Please, don't leave me alone here."

"If I can get away, I'll come back for you."

"Then you'll just become a slave again." She shook her head and averted her eyes.

"No, I won't. I don't know how yet, but I'm going to put an end to this nightmare. I won't leave you to die. But there's no way to take you with me. Do you understand?"

Sanina continued to avert her eyes from his, and was sobbing softly on the cot when Haflit returned from his duties. He gave her a questioning look but received no explanation as Strazis sat with his back against the wall and closed his eyes. He needed all the rest he could get.

It took nearly the entire following day for a squadron of guards to compel a group of fresh slaves to carry the skier out of the workshop and up the maze of sloping hallways. They finally deposited it on a stretch of waterway where both the inlet and outlet were guarded by tall, iron gates. A stream of water drained from a pipe jutting out of a wall that ran along the opposite shore.

Once on the water, the skier floated as though it had never been disassembled. Holding his breath, Strazis climbed aboard. He sat for a long time before hesitantly grasping the controls.

The craft immediately responded and started to move.

Jubilant, Strazis made several loops that sent plumes of water flying but worried about doing too much since the box apparently only had a single drop of fluid left with which to operate. He was certain that it was nearly out of fuel. It was a determination that he knew he should not reveal.

Looking at the gates on either end of the waterway, Strazis realized that Ameron had chosen the test area well, and there was no possible avenue of escape. His mind wandered back to a story Tanith Woanan had told him about how, on the day he was born, the Worldlord had literally flown his skier above the surface of the water. It lent credence to the legends about how the ancient skiers were powered not by fuel but by the spirits of their operators, and how those with the most powerful spirits could actually command them to fly.

Strazis moored the skier to the shore, his work done.

Returning to his cell, Strazis discovered that the junction where his hallway connected to the main passageway was missing the mirror that illuminated the way.

He stepped into the silent hallway, certain that nothing good waited there for him. There was still the light of dusk in the main hallways, so the darkness he faced was not total. He heard the sound of a folding knife snapping into place, followed by several more.

Then there came a stifled cry, and Strazis thought the speaker had tried to say his name. He had no doubt that the whimper that followed came from Sanina. The boom-

ing laughter that followed, he was certain, came from Cerry.

His eyes slowly adjusted to the darkness. He had spent many a night hunting with the wavana pack, which had sharpened his reflexes and instincts. His eyes too were now like the feral eyes of a wavana, and he could smell where danger was as much as he could see shadows that were a deeper black than the darkness. In the pocket of his tunic, he still carried the stones he had brought in case he had tried to get the skier cannons working. His hand closed around one of them when Sanina whimpered again.

"Cerry!" he shouted and then, reverting back to his persona as a wavana, exploded down the hallways like a killer descending on its prey, tossing stones at the heads of his ambushers. He seized a fallen blade and filled the hall with bloody carnage as he carved his way down the corridor with unbridled fury, striking killing blows without hesitation or mercy.

Screams from Cerry's gang filled the air, begging for mercy as he spilled their life's blood. The hallway was quickly cleared of every threat.

Pausing outside his chamber's door, Strazis listened intently. He could barely distinguish three figures inside. Haflit cowered on his cot, while what must have been Cerry and Sanina were a jumbled mass next to him.

Strazis dropped the knife on the floor with an intentionally loud clatter and called, "Cerry!" once more. Then he saw the mass separate as Sanina was pushed to the floor.

With a smile, Strazis attacked. His hands quickly found Cerry's throat and the wrist of the hand with the blade. The struggle lasted only the briefest of instants.

"I warned you," Strazis said before a loud snapping sound filled the room and Cerry fell to the floor.

Chapter Twenty-seven
Terms of the Fight

Throughout the long night, Strazis held the shivering Sanina as she cried.

"I didn't think you were coming back," were her only words.

The moans and begging of gang members dying in the hallway lasted until nearly morning, before they finally faded away.

After that, the only sounds came from their breath.

When dawn's light finally filtered down, someone replaced the missing mirror, and there was a brief commotion as the inhabitants of the other cells quickly scavenged anything they could strip from the dead. The husband of the wife next door loudly abused the bodies while expressing his anger at them and appreciation for Strazis.

Strazis peeled himself away from the clinging Sanina and tossed Cerry's body outside, where it was quickly picked clean.

The guards soon discovered what had happened and summoned Ameron.

Stopping the guards from applying discipline with their unfurled whips, Ameron strolled through the carnage to Strazis' cell and looked inside.

"This is your doing," he asked in a matter-of-fact voice, "isn't it?"

Making certain to stand far away from Sanina and Haflit, Strazis nodded.

"Very effective, indeed." Ameron smiled, then called for a physician and ordered an on the spot inspection of Strazis.

"He's untouched," the physician asserted.

"Not even a bruise?" Ameron confirmed with an even bigger smile, and began clapping his hands in applause. "This is much more than I expected. I compliment you. First, you get that skier working, and now you've proven that you're not just good in a fight, you're completely lethal."

Ameron reached into a pocket of his vest and pulled out the medallion belonging to Strazis, who hesitated only a second before snatching it from Ameron's outstretched hand.

"You arranged all this?" Strazis asked. "You wanted to know if I'm a killer."

"Let's just call this serendipitous good fortune."

Strazis was uncertain if he believed him.

"Anyway, it doesn't matter," Ameron continued. "What does matter is that I think you're ready for the contest Philandreas proposed when you first came to us. From what I've just seen, you don't need any training."

"What kind of contest?" Sanina asked, catching a look of horror from Haflit for having spoken.

Ameron saw Haflit's reaction and laughed.

"That actually is a good question," he said with a condescending tone. "Strazis, you're going to use that skier you've reassembled to fight one of Philandreas' slaves—another islander like yourself."

"What kind of fight?" Strazis asked.

"To the death. I hope you'll live up to my expectations," Ameron looked again at the bodies, "which you have now raised. I assure you, there will be rewards aplenty after you win."

"What kind of weapons?"

"Just your craft's, of course."

"I don't know if mine has weapons. I only just got it working yesterday."

A pall of concern spread over Ameron's face. Then he looked again at the bodies in the hallway, and patted Strazis on the shoulder.

"I trust your... animal instincts. You'll figure something out. Besides, the terms of the wager are already set. I'll have the proper apparel sent to you."

Ameron walked away, still inspecting the mayhem that the guards were instructing the other inhabitants of the hallway to clear, then he paused and looked back.

"Your skier," he asked, "is it tight?"

Strazis nodded.

"Good. Let's hope it's tighter than a woman of Arendahj."

Strazis found no humor in the laughter of the guards. He was about to fight to the death with a skier that had no weapons and was about to run out of fuel. Suddenly the times he had faced Eirlik's superior skier on the training waters of Kalikantari seemed like less of a mismatch.

Chapter Twenty-eight
Fight to the Death

"You're not coming back this time," Sanina sobbed. "I know it. What's going to happen to me?"

"Nothing, I hope," Strazis replied. "But whatever happens, hopefully I'll put up a good enough fight that Ameron will want to know what you've learned from me."

"That won't take long. You're a fisher-boy from the islands who thinks he's a Moon God."

Strazis caressed her face and wiped a tear away.

"I've never said that. Use your wits. Stall for time until I can return and put an end to this nightmare. Then I'll return you home."

"That's a lot of optimism for a man about to die," she replied. "Some might call it delusions of grandeur." Then she kissed him long and hard. "Please, come back to me."

Strazis was led away by a special escort of guards who were dressed in finer gear than any he had seen before in Arendahj. When checking for hidden weapons, the guard did something completely unexpected by pretending not to notice Cerry's folding blade hidden in Strazis' leather vest.

Taken to his skier, Strazis was pulled away from the mooring by ropes, dragged through the open inlet gate and down the waterway. He was certain this was their way of keeping a leash on him, but he was relieved to save his fuel.

Using a path that paralleled the waterway, the guards led him to a manmade lake surrounded by elegant gardens where a regal viewing stand was built on the very edge. There, Ameron lounged with Philandreas and others of their kind.

Ameron motioned the guard to bring Strazis to him, where another skier already waited without tethers. Far older than Strazis, this rider was definitely an islander, but Strazis could not guess which one he hailed from. By the expression on the rider's face, Strazis could tell that he had already been well corrupted by the vices of

Arendahj and was eager for fresh rewards. His opponent's skier was also ancient, showing no signs of previous damage, and sported a pair of cannons that spit liquid fire.

"Fight well," both Ameron and Philandreas said simultaneously to their skier.

Elsewhere all along the lake's shoreline, multitudes of spectators had gathered, and their voices hummed with loud anticipation. Behind the shoreline crowds, bleachers were filled to the top. Nowhere were there any slaves to be seen except for the occasional servant ferrying food and drink.

"Forgive me," Strazis said loudly the moment after his skier's ropes were pulled free. This shocked everyone present, it having been explained earlier in no uncertain terms that no contestant was ever allowed to speak. "I decline your offer to fight!"

His opponent on the other skier seemed stunned at Strazis' mock politeness and watched with his mouth agape when Strazis suddenly sped away.

Behind him, Strazis heard the moaned complaints of the crowd and Ameron shouting angrily for someone to stop him. Heading back the way he had come, Strazis shot through the waterway's gate before it could be closed.

An explosion of water off to one side warned him that the other skier was not only in pursuit but had quickly closed the distance between them. He was obviously riding the superior skier, as always seemed to be the case with every opponent Strazis faced on the water.

Then came the moment he had been anticipating. Certain that he was about to run out of fuel at any moment, Strazis pulled the throttle back full and closed his eyes to avoid any break in concentration when he approached the outlet gates. He felt the acceleration as his skier began skipping over the waves. Soon he couldn't feel the waves at all.

Hearing gasps of awe and certain that he should have already crashed into the gates, Strazis opened his eyes to discover his skier was hurtling through the air, skimming just over the upthrust spikes of the outlet gate. In a perfect arc, he dropped back down to the water and heard the cursing of the other skier when he was blocked.

Uncertain how he had accomplished the physically impossible, Strazis backed down on the throttle just enough to manage the twisting curves of the waterway until it led him to the river. Once there, he again opened the throttle full, hoping to build as much momentum as possible before his fuel ran out.

It never did.

After he had cleared the delta's mouth, Strazis continued far enough out to sea not to be seen when he circled around back to the shore.

Hiding his skier in the plants growing along a tributary, he climbed a tall tree and ate fresh fruit while watching a whole flotilla of ships head out in pursuit.

He hid there throughout the night, studying the stars to determine his course, and with the dawn set his compass bearing in the direction he hoped would lead to the Isle of View. He knew he was taking an incredible chance in trying to reach it before his seemingly unending supply of fuel ultimately ran out.

Once again, the impossible happened,

and he saw the Isle of View rise on the horizon just as dusk started to fall.

Strazis let out a jubilant wavana howl once he pulled his skier ashore but received no reply. He saw the white bones of the wavana who were slain the day he had been captured, lying half buried in the sands where they had bleached. Heading inland, he let out several more howls, but no reply ever came.

Suddenly, the Isle of View had become an empty and lonely place to him, and everywhere was evidence of repeated visits by the Shezendoa. He stayed only for the night, gathering food and hollowing out several gourds to fill with water.

With the first light of the new day, Strazis once more threw his fate to the mercy of the open waters and set out in an easterly direction that he hoped would lead him to the Teluchi Islands.

Despite the dangers from storms and denizens of the water, despite the likelihood of missing the widely-scattered islands entirely as he navigated without proper bearings, Strazis was still filled with an exuberance that he had not felt since his days of running with the wavana pack.

Chapter Twenty-nine
The Worldlord's Mercy

The scorched and ragged banners of Told Maton tilted in the wind. Maton's Tyle alliance had defied the Worldlord's alliance, and for a time, it appeared it might be a war that Maton could win, after newly independent Vanessa surprised everyone by allying with him.

Following their humiliating defeat at the hands of Ell Cee Baron's far inferior force,

the leaders of Vanessa decided on a new tactic, but it ultimately worked no better for them than did the last.

With his son Eirlik at his side, Dextran of Promessus eventually stormed Vanessa's capital and ruthlessly killed the ruling class. After that, all of Vanessa bowed down to Dextran and the Worldlord he represented, leaving the banners of the Tyle Alliance to stand alone.

Despite the devastating loss of life over the long conflict, the Issandran armies of the Worldlord finally shattered the Tyle armies and sent Told Maton fleeing from the island.

Hot in his pursuit, the Worldlord Eagal Ir Radin was determined to make a clear example, following Maton's remaining two thousand men far out into the unexplored seas of the western expanses with an army of five thousand at his back.

They had purposefully guided and goaded Told Maton into those treacherous waters, where the seasonal storms were due to appear at any time without warning—whipping up waves that no skier could survive. It was a tactic of fear: although the buoyant skiers always survived the rough seas, they would be found in the wake of such storms floating upside down, the fate of their lost riders a mystery. The western expanses were filled with an untold number of mysteries.

When Told Maton's armies were at their weakest, Eagal Ir Radin deftly maneuvered him into a trap between attack groups that struck from several directions. The battle horns were sounded, and all the pursuing armies of Issandra surged forth with their incomparable fighting skills.

The remaining legions of Tyle folded like a parchment.

Now Told Maton rode nearly alone with his sagging banner, with only his Royal Guard remaining at his side. The rest of his army had either surrendered, fled, or died.

Smeared with blood from the close fighting, Eagal Ir Radin circled the defiant knot of remaining skiers, keeping his warriors at bay to provide a final moment of respite and regret for the doomed men. While the Warlord of Promessus had achieved the honor of conquering Vanessa, it would be the Worldlord of Issandra who delivered the final blow to the rebellion.

Told Maton's massive body quivered with fear, which in turn caused his guards to shudder involuntarily as they watched the Worldlord circling them. Then he stopped, turned his skier to face Told Maton directly on, and raised his sword in preparation to signal.

Something to the west caught the Worldlord's eye before he dropped his arm. From out of the hazy distance, he saw a lone skier approaching, a silhouette framed by the sinking sun. This was unusual because there was nowhere in the west for someone to approach from.

Forgetting Told Maton for a moment, Eagal Ir Radin signaled for a squad to challenge the skier and learn his identity.

The stranger drew close enough for the Worldlord to see that the skier lacked any kind of markings, and when challenged, the rider refused to slow, shooting past the other skiers.

The strange skier was headed directly toward the Worldlord.

Eagal Ir Radin saw Ell Cee Baron move to intercept the newcomer himself, but he waved him off. He would handle this bold interloper himself.

As the unmarked craft drew near, Eagal Ir Radin squinted in the glare of the sun's last rays, trying to make out the figure of the rider. But before the Worldlord fired his cannons, the skier slowed and settled sideways on the rolling waves that carried him slowly closer. This man had the brightest bronzed skin that the Worldlord had ever seen.

"Strazis?" he gasped in disbelief, certain it must have been an illusion before him.

"Hello, father," the illusion said in a voice almost too manly to have been the boy he once knew. "You don't know how glad I am to see you. Your skier always stands out from the others."

For a moment, the Worldlord was at a loss for words. The man before him had a hardened body rippled with muscle tone and a mature face that he could barely recognize as his son, who had never shaved his head before, but his bronzed skin could belong to no one else. And the more he talked, the more familiar his voice became.

"Welcome back, my son," said the Worldlord, fighting back emotions that he could never display on the battlefield. "Tell me now, and tell me quick." He pointed at the skiers clustered around the Tyle banner that dipped ever lower. "Was Told Maton responsible for what happened on Kalikantari? Did he kidnap you?"

"No," Strazis shook his head. "I know exactly who made the attack and where to find them. It wasn't him."

The Worldlord turned and summoned Ell Cee Baron, giving him instructions to offer

Told Maton mercy if he immediately surrendered unconditionally. Baron was also told to inform Maton that this gesture was made in the joy of the Worldlord's lost son's return, and then report back on his reaction.

Without even waiting for the reply, the Worldlord set the nose of his skier in the direction of Issandra, and rode side by side with his son, who amazed him with his skill handling the craft.

Strazis told him about the attack by the Black Assassins, his capture and escape, his time on the island and as a prisoner in a previously unknown land called Arendahj. What the Worldlord found most amazing was how his son had crossed the western ocean alone, without weapons or defense of any kind.

"I did have a knife," Strazis replied.

They talked throughout the night and into the next day, never growing tired. Many of the things the Worldlord heard he thought might be exaggerated fantasies, they seemed so unreal. Strazis claimed to have accomplished deeds and survived incredible events that seemed too improbable.

But after they had reached the shelter of his Issandran tower, Strazis' details remained precise whenever retold, the facts never wavering. Eagal Ir Radin eventually lost all doubt.

"You've had a fantastic adventure," the Worldlord said when they enjoyed a private feast for two. "I am more than impressed. But I get the feeling that you're leaving things out. There's something you haven't told me."

Strazis took a drink of fermented grapes, his eyes widening from the taste and effects he had never experienced before. He then paused a moment, as though he were weighing what to reveal next.

"I told you about Arendahj," he took another drink, "and of the things they do there to islanders and others. I can see my rage mirrored in your face. And, while I have learned to do many things that I never imagined possible before, I realize that there are many things about which I still lack experience. I need to ask your advice."

"Ask it."

"While I was a slave in their pits, I made a vow not only to escape Arendahj, but to return one day and liberate it. That's not something I can do alone."

"How do you expect to accomplish that?"

"That's my question."

The Worldlord lifted his drink and downed the whole thing, then stood and put a hand on his son's shoulder.

"Strazis, to command an army, you must first prove yourself to be a leader—make those who follow you respect your name. You've taken a good first step in that direction. I could see my men were impressed when you came riding alone out of the west. No one has ever done that before. And the deeds you've accomplished will have everyone in the islands talking long after we're both gone. But the Teluchi Islands have just gone through a long rebellion that lasted many full cycles of the seasons, and we've lost so much putting it down. We need time to rest and allow tempers to cool before we declare another war."

"These people killed your children," Strazis said with a hint of confusion, "the grandchildren of every one of your allies."

The Worldlord sat back down.

"Let the storms on the western oceans blow until they've lost their strength. By the time a new solar cycle rolls around, my warriors will be restless again. That will give you time to tell them your tales and drum up support for a war against Arendahj."

"You make it sound simple."

"It's always simple to bend men to your will, if you know how."

"While we wait, how am I supposed to make them respect me?"

Eagal Ir Radin stood and drew his sword.

"Have you ever wielded one of these?"

"Only once," Strazis replied, "when I tried to protect Tanith. I failed. But I'm older and stronger now than I was then."

"You saw her die?"

"Yes. I saw her fall."

"Then now it's time to learn," the Worldlord growled, angered by the memory of her death. "Learn to make your blade into an extension of your arm. Train harder than anything you've ever done before. But realize this, we have other problems than distant Arendahj. Your old enemy, Eirlik, has proven both a proficient skier and fighter. I'm sure he won't be happy to hear that you've returned. You're going to have to face him one day, so learn well and practice hard. Every time you think you're being pushed too hard, and that you can't go on, remember what happened to you in Arendahj and use your anger to revitalize yourself. Keep pushing until there's no one who can match your skill, not even me. Can you do that?"

Strazis nodded.

"Then I'll teach you myself."

"I'm honored, father. I could have no better teacher. But there's something else that bothers me."

"What's that?"

"The Black Assassins knew too much about Kalikantari," said Strazis. "But their information wasn't complete, because my presence there confused them."

"What are you saying?"

"The Black Assassins are in league with someone here in the Teluchi Islands."

"That could have been Told Maton. He was quick to launch his rebellion."

"But the Black Assassins never did a thing to help him. Why would they abandon an ally that way?"

"Possibly misdirection," said Eagal Ir Radin.

"Could be," said Strazis.

"Ell Cee Baron said that Maton seemed confused when he heard it was your arrival that saved his life. He didn't know who you were."

Chapter Thirty
Master of the Blade

Strange sounds awakened the Worldlord earlier than usual. Life in Issandra had a routine set of noises that always occurred on a daily basis, which did not include the steadily repeating noise of metal on metal.

Eagal Ir Radin dressed and followed the sounds down to the docks by the Worldlord's tower, where he found Strazis had pulled his unmarked skier onto some pilings and was dismantling a section of it.

"You said you built that thing," said Eagal Ir Radin, "so why are you now taking it apart?"

"Trying to solve a mystery." Strazis pulled a black box from the very center of the inside of the skier. "And you're just in time." He put the box up to his head, shook it, and then handed it to his father. "Shake it and listen."

The Worldlord complied.

"Sounds like water has gotten in there."

"That's not water," said Strazis. "Don't ask me to explain how, but whatever is in there is what powers this skier."

"That is a mystery," the Worldlord replied.

"No. The mystery is that when I installed it, there was a single drop inside. The whole time I was riding that skier I kept expecting it to lose power at any moment. But it never did. And, after all that riding, it sounds like there's a lot more inside."

"That makes no sense."

Strazis agreed and reinserted the box, and then pushed the skier off the pilings and spun it to face open water.

"You left some parts out." The Worldlord looked at the pieces of outer metal casings lying about the dock.

"I'm testing a theory," Strazis said the moment before he fired both cannons into the water, creating massive plumes of water and explosions so loud that they woke everyone in the vicinity.

Without another word, Strazis pulled his skier back on the pilings and pulled the box back out. When both shook it, there was obviously less liquid inside than before.

"That decreased it," observed the Worldlord. "No one has ever figured out how these things really work."

"Have you ever heard of one exploding?"

asked Strazis.

"Sure," the Worldlord replied. "Not long ago, a few warriors who rode their skiers too often exploded, and I'm talking massive explosions that were far, far greater than the ones you just made. Then it stopped happening. No one knows why."

"It stopped when the war started?"

"I hadn't thought about it, but yes. It only happened when the islands were at peace."

Strazis gave the box another rattle, then reinserted it into his skier, this time reassembling all the parts and sealing the outer skin.

"It goes against any of the laws of nature that I've ever read," said Strazis, "But what if riding a skier actually builds up the fuel, like the sun charges a battery? Somehow it multiplies it with use. Then firing your cannons releases that charge. But... if you don't fire your cannons often enough, that charge overloads the container's capacity, and then you get an explosion?"

The Worldlord was astounded. His son had proposed an explanation for the workings of the skiers that no one had ever considered. That did not mean he was correct, but he certainly had an interesting hypothesis.

"That's something to think about," Eagal Ir Radin replied. "Come, it's time I showed you a secret I've been hiding."

Eagal Ir Radin picked up a couple of the tools lying about, stepped onto his skier, and pried loose the metal cover he had long ago hammered over the steering hub.

"Look at that," he said, "that's the same design as the one on your medallion. This is why I knew you were a child of the Moon

Gods."

Strazis instinctively put a hand to the medallion hanging under his chest gear.

"Whoever made this skier may have made your medallion. That's why I hid it after I found you. I didn't want anyone else to see it." The Worldlord stepped back on the dock. "There's something else that I want to show you. Walk with me." He led the way up the stone steps leading to his tower fortress. "Since I've made a revelation, now it's your turn. Tell me what's really been bothering you since you returned."

"I told you about my vow," said Strazis as they rounded the tower and headed down the path leading to the private armory in the rear.

"Yes, but there still is something else that's still bothering you. I can see it in your eyes every time you look at me."

Strazis stopped.

"What is it?"

"I told you how…" Strazis wetted his lips and hesitated before continuing, "…after my encounter with the white wavana, suddenly I could understand a language that I couldn't just moments before."

"Certainly. How could I forget?"

"Well, that's not the only thing she triggered in me. In Arendahj, I thought I was reading the lips of Ameron and Philandreas, but what if I was actually reading their minds?"

"I've never heard of such a thing."

"It seems that now you have. And that slave Ameron gave me. I always felt that whole situation was staged, even though she acted so appreciative and seemed to be fond of me, but sometimes when I looked at her—I could almost hear her plotting against me, preparing a report to give to Ameron."

"You were in a very stressful situation. It's only natural to have feelings of distrust."

"There's something else. I have no idea how it happened, but at the very moment of our reunion out there on the western waters, it was like I could see your memories of the morning when you first discovered me resting on stone hands in those watery ruins. Then when a hesitant Tanith Woanan decided to adopt me. I saw those memories manifest in your mind, as though I was standing right there in the room, in your place."

The Worldlord was stunned.

"I did think of both of those things when I first saw you again," he admitted. "How could you know?"

Strazis shrugged his ignorance.

"That's what's been bothering me. I don't know how I did it. What's happening to me?"

Eagal Ir Radin put a hand on his son's shoulder.

"Come with me. We need to clear your mind."

Entering his private armory, the Worldlord pulled a sword from all the others in the rack. It was unique, with a jewel-encrusted hilt that reflected a thousand prisms of color from the gems that lined it. He gently slid the marbled blue and silver blade out from its leather scabbard and handed it hilt first to Strazis, who marveled at its craftsmanship and perfect balance. The long blade had only one edge and a slight curve with a tapered point.

"This is a shakara, the kind of sword I carry," said the Worldlord as he pulled another pair of similar but nowhere near as resplendent blades from the racks. "There have been few swords ever made from the same material that our skiers are constructed from. It took my finest sword-smith months to create the heat needed to melt it, and then keep it flexible enough to hammer and fold over and over again. This was done while you lived on Kalikantari."

The Worldlord took the shakara away and handed Strazis one of the others.

"We'll be training with these. You don't practice with a blade like that. But it's yours whenever I decide that you're ready."

The training began immediately.

Eagal Ir Radin first taught Strazis the basics of grip, maintaining stance and balance while controlling the motion of one's body with the swing of the blade. He repeated over and over how wielding a sword was an art and not a task. He also explained why he favored a shakara over a double-edged blade, because the flat side was far better for deflecting your opponent's blade and didn't dull your own. Straight blades and those with greater curves like the Shezendoa carried, each had their own advantages when hooking a blade and knocking it from your opponent's grip. But for fighting on a skier, a long, thin blade easily outclassed those heavier blades that were too awkward for dueling. Plus, few men ever took the proper amount of time to train with them, over-relying on their confidence in their cannons for a combat situation.

The Worldlord quickly discovered that he did not need to repeat himself, for Strazis seemed to remember every instruction the first time it was given. He picked things up so easily that the Worldlord actually had to slow himself to keep from hurrying the training too quickly.

Once Strazis was shown a move, it became an instant skill of his, easily combining it with everything else he previously learned. Within days, the Worldlord was no longer keeping his own skills so much in reserve because his feints no longer worked. Their duels escalated into a frenzied pitch that offered ever greater competition to the Worldlord. All the while, Strazis took his injuries without complaint and always returned for more. He developed more skills each day than any other men learned in weeks or months.

Soon Strazis was dueling with the other sword-masters of Issandra, and defeating every one of them on his first try.

Eagal Ir Radin felt that this was proof positive that Strazis was indeed a blessing from the Moon Gods, and he decided to begin offering dueling challenges to the best swordsmen from other islands. No challenge was ever refused, with more pride riding on these affairs than anyone would ever claim.

When Strazis was matched against his first opponent, Calarn of Andera, he disarmed Calarn before he could even make his preliminary motion. An argument ensued that Strazis had struck early, but the judges ruled that his reaction had simply been faster than anyone had ever seen before.

During the subsequent banquet, Strazis stunned the guests with his stories of the terrible things happening to captive islanders beneath distant Arendahj, stirring the emotions of the crowd until every man present roared their outrage against Arendahj. They became the first pledges to Strazis' army of retribution.

But Strazis was not so quick to accept, warning them about how the Black Assassins carried cannons in their hands and traveled in massive ships like nothing the islanders had ever seen. He freely admitted that he did not fully know the strengths or weaknesses of the city. Then he told them how the denizens of Arendahj were firm worshippers of Neth and Nean, a cult that had often tried without success to infiltrate the Teluchi Islands.

The next day, Eagal Ir Radin handed the shakara with a jeweled hilt to Strazis.

"We've had four thousand men from Andera pledge to ride with you to Arendahj," he announced. "I think you've figured out how to build your army."

Strazis easily won dueling matches on four more islands, improving his perfect record against the best swordsmen alive, and the pledges to his army grew to ten thousand.

His next match was on the island of Keton, the largest in the Teluchi Islands and the furthest to the southeast. While they had remained steadfast in their treaties with the Worldlord, they had refrained from sending warriors to quell the recent rebellion. Like Vanessa, they were also suffering from overpopulation and were desperate to find new lands to settle.

Eagal Ir Radin was impressed with how his son had learned not to make the contests so quick. Instead, he defeated Nevil Daa Nara of Keton with a deft series of moves, always keeping perfect control of his blade and stopping the instant before a killing stroke was delivered. There was no argument this time over the outcome, and Nara thanked Strazis for his skill. In duels, accidents had been known to happen with swordsmen who could not control their blades so precisely. That was never the case with the Worldlord's son. His control was so perfect that no one feared to duel with him, and a dozen more challenges were made that same night, with every one ending the same. At no point did Strazis even break a sweat.

By the end of the festivities, the admiration for Strazis' skill was apparent, and the rumor of his Moon God heritage began to stir because of his bronzed skin. When he stood to speak, the entire hall listened intently as he brushed his short hair and told about how it had been forcibly shaved in the city of Arendahj. Then he ran his fingers over his still clean-shaven jaw and explained the reason he kept it that way was to remind himself, which drew a murmur of quiet surprise from everyone in attendance, all of them bearded. Strazis had learned not to press the issue of slavery since indentured servants were everywhere on the islands, and the issue did not resonate with many. But when he pounded a fist on the table and told of the crimes committed on Kalikantari and against islander women made prisoners in Arendahj, the outrage of the crowd became palpable.

Never did Strazis need to ask for volunteers. Warriors begged him to lead them, with Nara the first to pledge. The crowd became so roused that Strazis had to discourage them from riding out immediately, but he promised that the command would come soon.

By the time they left Keton, Strazis' army had swollen to twenty thousand strong, and there were still other Teluchi Islands left to recruit.

"Do not ask the men of Issandra to accompany you," Eagal Ir Radin told Strazis as they streaked toward home across the moonlit ocean. "The war of rebellion drained our army and economy. I'm certain men will still volunteer, but Issandra has treaty obligations for the whole of the Teluchi Islands to keep. As much as I would love to lead an Issandran army at your side, I need to remain here. We can't leave our lands unprotected with so much of our military absent."

"I understand," Strazis replied. "What about the islands that opposed you?"

"You don't need them. Your army is already so large that controlling it would be a challenge even for an experienced field commander."

Eagal Ir Radin knew that the upcoming crusade would be the supreme test where Strazis could prove himself as the Worldlord's rightful heir and successor. Conquering Arendahj on his own would cement his reputation.

"Then only Promessus is left," said Strazis, his firm voice clearly audible as their silent ships hurtled over the rolling troughs of water.

"It is. But be careful of Eirlik. Like you, he's developed an excellent reputation with a blade. He's got far more experience and more victories than you."

"Those all happened in Promessus," Strazis countered. "What kind of challenges could they have been?"

"Eirlik has shown before that he'll do anything it takes to win. Don't forget it and never let him take advantage of you."

Chapter Thirty-one
Eirlik's Disappointment

When Dextran of Promessus received Eagal Ir Radin's challenge to a duel with Strazis, he surprised Eirlik by not placing his son's name on the acceptance. Instead, the Warlord scheduled Stansar, a weathered veteran from the days of the Worldquest, who had only recently lost a duel with Eirlik.

Eirlik was certain that Dextran must have hoped another defeat for Stansar would help prove the decline of that once capable man. For his own part, Stansar was more than ready for another opportunity to restore his reputation in a fight against one of the next generation that was pushing him aside.

Absent without excuse on the evening of the contest, Eirlik watched from hiding as his father apologized for having to attend to duties of state, and made a show of riding away alone on his skier. Eirlik secretly followed him out.

Dextran rode only far enough into the dark of the freshly fallen night to be safely out of sight when he stopped his skier and drifted, listening intently to the waters around him, as if he sensed someone was following him. Eirlik likewise drifted, confident that the black colors he had painted his skier would keep him hidden.

There had been problems of late between Eirlik and his father, with Dextran insisting that his son ride to glory next to Strazis on his quest to Arendahj. Eirlik, for his part, wanted no part of pledging himself to the Worldlord's son.

As a result, Rhank, a warrior who had served Eirlik's father since the Worldquest, had been selected to be the first to pledge himself at the banquet that would follow the duel.

None of this made sense to Eirlik, and so he spied on his father, regularly nudging his skier so it continued to ride low in the rolling troughs of the ocean. It was the time of the cycle when storms ravaged the western waters, and while they rarely reached the Teluchi Islands, the whiplash they caused on the waters did. Eirlik kept a firm control over his skier as he bobbed up and down like a cork, constantly maneuvering so that he only caught a glimpse of his father with every third upward bob.

Even from a distance, Eirlik could see a sadness on his father's face as he watched the Shadowy Moons rise into the night sky. Then a score of skiers with the riders all dressed in black seemingly appeared from nowhere and surrounded him.

Eirlik silently moved closer so he could listen.

"I'm here," Dextran declared loudly. "Give me your proof."

One black-garbed man tossed a bundle into the Warlord's hands. From it, Dextran pulled fine cloth embroidered with colors from the banners of Promessus. Then he pulled a long, woven lock of golden blonde hair that sparkled so brilliantly in the moonlight that it could have only come from the head of Eirlik's sister, Phaedra.

"This is no proof," Dextran protested.

"Would you prefer a finger or an ear? How about her nose?" the other rider replied sarcastically. "You know those belong to her. If you don't do as we say, Phaedra will no longer be treated with the courtesy and care she's been shown so far. If you do as we ask, she'll be returned to Promessus, unharmed."

"Even if I did what you ask," Dextran argued, "I have no guarantee that you'll do what you promise. Do you think you're bartering with a fool?"

"You'll either agree, or accept my assurances that the men who've been keeping your daughter safe over the last few cycles will be rewarded—with her. To tell you the truth, I'm personally hoping you'll decline."

Dextran gave no reply, hesitating as he looked back up to the moons.

"You can do either what you want to do," the other rider pressed, "or what you have to do."

"What is it you want?" Dextran finally replied, but Eirlik drifted away and could not hear the instructions being given.

Not daring to draw attention, there was nothing else Eirlik could do, but he had seen enough. For the first time, he realized how weak his father had become. Regardless of whether Phaedra was their prisoner, Eirlik could not fathom why his father would ever agree to demands made by men who were most certainly the feared Nameless Ones.

Eirlik knew he had to become the strong leader that Promessus needed, sooner than he had ever expected. This would require doing things he despised.

"Michael Tierney is known to wear a mask when traveling abroad. His hobby is underwater photography—especially sharks.

Death and Renewal

By JIM BREYFOGLE

The Prince of Alomar has won a slave from the Bursa… Kat and Mangos must ensure the slave's silence at all cost, but on one condition: they cannot kill him!

Twenty-seven months after the fall of Alness.

The sun shone overhead.

Not the real sun, that had long set, but a crystal enchantment suspended on a golden chain slowly moving its way down the grand cathedral hall in imitation of the seasons. The sun was still in the first quarter of the hall, shining brightly to signify spring.

Mangos pushed through the room, lost amongst thousands of Alomar's citizens gathered in the vast indoor garden to celebrate the Renewal Festival. He ignored the women in their colorful dresses and the men in their finest tunics as he searched for Kat.

Instead he saw the Bursa, the man who hired him, seated in a high-backed chair near one of the great columns that marched down the nave. The Hand, his administrative assassin, stood behind him, half in the shadows.

The Bursa lifted a hand, beckoned him with his fingertips.

"Damn," muttered Mangos, wondering what could be said that would help. He pushed his way forward, shoving harder than he needed, but angry that he didn't know the answers to the questions the Bursa would surely ask.

"Mangos, my friend," said the Bursa.

"Bursa, you have news?" Mangos asked to forestall any of the Bursa's questions.

The Bursa chuckled, but without humor; worry lurked in his eyes. "I hoped you had news for me. You haven't much time." He pointed to the crystal sun. "At the end of winter, when the sun reaches the end of the gallery, the mute spell on Manchil breaks, and he can talk again."

Mangos nodded. He knew this. He knew somehow the gladiator/slave Manchil had passed from the Bursa's ownership to the Prince of Alomar. The Bursa had already made it clear Manchil could not be allowed to give information to the Prince—something that would be possible at the end of the celebration. Mangos didn't want to hear it again.

"I have no doubt Kat is doing her part as we speak," Mangos said. *I just don't know what it is. So don't ask.*

"No doubt, no doubt," said the Bursa, obviously not convinced. "A bright girl, Kat, and I'm already in her debt. But it's worth remembering, yes, it is; it's worth remembering if the Prince can move against me, I won't be able to pay my debts. That is certain. But," he hunched in the chair, leaning forward, "I can make sure those who failed me share my downfall."

Mangos ground his teeth as he forced a

smile on his face. *Don't threaten me, old man,* he thought, *I'm not in the mood for it.* "I can make sure Manchil never talks again."

Shaking his head, the Bursa replied, "No, no, no. My Hand should have made that very clear." He twisted to look up at the Hand, who nodded. "Yes, very clear," the Bursa continued. "The Prince said if Manchil dies—no matter how he dies—I will be held responsible. And again I will—"

Make sure those who failed me will share my downfall, Mangos thought, not even listening as the Bursa spoke the words. He knew this! Hearing his problem didn't help him find a solution. *We've been hired to kill a man we're not allowed to kill.*

The Bursa smiled. "I hope you succeed. I really do. So does my Hand."

Mangos didn't trust himself to speak. He lowered his head, just a bit, to give the impression of respect, then spun to go.

He climbed the stairs to the first balcony and looked down the length of the cathedral's five hundred foot long nave. He could not see into the transepts, each large enough for its own permanent festival functions. The northern one held a gladiatorial arena with seating for hundreds; the southern currently held a runway stage used for theater and the fashion show.

With a sigh, he glanced up. He imagined the stained glass windows would be beautiful during the day, but at night they were flat and dark. The crystal sun illuminated frescos painted between the ribs of the vaulted ceiling, scenes of the gods and the seasons.

"Go, look around," Kat had said. "Enjoy the festival. I have an idea I want to work on. Be ready, I'll get word to you."

By the Gods of Eastwarn, she can be frustrating! he thought.

"I've a note for you."

Mangos turned. The Hand stood next to him, a folded piece of parchment in his hand, which he held out. Mangos took it.

He unfolded the paper.

It has been arranged for you to fight Manchil during the gladiatorial contests in late summer. You are NOT to kill him. He must be embarrassed.

—Kat

Spring fashion, summer games, autumn feast, winter dance; that was the order of the Renewal Festival.

He crumpled the message. They had not been hired to embarrass Manchil. How would this solve their problem?

If they could make Manchil disappear… Without a body, maybe the Prince wouldn't punish the Bursa. Then everybody (except Manchil) could enjoy the festival. He sighed. Things didn't work that way in Alomar.

Where was Kat? He had been around the hall twice without finding her.

"Everything in order?" the Hand asked. He leaned on the balcony rail, smiling slightly and looking the length of the hall.

"Why aren't you the one taking care of this?" Mangos demanded.

"I presented three plans to the Bursa concerning Manchil. He chose the third."

A smile curled the edges of Mangos's mouth. At last he would find something out. "What is the plan?"

"To hire the Mongoose and Meerkat."

"What?" Mangos's good humor vanished. "That was your plan?"

With a shrug, the Hand said, "I came up with nothing. It is a cunning trap. In truth, the Prince thinks he has won and is enjoying the Bursa's discomfort. By showing Manchil in public, he mocks the Bursa."

"How did the Prince get Manchil in the first place?" Mangos asked. "And how did the Bursa cast a spell that would keep him silent, and why is the spell only good until the New Year?"

"I'm not the one telling you, but it involved too much brandy, what the Bursa thought was a winning hand of cards, and a hurried spell by a less than competent mage."

Drinking while gambling. Mangos could understand that.

He let out an angry breath. It didn't matter, anyway. They had taken the job. "Where's Kat?"

"She went to see Snader," the Hand said, referring to one of Alomar's more powerful wizards. "I think she wants to know if the mute spell on Manchil can be made permanent, or another laid on top of it." He shook his head. "She'll be disappointed. I already checked.

"Come," the Hand clapped Mangos on the back. "She said she'd be at the fashion show."

Mangos twisted away from the Hand's grip, glaring, but followed down the steps, returning to the main floor.

"The Prince will be at the show also," the Hand added. "Have you ever seen Manchil?"

Mangos shook his head, realized the Hand wasn't looking at him, and said,

"No."

"Now's your chance."

They made their way into the south transept, working through the crowd to emerge just behind the reserved seating.

A temporary runway jutted from a doorway on the south wall, extending into the transept so the models could be seen from three sides. Extra lights, bright burning "sunflower" lamps, shone onto the runway, making everything else dim by comparison.

The show set the tone for Alomar's fashions for the next year, Mangos knew. A well-received design meant sales, and sales to Alomar's elite meant wealth. The worlds of high fashion, treachery, and murder intertwined in Alomar. Two designers had been killed in the last month, and another's studio burned.

"Do you see Kat?" Mangos asked the Hand.

Instead of answering, the Hand said, "The Prince has taken his seat. The show will begin soon." He nodded, drawing Mangos's attention to the Prince and the favored slave beside him.

Mangos could only see the top of the Prince's head over the back of the throne facing the runway. He had a better view of Manchil, whose chair lacked the high back of the Prince's throne.

Manchil hulked in his chair, neck as thick as his head. The edge of a tattoo showed above his silk shirt—an incongruously light yellow shirt. He was bald and missing half an ear. Even from the back, he looked like what he was—a gladiator. Unfortunately for Mangos and Kat, he was also a slave who knew too much information about a former owner.

Embarrass Manchil? Manchil was the most dangerous gladiator in Alomar. Embarrass him? Seeing Manchil, Mangos couldn't help but think, *I'll be lucky to survive, and Kat's instructions be damned.*

"The show is going to start," the Hand said.

I need to learn that trick, Mangos thought, *how to be so unconcerned.* It was clear that if the Bursa fell, he would take not just Mangos and Kat, but the Hand, too. Yet the Hand seemed only interested in the show.

The tip of a sword parted the curtains. The rest of the curved sword followed, then a slender, white-gloved hand. It rotated, making the sword spin and twirl, sparkling in the light. Another sword-wielding hand joined it, and the two weapons performed together for a few moments before parting the curtains to allow the model to walk out, still twirling the swords.

"Can't I just make it an accident?" Mangos asked. "Do it, some way the Prince can't possibly blame on the Bursa?"

The Hand snorted. "The Prince made it clear if *anything* happened to Manchil he would hold the Bursa responsible. I think that's why Kat wanted you to fight Manchil—to make sure somebody else doesn't kill him." The gladiatorial games were timed so they didn't overrun their season, but there was a death bonus if one gladiator killed the other before time expired.

Mangos blew out his breath, frustrated. He seemed to be doing that a lot lately.

The model performed an empty routine designed, not to show her prowess with the swords, but her beauty and that of her dress. She was beautiful, and so was her dress, though Mangos no more than noticed. The crowd applauded politely when she finished.

"Maybe I should make a renewal offering," Mangos said. "For luck." He didn't have anything else on his side; he may as well have luck. The Temple gathered small gifts early; would luck begin when he gave the gift or when it was presented to the gods at midnight?

The Hand glanced at him. "Did you bring anything?"

"No, but I can give something and buy it back when they sell the gifts." Many temples sold donated items so they could pay expenses.

"Don't give anything you want," the Hand said. "You'll never get it back. *This* Temple doesn't sell anything for revenue and, once given, gifts are beyond anybody's influence."

"I can't even buy luck for this job," Mangos muttered.

The next model walked out, a man dressed in tight-fitting trousers that flared out at the cuffs. A circle of wire held each cuff in shape and made it look like he wore two cones. He had to bow his legs to keep the cuffs from rubbing together. The sleeves of his shirt flared in a similar fashion. Swirling shades of orange and green covered both trousers and shirt.

A man behind Mangos murmured, "I'd never wear that."

Mangos endured a steady procession of men and women in clothes he could not comprehend. A few he thought were dressed to appeal, but others, like the woman with stuffed, purple-dyed lemurs on each shoulder, mystified him.

Where's Kat? He could not find her in the crowd and started to move to see the other spectators better. Everybody gasped, and he looked back to the runway.

A woman had come out and seized the attention of every person watching. She wore a cape of snow lion fur, luxurious white and three-quarter length that caressed her as she walked. All else that she wore was swim clothes, two small pieces made of snow snakeskin, mottled white and cream, and a mask over her eyes.

Her hips swayed as she walked, and walking was too pedestrian a word. She had a feline grace, an elegance that held the crowd spellbound. She stopped to twirl, causing the cape to lift and the audience to draw in its breath. She flashed a smile and a wink at the Prince.

Mangos had never seen a woman so captivating—or had he? Could that be—Kat? He cursed under his breath. It could be, because it was, but it was also true that he had never seen a woman like this.

Kat had always felt like a sister, had always been ignored by men. This—this was *so* different. Every *person*, but especially the men, stared. The air practically dripped desire.

Kat ran her hands down her sides, over her hips, pushed them out, and rotated them. The rotation traveled up her arms, through her chest, and down. Mangos swallowed, conscious that he suddenly felt warm. He had a hard time believing those limbs were the same that fought and killed so effectively.

Kat raised her arms, inhaled. The man next Mangos whimpered softly.

That's my partner? Mangos thought. When Kat wrapped the cape around herself, it was almost as if she were giving the audience permission to breathe.

She sashayed up the runway, looking coy above the thick fur. She reached the curtains, drew one across her as she let the cape fall back, so only her head and bare shoulders showed. With a smile, a wink, and a wave, she slipped out of sight.

Applause thundered through the transept like a spring tempest. Mangos closed his mouth. He hadn't been aware it was open.

From the whistles and calls, it was clear everybody wanted to see Kat again, and Mangos knew he had an excuse.

What had changed, and why? He didn't know if it was because of their job or an instinctual reaction, but Mangos needed to see Kat, and quickly.

He finally found her seated next to the Prince outside the transept. The Prince was a lean man, about fifty years old, with a long face and high forehead. Manchil stood behind them while four palace guards kept people away.

Kat and the Prince burst out laughing. Manchil shuffled his feet and looked down, the top of his head red.

Kat still wore her modeling clothes, little though they covered her, and the guards couldn't keep the stares from her. The Prince did not seem to mind that her garb drew attention from his flamboyantly colored tunic. He was clearly more interested in flattering her with his undivided attention. She, in return, appeared to be entertaining him at Manchil's expense.

Mangos started toward them only to have a guard drop a spear in his path. "No one approaches the Prince," the guard said.

"I could care less about the Prince, I want to talk to the woman."

A sly smile crept across the guard's face. "You and me both. But you can't compete with the Prince."

"You miss my intention," Mangos said while trying to catch Kat's attention. She finally looked up and saw him. She laid a hand on the Prince's arm. With obvious reluctance, the Prince called for the guard to let Mangos approach.

"What are you doing?" Mangos demanded. Beside Kat the Prince stirred, frowning at Mangos, but Mangos didn't care.

Kat cut him off, presenting him to the Prince as etiquette demanded. "This is Mangos of Arnelon, a formidable adventurer and sometime gladiator." She laid her hand on the Prince's arm again. Mangos ground his teeth. "And this," Kat said with a flick of her hand, "is Manchil, the greatest gladiator in Alomar, which is good because he isn't the smartest man I've met."

Manchil flushed bright red, and Kat laughed. "Isn't that cute? It just goes to show wits aren't everything."

She did not introduce the Prince, which reminded Mangos of the expected manners. "An honor, Your Grace," he said. The Prince merely inclined his head.

Mangos glared at Kat. "A word?"

"You just took two, and you want another?"

The prince laughed as Mangos blushed. Kat smiled, "Just one."

Kat stood, turning as she did to face the Prince. His eyes seemed glued to her chest as she rose. "I'll be right back," she said.

Mangos stalked away, sure she would follow. Once far enough away he turned, "What are you doing?" He felt anger, and if he were honest, jealousy boiling inside him.

"Why aren't you getting ready?" she demanded, not answering his question.

"That's not the question! What do you think you're doing dressed like this, playing up to the Prince? Do you think he will give you Manchil as a gift?"

"No," Kat said. "Manchil's too valuable both as a gladiator and informant against the Bursa."

"Then what?"

"I've been baiting Manchil, making him look foolish."

Manchil glowered in his seat while the Prince looked from him to Kat, an unhappy expression on his face. Mangos frowned, not sure how this would help kill Manchil. The prince wouldn't forgo retribution just because Kat made Manchil look stupid. Even if Kat convinced him Manchil *was* stupid, it wouldn't help.

Kat struck a pose and took a deep breath. "Do you like the latest fashion?"

His eyes snapped back to her. "Yes! NO!" he said, he didn't know what to think, how to react. It made no sense that Kat should suddenly become so appealing.

Kat laughed softly, enjoying his discomfort. She looked up at the sun. "It's almost mid-summer. Prepare."

"Manchil hasn't prepared, and I'm a better warrior than he is."

"This isn't knives in the dark or hunting worms. Nobody knows the arena like he does," Kat said. "This is the most dangerous gladiator in Alomar, and he is very angry right now."

"I'm not happy myself."

"You must not kill him," Kat said. "You must *humiliate* him."

"The Bursa wants him—"

Kat interrupted him. "You must not kill him."

"Just tell me your plan!"

She glanced over her shoulder at the Prince. "No time. The Prince *mustn't* get anxious." She returned to her seat, brushing against the Prince as she sat down. She spoke in quiet tones, laughing and ignoring Mangos until the Prince relaxed.

"But I want to kill him," Mangos muttered, and he would have been perfectly happy if the Prince were in the arena too.

Humiliate without killing? Did she even know what she asked? He sighed. She usually did. Well, he thought, he wouldn't beat Manchil; he would mock him. He might get killed doing it, but it would be funny.

The sun was yellower, now, losing some of the warmth of high summer. The crowds had moved to the arena—Mangos looked up from the sands, understanding finally that this was different from his normal fighting. Seeing the crowd told him how alone he was in the arena. Nobody could help him; the hourglass timing the fight would not stop to rescue him. His only friends were those he brought with him: his sword and the whip fastened to his belt.

Kat sat in the Prince's box; he had no idea how she had arranged this fight. The Prince pointed toward him. Kat began to clap, and those near her took it up. The applause barely overcame the buzz from hundreds of people talking. He had hoped for more, from her and the crowd.

Manchil stepped out onto the sands, lifted his arms to the crowd who stopped talking to cheer their approval. He no longer wore the light yellow shirt; instead, he wore a full brassard on his right arm. A tattooed dragon coiled from under his left arm to climb over his shoulder and out of sight. He wore a short loincloth fastened with a golden clasp and carried a wide sword in his left hand, a short-handled scythe in his right.

Well, Mangos thought, *time to begin.* He pointed at Manchil, lifted his own arms in the air, and began to wiggle his butt like a cheap tavern whore. The crowd roared.

Manchil clashed his sword and scythe together. He looked like he would like nothing better than to measure the length of Mangos's intestines.

Mangos blew him a kiss.

The bell sounded. Manchil charged forward, intent on killing.

Mangos caught the sword with his own and let the force of the blow push him back as he dropped and rolled out of reach of the scythe. He sprang up, Manchil already on him, swinging again—appallingly close.

Mangos parried the sword, parried the scythe, and danced away from the kick Manchil aimed at his knee. The crowd roared, but he didn't know for whom. Again, Mangos had to parry, once, twice. Pain shot through his arm, and the crowd roared louder.

Blood flowed down his arm. The point of the scythe had curved around his sword guard and, though he parried, cut into his forearm.

He parried the sword, parried the scythe. Manchil kicked, lifting sand into his face, into his eyes, blinding him. Mangos leapt back, blinking, wiping his face, backpedalling, moving to avoid the blur that was Manchil until he could see again. He parried and knew he was lucky.

Who's getting embarrassed now?

His eyes stung, but he could see well enough to parry again. He was starting to get the rhythm of Manchil's attacks. Sword, scythe, other. Unbelievably fast, fueled by Kat's poor treatment of him before the Prince. Sword, scythe, other.

Mangos readied a parry, disengaged, which fooled Manchil into over swinging. Mangos put his free hand on Manchil's shoulder and pushed, turning him further and exposing his back. *I could kill him now.*

Mangos took two steps and leapt, one foot on Manchil's back and a quick step up to stand on his shoulders. Mangos threw up his arms in triumph and jumped away as Manchil ducked and flailed his sword. Waves of laughter rolled down from the crowd.

Manchil spun, attacked, nearly purple with rage. Sword, scythe, scythe. Sword, scythe, kick. Even knowing the pattern Mangos could barely parry.

Be patient, Mangos told himself. Sword, scythe, sword. He knew the pattern and couldn't believe Manchil didn't realize it. Surely everybody realized it. Manchil was well trained for sure, but stupid. *Wait for the right moment.*

Sword, scythe, and the kick for his knee. *There.* Mangos rolled away, planted his hands and one foot, kicked the leg Manchil stood on. Manchil collapsed.

Mangos rose, stepped away, and took his whip from his belt.

Manchil stood, favoring his leg, moving slowly.

With a quick flick of his whip, Mangos snapped the clasp at Manchil's waist. Manchil's loincloth fell to the sand, leaving him naked and vulnerable to the crowd's laughter. Mangos straightened to attention and gave his foe a mocking salute.

The hourglass ran out, and the bell sounded, ending the match. Mangos had done what Kat wanted, but he still didn't know how it would solve their problem.

Mangos feasted well. While he hadn't killed his opponent, the crowd feted him like a king, moving him to the second table where he could be lauded by all and served immediately after the first table.

Two priests, a man in black representing the old year, and a woman in white representing the new, sat in the center of the first table, presiding but not eating. The Prince and his guests filed to the chairs on either side. The Prince was still dressed in his flamboyant tunic. Kat still wore her snow lion cape, but she had changed into loose cream-colored trousers and a light green blouse; a blouse, Mangos knew, that would bring out the color of her eyes.

Manchil sat with them, looking both angry and despondent. He wore a restrained maroon shirt, open at the neck, with leather bracers, and charcoal grey trousers held up by a broad leather belt. Mangos couldn't help smirking as Manchil stared down at the table.

Kat would not meet his eyes. She spent her time flirting with the Prince, laughing, laying her hand on his arm, batting her eyes. When she wasn't doting on the

Prince, she consoled Manchil. She leaned against him to whisper in his ear. This seemed to cheer him some but appeared to frustrate the Prince, and it infuriated Mangos.

A poison, he told himself, *she's going to poison him*, but he didn't believe it, for there would be no point in embarrassing Manchil if she just meant to poison him.

Mangos wondered if it was too late to donate his sword. He wouldn't need it anymore tonight, and could use all the luck he could get.

The sun passed beyond autumn as the revelers rose from the table. Some headed toward the southern transept where the runway had been cleared away to make room for dancing. Others wandered up and down the nave where entertainers performed.

Mangos found himself with the dancers, not that he felt like dancing. Kat would be there. They could run away. They'd never walked away from a job before, but they'd never had a job like this. And he'd never felt such attraction to Kat, either. It was affecting his thinking.

It must be the festival. Once they got away from Alomar, they could return to just being partners. Right now, he wasn't sure if that was what he wanted—he wasn't sure of anything.

The dance floor was awash in colors from the expensive gowns and jewels as couples spun to the music. The press of dancers parted, and he could see Kat walking toward him.

She was stunning. She wore a long, cream-colored gown that hugged her tightly. It had one shoulder strap and no belt, though it fit her waist perfectly. Jewels sparkled as she walked, priceless leopard-eye emeralds at her throat and on her ears.

Mangos smiled as he saw her, his heart beating faster. "By the gods of Eastwarn," he murmured. "By the gods of Eastwarn." He moved across the floor in a daze, noticing others just enough to avoid them as he held out his hand to take her in his arms and dance.

While he was still ten feet away she turned her head, lifted her hand, and swirled away in the arms of Manchil.

It felt like being struck in the gut. He dropped his hand. The dancers closed in around him, Kat and Manchil vanished in the crowd, and he shuffled off the dance floor.

Anger built as he stepped off the floor and turned to look over the dancers. The Hand came to stand next to him.

"Peace," the Hand said. "Find another woman for dancing. She is not the only one here."

Mangos shook his head. "I have saved her life countless times. We've traveled far lands together. Yet *she will not dance with me!*"

The Hand smiled, a tolerant smile. "If it makes you feel better, she would not dance with me, either."

"You asked her?"

"I, and every man here," the Hand said.

"But she dances with that fool, whose intelligence she mocked and whom I exposed as fraud in the arena!" By chance, he caught sight of Kat through the press of dancers. She was pressed against Manchil with every appearance of intimacy. "I'll kill him."

The Hand grabbed his shoulder before he could move. "And the Prince will visit retribution on the Bursa," the Hand said. "Here comes the Prince now."

The Prince cut in, taking Kat from Manchil's arms. He tried to draw her close, which she allowed, though not as close as she allowed Manchil.

A popping sound surprised Mangos, and he realized it was his knuckles as he clenched and unclenched his fists.

"You will not kill *him*, either," the Hand said, nodding toward the Prince.

"No," sighed Mangos, feeling hollow. "Gods, how can she do this? What happened?"

"The Bursa hired you," the Hand replied.

"And damn him for putting us where she would meet them."

The Hand nodded toward some chairs where the Bursa sat with a frustrated and angry expression. "Carefully," the Hand said.

Mangos curled his lip, sneering at the entire situation. The Bursa would fall; he saw no way around it. But Kat was safe; the Prince would protect her. She was making sure of that.

If he was honest, he really didn't care. The image of Kat dancing close to Manchil burned into his mind. He wanted to get very, very drunk.

The Hand stood next to Mangos, watching as the priest started the offering ceremony. "When the offering is completed, the new year begins," he said.

"I know," Mangos said.

The priests approached the altar. Behind them, a pair of slaves drew carts of offerings—small coins, pottery, a cage of chickens, Mangos's sword—the gifts of people not important enough to present them individually.

"When the new year begins, the spell is lifted from Manchil," the Hand said. "He will be able to speak."

"I know," Mangos said. Why not just say they would have failed?

"If Manchil can speak, the Bursa will make sure you feel his pain."

Mangos snorted. There was a time this would have intimidated him. It might be true, but he'd be damned if he suffered alone. "It's your plan," he said. "You hired the Mongoose and Meerkat."

"The Bursa reminded me of that, too," the Hand said.

Neither spoke as devotees approached the low altar wall separating the nave from the chancel. The black-robed Old Year took their offerings and bore them to where the white-robed New Year sat enthroned at the altar.

These were costly gifts; given by prominent citizens, but except for a few given by the truly devoted, Mangos didn't see anything that would be missed. Alomar didn't take the gods *that* seriously.

The Prince stood next to the altar wall; it was customary that he be last. Manchil waited next to him, holding an iron-bound chest that contained the Prince's offering. Kat stood too close to Manchil for Mangos'scomfort. He was not the only one, either. The Prince glanced from her to Manchil, frowning slightly, before looking back to the ceremony.

Maybe, Mangos thought, she's going to

kill Manchil and trust the attraction the Prince feels for her to protect them. But the Prince would cheerfully ignore Kat's role (if it pleased him) and cast the blame on the Bursa as he promised.

The sun, now dim, approached the back of the chancel. The last citizens brought their gifts, and all eyes turned to the Prince. He stepped forward, Manchil trailing after him holding the coffer.

"This plan didn't work," murmured the Hand.

The Prince lifted the coffer from Manchil, tucked it under his arm—and pushed Manchil past the altar wall.

Manchil looked back in confusion. Murmurs ran through the crowd. The priest of the old year took Manchil's arm and guided him to the altar; he followed like a bewildered child.

Mangos blinked. "What happened?"

The Hand laughed quietly. "The Prince just donated Manchil to the gods. He's a temple slave now!"

"But he's not dead..." Mangos trailed off.

"He may as well be. As temple property, he is immune to the laws of the city. He is beyond the Prince's reach. That will satisfy the Bursa."

The light in the crystal sun went out, and fireworks lifted off, filling the vaults with explosions of color and light, signaling the successful renewal and anticipation of the real sun rising again in the morning.

Not knowing whether to be happy they fulfilled their contract or despondent that Kat had barely talked to him, Mangos drank. He was trying to convince himself it was all a bad dream, but three ales in he wasn't making much progress.

The true sun would rise in a couple of hours, bringing a new day and a new year. He couldn't care less. The bar was empty except for him. Even the barkeep had gone to bed.

The door opened, and Kat came in. Sat down across from him. The old Kat, hair drawn back, dressed as she used to dress. As beautiful as any work of art, and one that he could view without a trace of desire.

Mangos looked at his mug, wondering if he were drunk now, how to interpret earlier. He looked at her, trying to conjure up the desire and jealousy he had felt. He couldn't do it.

"You did perfectly," Kat said.

"I don't understand." *About a lot of things, which is*, he thought, *an understatement.* But it was safest to ask, "Why did the Prince donate Manchil to the Temple?"

"What good is a weak, stupid slave?" Kat asked. "You might keep him because he's expensive, but when he's also a competitor for the attractions of a woman..." She shrugged. "It's better to just to get rid of him."

"So you made the Prince—"

"It's easy to make powerful men jealous," Kat said.

Pushing the mug away, Mangos sorted his thoughts. "Making Manchil look stupid made the Prince doubt his ability to give evidence against the Bursa."

Kat nodded. "And in the arena, you made the Prince doubt Manchil's value as a gladiator.

"And he wanted Manchil out of the way," she continued.

"*I* wanted Manchil out of the way too," Mangos admitted.

"For the same reason, maybe," Kat said. Mangos couldn't read the expression in her eyes. It seemed less important now.

"He couldn't kill Manchil himself," Kat continued after a moment, "because he would still have to punish the Bursa for Manchil's death—which would be too much even for Alomar."

Mangos laughed. He couldn't help it. "I bet he thought he was clever when he decided to donate Manchil."

"I'm sure."

Mangos toyed with the mug, spinning it idly on the table but not drinking. The world was a more familiar place now. "You had Snader place a glamor on you to become more desirable?"

"No, quite the opposite," Kat said. "But the job is done, and all is returned to normal—no matter anybody's desire otherwise; mine, yours, or the Prince's."

Jim Breyfogle's Tale of the Mongoose and Meerkat continue in our next issue with Fight of the Sand Fishers! In addition to his fantasy romance, The Paths of Cormanor, and the first volume of Mongoose and Meerkat, Cirsova Publishing will be releasing a second volume collecting Kat and Mangos's adventures later this year.

What Price the Stars

By JEFF STONER

Jørgen Pangloss offers the promise of the unthinkable: faster-than-light travel! To what lengths will potential investors go to win Jørgen monopoly... and its fetters!?

Chapter 1
The Demonstration

Michael Von Ekaterinburg noticed the strange spacecraft as soon as he arrived at the Montevideo Grand Hotel. Parked on a little greensward, it looked exactly like a flying saucer from an ancient twodee, complete with spindly landing legs and a metallic silver paint job. The young Novaruskeen industialist chuckled at the sight and made a mental note to take a closer look after his business was complete.

Michael's business was mysterious in itself. Months ago, a strange man had approached him on the street and silently presented an invitation. He held the selfsame card in his hand. It was no less cryptic now than it had been when he received it.

Mister Jørgen Pangloss
Cordially requests the presence of the Estimable Michael Borisovich Von Ekaterinburg, Esquire, at the Grand Hotel, Montevideo, on Twelvemonth 1st at 1300 for a technology demonstration.
A complimentary afternoon tea will be served afterwards at Madam Shigueva's Tea Room, Pournelle City, New Earth. Sun protection is recommended.

The invitation was absurd on its face.

New Earth was humanity's only interstellar colony. It orbited Gliese 832 in the constellation Grus. The only way to get there was a century-long voyage by sleeper ship. Inquiries after Jørgen Pangloss had come back empty. There was no such person, either on Earth or Mars. Michael had chosen to attend anyway. His family's fortune was built on following the road less traveled. If this was a prank, at the worst he would spend a balmy summer day in South America.

Leaving the flying saucer behind, Michael entered the hotel. The gathering was in the main ballroom. A handful of people were already inside. All but one were familiar, an old man with a cheap straw hat pulled down over his eyes. He sat by the patio doors with his back turned, probably a local sheltering from the blazing heat outside. Michael promptly forgot about him when a familiar female voice hailed him.

"Mishka! I didn't imagine I'd see you here," said Alexi Petavia, the tall blonde CEO of Petavmash Combat Systems, a schoolmate of Michael's and his most attractive competitor.

"I might say the same to you, Alechka. My invitation doesn't mention anything that explodes," he replied playfully.

She grinned. "I'm just here for the free

89

funjuice."

A genial elderly gentleman cut into their chat. "You're curious. We all are, or else we wouldn't be here," said John Roerich, a renowned Martian habitat developer.

"Do you have any idea what this is all about?" asked Alexi.

"No, but I couldn't help but notice the implication. Do you suppose we are going to see a hyperdrive in operation?"

"That was also my impression," agreed Tuan Li, the stern little president of Daiginga Spacecraft Corporation. "I'm skeptical. Everyone knows that objects with mass cannot break the light barrier. You can't fool the gods of the Unified Law."

"But you can always fool people, hence this charade," announced Professor Chandra Rosencrantz, Dean of panspectrum holography at Tycho University. "Ibn Yaghi's principle of unified scalar progression is thoroughly tested and confirms Einstein. The light barrier is unbreakable. What intrigues me is how this Pangloss character intends to trick us. We are the smartest people on the planet."

By this, Rosencrantz meant that *he* was the smartest man on the planet. He made no secret of his voluminous credentials, and his mastery of nonstandard dynamic holographic geometry was uncontested. Nevertheless, he was out of his depth in the present company. Michael's most charitable estimate of his business acumen put him below a common street vendor.

The snick of a latch drew the group's attention. The man Michael had taken for a local locked the lobby door and laid aside his battered hat. He was not aged. Though his hair was white and he wore a crisp black suit in a style not seen for centuries, his frame was hale, and his uncanny silver eyes flamed with the vigor of youth. His voice commanded attention. "Good afternoon. Thank you for coming. I am Jørgen Pangloss. While it is disappointing that only five of you chose to attend, it will make your contest all the shorter."

"Contest?" snapped Li. "Mister Pangloss, we are executives and scientists. Our time is valuable. We are not here to play parlor games but to see the technology demonstration you promised."

"No one's time is as valuable as mine," Jørgen replied. "But I must beg your pardon. The demonstration of my starship's capabilities is but the prelude of a contest that will definitely interest you. The winner will obtain unlimited success and a place in history alongside Newton, Einstein, and Ibn Yaghi. The rest of you—assuming you survive—will be returned here with no memory of the next twenty-four hours."

Alexi laughed. "Assuming we survive? Do you really expect any of us to agree to those terms?"

"I do. But we will waste no more time here. We shall travel swiftly, but not faster than Madam Shigueva will cancel our reservation if we are late for tea. Come, my ship awaits." Jørgen opened the patio door and stepped outside.

Michael followed, but Alexi grabbed his wrist. "Mishka, no. He's insane."

"Aren't you even the least bit curious about his spaceship?"

Rosencrantz scoffed. "It's just a prop!"

"What did you say earlier? If he thinks he can fool us, he must have a good scheme. I want to see what it is."

"As do I. I am going," Roerich declared.

Alexi shook her head. "If all of you are going, I suppose I will, too. If it's a con, I might learn something from it. If it's for real..."

Li completed her sentence. "If it is real, we would be fools to walk away."

Michael chuckled to himself. Charlatan or no, Jørgen had them hooked.

They caught up with their strange host on the greensward. A ramp had lowered from the looming silver saucer. Jørgen motioned towards it. "I present the Inscrutable."

"I've never seen anything like this. Who makes it?" Li asked.

"She's my own design. Twin fusion motors, dual redundant zed reactors, luxury accommodations for ten, gourmet kitchen, wet bar, and a fully operational Spooky engine."

"A *what*?"

"It does no good to describe it. You must see it in action."

"By traveling five parsecs before teatime?" teased Alexi.

Jørgen nodded. "Just so."

The titans of industry exchanged dubious glances, but all five of them followed Jørgen up the ramp.

Chapter 2
The Flight of the Inscrutable

Inscrutable was incredible in every way. Her hull was a one-way transparency that gave a commanding view of her surroundings. In lieu of a cockpit, a mobile halo of virtual holographic controls encircled Jørgen as soon as he alighted on the deck. But her strangest fixture was a huge cylinder that squatted in the center of the main deck, its golden skin festooned with arcane hieroglyphics. They changed right before Michael's eyes, flowing silently across the metal like ripples on the surface of a pond. Curious, Michael reached out to touch it. He was thwarted when his fingertips encountered an invisible wall of force.

Roerich appeared beside him and tried his hand. The same thing happened.

"That equipment does not care to be touched," Jørgen called from across the compartment.

"What a strange turn of phrase," Roerich mused.

Michael now noticed something even more alarming than the cylinder. Jørgen's hand was resting cozily on the small of Alexi's back. Alexi ordinarily did not allow such cheekiness. Whatever the true stake was, Michael wasn't willing to concede the contest *that* easily. He moved in behind them and leaned in as if inspecting Jørgen's traveling control constellation. Jørgen discreetly withdrew his hand, and Alexi glared daggers at Michael.

Jørgen took no notice of the drama playing out behind him. "I hope all of you are ready for launch. We will climb to altitude under conventional power before I demonstrate the Spooky engine. Please find a seat and enjoy the view."

Inscrutable filled with the familiar hum of lift engines. The party scrambled to find good seats. Michael settled beside Alexi on a couch. She stared straight ahead as Montevideo vanished beneath clouds. "Are you okay?" Michael finally hazarded.

"Never better. No thanks to you."

"Alexi, you don't know a thing about

Jørgen. Just a few minutes ago you called him insane."

"So what? He knows how to treat a woman."

"He knows how to take advantage of the situation."

She snorted mirthlessly. "He took no more than I offered. I don't need a chaperone, Michael."

"Not a chaperone, a counselor. If I were you..."

She angrily cut him off. "You aren't me, and I'll flirt with the old goat if I want to. Now, if you'll excuse me." She stalked away in a huff.

"Trouble in paradise?" came Rosencrantz's unwelcome voice. Without waiting for an answer, the wispy man took a seat next to Michael. He dandled a jigger glass in his right hand. "If you ask me, she's a fool. The madman can't possibly deliver. She'll exchange her virtue for nothing."

"Are you sure?"

"Of course I am. Li is right. The Unified Law is tried and true. Pangloss is a fraud."

"I thought so too, but I'm beginning to wonder."

"This ship impresses you? I must admit it's better than I expected, but not beyond the means of a professional confidence man. His schnapps is first-rate, too." He downed his glass with a chuckle.

The sky outside was growing black. Without warning, crushing thrust mashed Michael and his unwanted guest into their seats. Rosencrantz was terrified. "Why are the motors at full power?" he shouted.

The scene outside abruptly overturned. The broad blue expanse of the Atlantic loomed ahead of them. A bright corona of superheated air coalesced and roughly embraced the hull. Tiny dots on the sparkling sea swiftly grew into rugged pinnacles of black rock. Pinned in place by massive gees, Michael jammed his eyes shut and waited to die.

His stomach lurched, and the brutal thrust vanished. Hardly daring to hope, Michael opened his eyes. He saw no rocks, no ocean, and no Earth. Inscrutable was flying free in empty space.

Rosencrantz was curled into a fetal position on the deck. Michael prodded him. "You can relax. We're not dead."

The professor uncurled. "What happened? Where are we?" he whimpered.

As if in answer to his question, a world hove into view outside, all azure blue and ocher. Unfamiliar continents peeked out from beneath a filigree of silver clouds, and a brace of stark white crescent moons hung in the distance behind it.

"Lovely, isn't she?" said Jørgen Pangloss from behind the couch, where he stood with Alexi draped decorously on his arm like a gangster's moll. Li and Roerich flanked them, eyes wide.

"My incomparable lady, gentlemen, I give you New Earth," Jørgen announced, a conqueror's smile on his thin lips.

Chapter 3
Go Climb a Tree!

The ruby sunlight of Gliese 832 sparked in the pools of Glorious Founders Park like a million welding arcs. Michael wished he'd heeded Jørgen's warning and brought sunglasses. Only Jørgen and Roerich had come prepared, but Jørgen had immediately surrendered his antique sunglasses—

Wayfarers, he called them–to Alexi. She walked close beside him, their fingertips occasionally brushing. Li stalked along next to Michael, alert but stonily silent. Rosencrantz brought up the rear, grumbling and fussing to himself. "Intolerable!" he suddenly exclaimed. "Haven't any of you realized why we took that swan dive?"

"Not this again," Alexi retorted irritably. "There's a huge velocity difference between New Earth and old Earth. Jørgen compensated for it."

"Nonsense. It was a distraction, so we wouldn't notice when we were jacked into a simulation."

"You can't be serious!"

"I am deadly serious. Not that I'd expect you to take a rational view of the situation. It would interfere with your puerile sex ploy."

Alexi's jaw dropped. "*Ty chertovski pedik!*" she snarled.

Jørgen laid a soothing hand on her shoulder. "Peace, peace. He is right to demand a proof. Professor, what would suffice to overcome your doubts?"

"A controlled experiment."

Heads wagged in agreement, including Michael's. Absent evidence to the contrary, Rosencrantz was probably right. Even Alexi fell silent. She kicked at the dark pebbles of the path, as if to prove to herself that they were solid.

Roerich cleared his throat. "I may have a solution. When I was young, I had a foolish habit of carving my initials. Jørgen couldn't know where I put them. As luck would have it, some are nearby. If we find them, your simulation theory will be disproved."

"Would you be kind enough to lead us?" asked Jørgen.

"No offense, but for it to serve as a proof, you must remove yourself. We will make the search and report."

"No offense taken. But who will go with me, to make sure I don't interfere?" Jørgen's brilliant eyes shot to Alexi.

Li coughed. "I will."

Jørgen took the imposition in stride. "Excellent! The local brews are good, and I know a place nearby. Please join me."

Li nodded and followed Jørgen down a side trail. As soon as they were out of sight, Roerich pointed in the opposite direction. "It's in there, past the drumhead plantation. Don't mind the drumbeater bugs. They eat drumhead spores, not people."

With Roerich in the lead, they plunged into a stand of blobby alien trees that thrummed from the drumming of hidden insects. Michael deliberately lagged behind, the better to speak with Alexi. "Don't start on me, Mishka," she hissed. "I know what I'm doing."

"How far will you go?"

"Do you need to ask? Jørgen's got a working hyperdrive. The company that gets it will control the interstellar economy. I'll sell my soul if I have to, but I'm going to win it for Petavmash."

"You don't think Rosencrantz's theory is right?"

"Not for a minute."

"Well, whatever happens, be careful. I don't know what Jørgen's game is yet, but he's formidable. He certainly knows what you're up to. I'd hate for you to get hurt."

Alexi rolled her eyes. "Thanks, but I'd hate to lose."

They emerged from the drumhead plantation into a broad park. "Up there," Roerich announced, pointing to a colossal alien plant. It resembled nothing more than a ten-story bronze carrot.

Rosencrantz drew up short. "I thought we were looking for initials?"

"I carved them up where the main trunk branches. I was more agile in those days, and the tree smaller."

"It's twenty meters high, at least! How can we see them?"

Michael laughed. "We climb, Professor. Come on."

The group circled the towering tree. Michael soon found an ascent route. It followed the line of a deep, spiraling rupture in the trunk. The ragged bark offered ready-made handholds. He hauled himself up, with Alexi close behind. But Rosencrantz and Roerich stayed put at the base of the tree.

"Are you coming?" called Alexi.

"Ah, well, no," Rosencrantz replied timorously.

"I hope you will forgive me, but tree climbing is for the young," Roerich said.

"Lazy men!" Alexi grumbled.

The climb was difficult. The craggy bark scuffed Michael's hands and ankles. Alexi's fashionable boots protected her shins, but they were swiftly ruined. She bore the indignity with stoic calm, which she maintained until the drumbeater bugs began to buzz around her. "Do I look like a drumhead tree?" she huffed, pausing to claw one of the golf ball-sized creatures out of her hair.

"Don't smash them. It'll draw a swarm," Roerich hollered from below.

"Now he tells us," Alexi groaned.

At the top of the trunk Michael found a wide hollow fringed by stout branches. He helped Alexi over the lip. They collapsed together, tired and panting.

"I hope the tea house has a washroom," Michael said.

"And a first aid station," Alexi said ruefully, rubbing her bloody hands.

"We're going to need it. Let's find those initials and get this over with."

They began a slow circuit of the hollow. The going was treacherous, but the search area was small. They soon found a branch cut with a jumble of old scars.

"This has to be it," said Alexi. "Can you make out what it says?"

"I see a 'J'. That's for 'John'."

"But is the second initial 'B'?" Alexi asked, peering under her borrowed glasses.

Michael called down to Roerich. "John, did you carve 'JB' instead of 'JR'?"

"No. It has to be 'JR'."

"Sorry. It's 'JB'." Alexi confirmed.

"Does the lower loop of the 'B' look like an addition?" Roerich replied.

Alexi scrubbed the second letter with her heel, revealing the ghostly front foot of an 'R'. She pumped her grimy fist. "You're right! It's a 'B' carved over top of an 'R'."

Roerich roared with laughter. "That bastard!" he exclaimed. "My best friend was Javer Bylok. He came behind me and defaced my initials with his own!"

Michael was impatient. "I don't think we'll get better proof than this. Professor, are you satisfied?"

Rosencrantz dithered far below. "I'm not convinced. Perhaps this rogue here is in on the plot!"

Alexi flew into a rage. "Really? Do you think this was easy? If you want a better proof, find it yourself!" As she shouted the last, an errant drumbeater bumbled into her face. She angrily swatted it. Pungent yellow goo splattered her breast. A cloud of the golden bugs immediately dropped from the canopy overhead and swarmed over Alexi. She flailed, vainly trying to swat them away. Before Michael could reach her, she stumbled into open air.

Michael lunged for her. He caught hold of her wrist, but his hand was slimy with muck. "I can't hold on! Grab the tree!" he shouted, but it was too late. Alexi slipped away with a shriek.

Thrown off-balance, Michael almost tumbled after her. He scrabbled for hand-holds, barely managing to catch himself on a branch. His lacerated fingers arced with pain, but no physical sensation could compete with the anguish in his soul. He could hardly bear to look below at what had become of Alexi, but he did. To his almost infinite astonishment, he saw Alexi very much alive, unharmed, and cradled safely in the arms of Jørgen Pangloss. It was impossible. No man could have caught her out of the air, or broken her fall without injury, or appeared out of nowhere to do it, for that matter.

Who is he? Michael wondered, and not for the last time.

Chapter 4
Tea, Five Parsecs From Home

Madam Shigueva's Tea Room reminded Michael of a museum. In lieu of decoration, the walls played out holographic scenes of the colonization of New Earth.

Great rockets landed, heroic voyagers emerged, and bright flags were planted in eerie silence. The teacups were shaped like bulbous space helmets, each emblazoned with the name of a founding cosmonaut. Roerich grinned. His bore the legend 'Bylock.' "I can't shake the bastard," he joked.

Michael laughed as politely as his itching hands would allow. His tattered skin was healing beneath a protective layer of pink nanoplasm. He could hardly wait to peel it off after tea.

Alexi sat across the table at Jørgen's right hand. Unlike Michael, she'd received no medical care, but her hands were perfectly healed notwithstanding. On a hunch, Michael dropped his napkin. While retrieving it, he confirmed that Alexi's formerly shredded boots were as good as new. It was obvious that she'd found favor with their strange and powerful host.

Jørgen headed the party with effusive grace, as if nothing was out of the ordinary. When the dessert was delivered, he uncovered a plate and passed it to Li. "I cannot recommend these scones highly enough. They pair well with the milaya-infused tea."

Li sat the dish aside. "How does it work?" he demanded.

Jørgen blinked. "You'd have to ask Madam Shigueva, but I gather her recipes are a family secret."

"Not the food! The Spooky engine."

Jørgen replaced the serviette and leaned back, tenting his fingers behind his head. "That's a good question. I don't know."

"Do you mean to say that we risked our lives aboard a ship that moves by an unknown principle?"

"The method may be unknown, but the principle is not. Two unrelated objects may undergo a simultaneous state change, even if they are light-years apart. Einstein called this 'spooky action at a distance'. The Spooky engine uses it, causing a spaceship to exist in two places at once. Neither is a duplicate. Both are instances of the exact same vessel. Because the universe must conserve mass, the original instance immediately vanishes in a puff of luxons. Travel is instantaneous and perfectly safe."

"Fascinating. Preposterous, but fascinating," Rosencrantz declared.

"How are the engines made?" Li asked.

"We can visit the foundry if you like."

"I would," said Li.

"Me too," Alexi seconded. Michael nodded, to be polite.

Rosencrantz waggled his tiny petit-four fork at Jørgen. "Not so fast. Assuming your engine works as you say—which I doubt, mind you—you must share it with all humanity."

"I'm doing just that."

"Don't make me laugh. If one of these paragons of avarice gets it, they'll have an overnight monopoly on interstellar travel. They'll demand a premium price for the engines, ensuring that only people like themselves can reach the stars. Wouldn't it be better to give it to a responsible custodian who will distribute it equitably, for the betterment of humankind?"

"That would be you, of course."

"I didn't say that."

"You didn't have to. But if the equitable distribution of my engine is so important to you, you should try all the harder to win."

"You still haven't described the contest. When does it start? What are the rules?"

"It began the moment you entered my presence. The rules are entirely up to you. I am but the judge."

Michael was not surprised, and judging by Li's stony brow and Alexi's smug grin, neither were they. But Rosencrantz was taken aback. "It's a sham, then!" he protested. "You'll do whatever you please, humanity be damned."

"I have always done so, and there is none to stop me. But the contest is well underway. What intrigues me is that none of you have asked if there are conditions."

"There are conditions?" Alexi asked.

"Of course. The means of production shall forever be mine and mine alone. I will provide the necessary equipment and staff. My involvement must be kept secret, even from your closest associates. Lastly, the winner and his progeny shall be my servants in perpetuity."

Alexi's eyebrows went up. "Your *servants*?"

"Aye. Retainers, if you like. Slaves if you choose not to mince words."

"I'm not surprised," said Li. "But what do you mean by in perpetuity?"

"Forever, until the end of time, world without end, or however you might choose to formulate it."

Rosencrantz squelched derisively. "Such presumption! Your conditions won't hold sway over anyone when you're dead and gone."

Jørgen smirked, an expression that gave his sharp features a positively lupine aspect. "Perhaps not. But in my case, death is already extraordinarily tardy. I believe he may be afraid of me. If you are counting on my demise to release you from your obligations, you will be sadly disappointed."

"Are you claiming to be immortal?"

"As men measure life, I am."

A giggle cut off in Alexi's throat. Someone coughed. Despite the warmth of the room, Michael shivered. "What would happen if one of your conditions was broken?" he asked.

Jørgen leaned forward, his argent eyes filled with living fire. "I would be very, very angry. Tea time is over. The foundry awaits us. Shall we go?"

Everyone followed, except for Roerich.

"Is there something you'd like to tell us, John?" Jørgen prompted.

Roerich nodded. "If it's all right by you, I'd like to stay here. Riches and power may tempt the young, but I'd rather spend my few remaining days in the home I never imagined I'd see again."

Rosencrantz erupted. "You accepted the invitation only to return to New Earth? With that kind of faith, you're no better than a religionist."

Jørgen cleared his throat. "Perhaps the professor is right, but faith deserves a reward. John Roerich, you may stay, with my compliments and goodwill. Long may you dwell in your childhood home." He laid a hand on the old man's head. It might have been a trick of the light, but the lines in Roerich's face seemed to flee from Jørgen's touch, and did not return.

Their host had strange powers, and Michael no longer doubted that he could deliver on his promises. But Michael pondered his own soul, and what price it might sell for.

Chapter 5
A Safe Harbor

The stars outside changed. Michael's stomach flipped. The scone he'd eaten at tea jumped to the back of his mouth. He gulped it back down with effort. Alexi was less lucky. The remains of her meal splattered across the Inscrutable's deck. Jørgen rushed to drape his jacket over her shoulders. "I'm sorry," he said. "The discomfort that accompanies a ghostride is unavoidable. Some people are more sensitive than others."

"What causes it?" asked Michael.

"Minor spiritual trauma. Unlike matter, pneuma cannot be instantiated. During a ghostride your soul is stretched between your origin point and your destination. When your origin instance is voided, it snaps back, causing psychic whiplash."

Rosencrantz snorted. "Psychic whiplash? Tosh."

"Professor, I invite you to come up with a better explanation."

"I shall."

"I await it, but here is our destination." Jørgen yawed the Inscrutable to port. A steely gas giant world hove into view, banded and bruised with indigo storms. So swift was the planet's rotation that it was visibly flattened. A flotilla of moons compassed around it, at this range little more than a stately escort of colorful dots.

"A super Jupiter," Li marveled. "There are none near the solar system. Where are we?"

"This world has no name on any charts. But its inhabitants call it Sanctum Dominio."

The approach would take some time.

While Rosencrantz and Li peppered Jørgen with questions, Alexi retired to the lavatory, and Michael slipped away in search of a different sort of comfort. Fortified by the bar, he settled onto a couch and tried to calm his nerves without success. The four of them were utterly at Jørgen's mercy, and Jørgen was a closed book of the most dangerous variety. Alexi might trust him, but Michael did not. Ever since she'd slipped out of his grasp, Michael could think of nothing but keeping her safe. But how could he? Jørgen was the sun to Alexi's Icarus, and all Michael could do was watch her climb to her doom.

Someone gently touched his shoulder. He looked up, expecting Alexi. Jørgen was there instead.

"May I join you?"

"Yes," Michael replied, his actual feelings notwithstanding. "I'm surprised Tuan and Chandra let you go."

Jørgen chuckled. "My tormentors are arguing, so I excused myself. I've wanted a word with you. You speak little but listen well. I would hear your thoughts."

"You may be disappointed. I was thinking of Alexi."

"That disappoints me not at all. She is an exquisite creature, worthy of much contemplation. If I may be so bold, what bit of her occupies your thoughts?"

Michael was emboldened by the last of his drink. "Her hands."

"Aye. Matchless works of the Creator's art, delicate yet strong, and quick, I think, to ball into fists. From them I would treasure sweet caresses or savage blows, it matters not which. That's why I restored them when they were sadly battered."

His candor cut right through Michael's buzz. "You admit it. Would you mind explaining how?"

Jørgen shook his head. "A man may keep a few secrets, don't you agree?"

"I suppose. Thank you, by the way. Alexi is a dear friend of mine."

"More than a friend, I think."

Michael refused to take the bait. "What else would you like to discuss?"

"Do I guess rightly that you are not interested in the contest?"

"Yes," Michael replied. "My chief concern is..." he stopped when a refreshed Alexi appeared at Jørgen's side. She turned mischievous eyes on Michael.

"What are you concerned about, Mishka?"

"Our welfare." *Your welfare*, he said to himself.

Alexi giggled. "You are such an old man, Michael Borisovich!"

She peeled languorously out of her borrowed jacket, now liberally daubed with her favorite perfume. Receiving it, Jørgen took a deep breath and smiled. "Thank you, Lapooshka. It has returned to me better than ever, and warm!"

Lapooshka?

"Where there is warmth, there is fire," Alexi purred.

Michael's glass shot to his lips. It was empty.

"Perhaps I could get you something?" Jørgen offered.

"No, allow me," said Alexi. "I know Mishka's poison. What would you like, Jørgen?"

"As my lady chooses."

"One Venus's Endless Climax coming

right up," Alexi announced. She strutted away with a fantastic roll of hips.

Michael could stand no more. "You must know that it's all an act," he hissed.

"Beyond doubt. A cunning woman races her fastest horse first. Shrewd Alexi's mare is passing swift."

"Do you think so? I'm ashamed for her. Alexi is so much more than a mere temptress."

"There is no such thing as a mere temptress. A sword may slay a thousand men, but the loins of woman consume worlds and disgorge new ones in their place. The feminine is first among the temporal powers. Only the divine is greater."

"How archaic of you."

Jørgen smiled slyly. "Archaic is not necessarily wrong. The wise once held that the hand that rocks the cradle rules the world. They were right. But hush! The huntress returns."

Alexi appeared with a beverage tray. She handed Michael a mundane vodka but presented Jørgen with a fantastic pink concoction.

Jørgen took a taste. "A peerless choice," he announced.

Alexi licked her lips. "It's a pity that endless climaxes are reserved for stodgy old Venus."

"Are you quite sure of that?" Jørgen replied softly. Hot blood rose in Alexi's cheeks.

A chime interrupted. "We're being hailed," Jørgen said. He waved open his corona of holographic controls. One was blinking. He thrust a finger into it. A life-sized holo of a man appeared before him, wearing the robes of an ancient monk, complete with tonsure and an over-sized Latin cross.

"Dominie Pangloss, it's good to see you," the monk said.

"Thank you, Fra Grimaldi. Is the foundry prepared for our visit?"

"Yes. But won't you join us on Sacra Cor first? His Holiness has been asking after you. The shield girdle you provided has stopped working, and as you know, he is a cautious man."

"I will fix his girdle when I'm finished with my business. Until then, he may shelter inside his armored Popecarrier, unless that is defective, too."

"Oh, about that. It's in good working order, but the interior palette is that of Boniface the Ninety-Fifth. I hesitate to report that it clashes badly with His Holiness's favorite shoes."

"A pity. He will have to make do for now. Please inform the Abbess of Wrightstown that I'll be arriving soon."

"I shall, Dominie Pangloss. I daresay she will be glad to hear it. Good day to you."

The hologram vanished. The contestants stood astounded. Rosencrantz spoke first. "Please tell me that was some sort of charade for our amusement."

"Not at all," Jørgen said. "I have known Fra Grimaldi since he was a neophyte. He is tirelessly industrious. When I have my way, he shall be a Cardinal."

"What is the church doing here?"

"They shelter in the safe harbor I provided. Without me they would have died out long ago."

"A fine thing that would be! You've nurtured a hive of superstitious primitives! How can you make the engines here?"

Michael thought he knew. "It's obvious, Chandra. The church is running the foundry. They are the staff the winner must accept."

Jørgen nodded. "Very astute, Michael Borisovich. The Diaspora Catholic Church renders superb service. The winner will discover that they are literally indispensable partners."

"Partners?!" Rosencrantz exclaimed. "They are nothing but a liability! If the government learns of their survival, they'll send an armada to collect reparations."

Jørgen's eyes flashed. "They would find this place very well defended, indeed. I have promised the Church safe dwellings, and I do not break my word."

Rosencrantz bit his lip and said no more.

"Jørgen, the foundry cannot be on that gas giant, can it?" asked Alexi.

"It is not," Jørgen replied, working the controls. Inscrutable banked, and an Earth-sized moon appeared to starboard. It was no frozen rock, but an inviting blue marble brushed with swirls of white cloud. It had its own satellite, a metallic copper orb the size of a large asteroid. Jørgen steered straight towards it.

"We have arrived," Jørgen said. "Here are Sacra Cor, the home in exile of the Diaspora Catholic Church, and the foundry moon."

Chapter 6
Monsters

"This is a disaster," Rosencrantz grumbled as the party tromped down the Inscrutable's ramp.

"Please keep quiet. You're ruining the mood," Alexi scolded.

Michael was too interested in their surroundings to pay attention to the other's bickering. The foundry was unlike any space station he had ever seen. The fabric of the place was a translucent golden matrix that was neither metal nor plastic. Currents and eddies swirled in the floor beneath their feet. Suggestive shadows moved far below, lazily navigating the depths of presumably solid matter like whales beneath an amber ocean. Michael quickly averted his eyes from the nether abyss lest he succumb to vertigo.

Jørgen led them to an immense archway blocked by a single featureless door. Large enough to admit a brace of spaceliners, the lintel above it was a slab of...something. It was alive with motion. A swarm of immense eyes coalesced on it and focused on the group. Michael's feet moved slower and slower, as if they had a mind of their own. Li and Rosencrantz drew up short beside him, gaping in awe at the haunted door. Alexi noticed the men were no longer following. "What's wrong?" she said.

Rosencrantz pointed at the mobile, interested eyes on the lintel. "That. What is it?"

Alexi shrugged. "Unless it makes hyperdrives, who cares?"

"It seems rather more intelligent than a door should be," Rosencrantz stammered.

Alexi laughed. "Such bravery! You rail against superstition, but a door frightens you? But don't let me encourage you. If you stay here, I'll win by default."

Michael hurried to the door with Li and Rosencrantz hot on his heels. He caught up with Alexi and Jørgen just in time to catch a snatch of quiet conversation.

"...but what is it, really?" asked Alexi.

"Some call it the Watchman, for obvious reasons."

"But what does it do?"

"It watches, Lapooshka."

Michael chuckled to himself. For all Alexi's shameless flirting, Jørgen was as glib with her as he was with anyone else.

"Open, please," Jørgen said. The immense door withdrew slowly into the floor. The party gasped in unison. The arch opened on a vast, dim cavern. The ceiling was invisible in the gloom, and the far walls were lost in leaden haze. The amber floor was smooth, save for random, knee-high blocks of glass. An isolated cluster of boxy buildings squatted a little distance off. They looked lost and out of place, like a tiny sand castle on an empty beach. "There is Wrightstown," Jørgen said, striking off toward it at a brisk clip.

"Where are we?" Michael called, puffing to keep up.

"This is called the Hall of Receiving," Jørgen replied. "The Himalayas would fit inside with room to spare."

"What is received here?"

"Your guess is as good as mine. No one knows."

Winded, Rosencrantz staggered to a halt. He leaned heavily on one of the blocks of golden glass. "Enough!" he wheezed angrily. "This is your space station. You must know the purpose of all its parts."

"Why should I? I didn't build it," Jørgen said.

"Who did, then?"

Jørgen pointed down, at the block beneath the professor's hands. "Why don't you ask him?"

All four of them came close and peered into the murky block. At first, they saw nothing. The dark glass roiled with lazy currents of living shadow. But a colorless eddy soon swept by, revealing the occupant. It was not human. Huge eyes with pinpoint pupils stared sightlessly from its narrow head. At the base of the creature's long neck there was an enormous, ragged wound. Whatever it was, it had died a violent death.

A flow of honey color obscured the ghastly vision. The contestants looked up to find Jørgen grinning at them. "Unfortunately, he's not very talkative," he said.

"Is this an *alien*?" Alexi quavered.

"It is called a Grig. For ten billion years, the Grig watched over the universe. It was here that they conjured the engines that enabled them to leap from world to world."

"A Grig," Alexi said slowly, turning the strange word on her tongue. "Why haven't we met them?"

"None remain. They were consumed by their folly."

Rosencrantz cleared his throat. "A hyperdrive. A surviving church. Intelligent life. These things are enormous. When word gets out, everything will change."

"That is why they will be spoken of carefully, and in the case of the Grig, not at all. There are some things that mankind is not yet ready to know."

"Why is that?" Rosencrantz demanded. "Up until now, we've found no evidence of intelligent life. You turn up with an alien space station the size of Mars and expect us to keep it secret."

"The size of Pluto, actually," Jørgen said.

"Pluto, then! It doesn't matter. What

gives you the right to hide it?"

"Ownership, of course. The foundry moon is mine."

"Someone will certainly talk," observed Li.

Jørgen shook his head. "Not so. One of you will speak only as I command. The rest will remember nothing of this place, nor of the contest, nor of me."

Rosencrantz blanched. "Even worse! That would be pure exploitation."

"What else does one do with property?"

"People are not property," Li replied.

"Nonsense. Men are naturally chattel. All their lives they seek for an owner, but most find no lien-holder but their own miserable vices. Lucky is the man who finds a worthy master."

"Only a monster could believe that in this day and age!" Rosencrantz said.

Jørgen shrugged. "I am what I am, the times notwithstanding."

Michael noticed a group of human figures coming toward them. Their timing could not have been better to end this uncomfortable conversation. "I think we have company," he said.

"Excellent!" Jørgen said. "This will be the Abbess. I caution you to show her only the greatest respect. She is a maestro with the neuron flail."

"Is that the voice of experience?" Alexi teased nervously.

"Aye, it is. But she bored of me quickly. My groans and pleadings lack the authenticity that her satisfaction requires."

A squad of guards wearing powered armor and particolored cockades on their helmets arrived, headed by the Abbess. A hawk-nosed woman in a steel gray habit, she was obviously pregnant. "It's good to see you again, Reverend Mother Dumiel," Jørgen said, scraping low.

"The pleasure is all mine, Dominie Pangloss," she replied warmly. "My staff is prepared to meet your every need."

"That is unlikely. On the other hand, you have always exceeded my expectations."

The Abbess blushed but recovered quickly. "You flatter me, Dominie Pangloss. On behalf of the Ancient and Holy Order of Drivewrights, I welcome you and your guests to Wrightstown. Our home is your home, such as it is."

"Superb!" Jørgen replied. "We must soon take advantage of your generous hospitality. We will require food and a place to spend the night."

"Your guests may have the bunks in the safe room. A late meal will be served in the commons. I can promise abundance, but little else. Our table is simple, out of necessity. The kitchens are incomplete. All of our food must come up from Sacra Cor."

Jørgen laid a cheeky hand on her stomach. "I am pleased that you have not wanted for sustenance. Your twin boys are healthy and vigorous. Have you named them?"

"Andre and Bleriot. Our custom is to follow the alphabet. Perhaps next time I shall bear a girl. I dearly love the name Capucine."

"A beautiful name, and a lovely flower. Do you prefer the red or the gold?"

"The gold."

Jørgen traced a strange sign on her belly with a swift finger. "When beloved Capucine comes, she shall be fair, unlike her dusky brothers."

The Abbess gasped in delight. Michael was astonished. Jørgen promised fantastic gifts to his favorites.

Ever one to ignore the sublime, Alexi cleared her throat. "Ah, excuse me, Mother," she said awkwardly, "I'm no historian, but I didn't think the religious were permitted to make babies."

"It was true, long ago," the Abbess replied. "When the Neosoviets drove us into hiding, our vows were relaxed lest we die out. When Dominie Pangloss gave us a new home, procreation become a meritorious work. We bear joyfully so that Sacra Cor may be filled with life and worship."

Alexi opened her mouth to reply, but she wasn't given the chance. There was a huge explosion behind them, near the archway. Gigantic fingers of orange fire clawed the dim air of the Hall of Receiving. Michael pulled Alexi to the ground. But no shock wave came, and no debris fell.

"Stay here," Jørgen commanded. The Abbess's armored bodyguard lifted into the air and roared off toward the source of the blast. Jørgen rode the leader like a mounted knight, his black jacket flapping in the slipstream.

"What just happened?" Michael wondered aloud.

"Bad business," replied Li, who remained standing and curiously unruffled.

Michael helped Alexi to her feet. "Are you okay?" he asked.

"I'm fine," she said, dusting her knees and elbows. "Thank you, Mishka. I wasn't expecting that."

"You still think the contest is worth it?"

"I do," she said, squinting after Jørgen.

"I can't tell what's going on. Did you see where Rosencrantz got off to?"

The light changed. The Abbess screamed.

Michael whirled to behold a huge black monster. Tatters of shadow hung from its hulking husk like the wrappings of a mummy. But its face was the queer fishy visage of a Grig, and it reached out for Mother Dumiel with immense, iron-clawed hands.

The Abbess stood her ground. She withdrew from her habit a device like the hilt of a knife. A neuron flail, just as Jørgen had warned. The entity took a menacing step toward her, and she fired. Unfazed, the monster charged. Mother Dumiel gave back but slipped on the glassy pavement. She fell, landing hard at the feet of the apparition.

Help came from an unexpected quarter. Professor Rosencrantz dashed out of nowhere and stood over her, arms outstretched. "Begone, you alien thing!" he screeched in his reedy voice.

The monster halted and abruptly lumbered away into the gloom.

The guard returned in a roar of jetpacks, bearing an angry Jørgen. He dismounted and rushed to the Abbess' side. "Mother, are you hurt?" he asked earnestly.

She shook her head. "I don't believe I am. What was that creature?"

"It looked like a Grig," Rosencrantz declared.

"That cannot be," Mother Dumiel replied. "But thank you very much for rescuing me. You are very brave."

"Our good Professor is full of surprises," Jørgen said, but the look he gave Rosencrantz was peculiar indeed.

While the others comforted Mother Dumiel, Michael cautiously followed the monster, but it had vanished into the gloom. There was nothing as far as the eye could see, except for countless low Grig tombs that could not have hidden a man, let alone a giant.

Perplexed, Michael turned back. A shiny object like a coin caught his eye. It was unfamiliar: a crystal disk with a cluster of plastic studs protruding from its narrow edge. Whatever it was, it seemed like a clue. Michael put it in his pocket and returned to the others. But he chose not to tell them what he had found.

Chapter 7
Into the Depths

No rail guarded the foundry's rostrum. The kilometers-wide pit was suffused by a golden glow welling up from the depths. Rosencrantz leaned out over the yawning chasm as far as his courage allowed, which was very little. "I can't see anything," he complained.

"Of course you can't," Jørgen replied. "The working floor is a thousand stories below us."

"I see no way to descend," Li remarked.

"There is an elevator. But before we ride it, we must have a short council," Jørgen said. Heads nodded, and someone–probably Rosencrantz–groaned. Jørgen continued. "Beyond this point, none may ordinarily go."

"Why not?" asked Rosencrantz.

"'Bloody hand stains the paten', or so the wrights say. They will not risk contaminating the rostrum. An exception has been made for us. But beware! Inside the rostrum you must follow me closely, and touch nothing."

"Is it dangerous?" Alexi asked.

"You would not believe how dangerous it is even if I told you. There are a thousand ways to die in the foundry. Worst of all, there is danger to the place itself. One misstep, and the foundry might cease to function forever."

"You obviously need safety oversight," Li said.

"No oversight is possible. You will understand in a few minutes. Follow me," Jørgen said and stepped backwards off the cliff.

Alexi gasped and dashed to the edge. Michael joined her. He was astounded to see Jørgen standing upright on empty air, falling slowly toward a terrifyingly remote landscape. He gestured impatiently for them to follow.

"How much do you trust him?" Michael asked Alexi.

"Enough," she replied and jumped off the precipice. Michael grabbed for her, missed, and fell forward. He found himself floating slowly downward, half a meter above Alexi's head. She laughed happily. "This is better than the Gravity Well ride at the Lagrange Circus."

"This isn't ordinary gravity inversion, is it?" Rosencrantz shouted down from above. He and Li were suspended in midair above Michael.

"There are dual opposing gravity fields circling the entire perimeter of the rostrum," Jørgen replied. "When you enter at the top, the field below is slightly stronger. When you enter at the bottom, the reverse is true. Before you ask, no one has been able to reproduce it."

"Interesting. What is the capacity of the system?" asked Li.

"Quite small. It was probably intended only for foot traffic."

"What happens if you overload it?" asked Alexi.

"The terminal velocity rises. If enough mass got into the system, the ride down would be no different from a fall."

"Oh," she replied.

The descent was slow and nerve-wracking. Michael distracted himself by taking in the lay of the land. The rostrum was perfectly round. It was dominated by a central peak, a pyramid wrought of gleaming gold. It was connected to an encircling ring of low buildings by shimmering pipelines. It vaguely reminded Michael of an ancient circuit board, but it was obviously not manmade. The proportions were wrong, and the execution thoroughly alien. The only familiar objects were a scrum of heavy cargo lifters parked directly below. Michael knew them to be gargantuan, but from his vantage point they looked like a school of silver minnows at the bottom of a lake.

Many uneasy minutes later the party alighted on the floor of a cyclopean factory. Rows of immense golden cylinders floated on antigravity conveyors, attended by workmen who wore green stoles and clerical collars over their bulky waldo suits.

"Welcome to the rostrum," Jørgen said. "This is the working floor of the foundry. Here, the engine vessels are prepared for filling, and the completed units are packaged for shipment."

Michael pointed to the golden cylinders. "These are Spooky engines?" he asked.

"Yes. You saw one aboard Inscrutable."

"What do you mean by 'filling'?" asked the professor. "You make it sound as if they are containers."

"They are."

"Whatever for?"

"I must show you something before I can explain. Come." Jørgen led them to a broad track painted on the floor. As soon as Michael stepped onto it, he levitated a few centimeters and began to accelerate. Soon the rostrum was streaking by in a golden blur. But there was no wind, and he could walk as if he were on a solid floor.

Alexi sidled close to him and grinned. "When I win, I'm going to have this thing reverse-engineered. It will sell just as well as the engines."

"You're pretty sure of yourself, aren't you?"

"I am. Aren't you?"

Michael shook his head. "No. Something's wrong."

Alexi giggled. "My babushka has bigger balls than you! If Jørgen wanted to kill us, we'd be dead."

"It's not just Jørgen. This place isn't for us. We shouldn't be here."

"Don't be a superstitious ninny, Mishka."

"You think I'm being superstitious? Why don't you tell me why priests must run the foundry? By temperament and training, they're rigid and resist change. With staff like that, how can you innovate? Even streamlining processes will be difficult."

"Maybe they were the only workers Jørgen could find. What are you getting at?"

"The foundry is an alien machine that makes hyperdrives. I don't think the wrights do anything themselves. They're here to serve the machine."

Alexi nodded slowly. "You know, Jørgen said as much. But does it matter? I don't care who or what makes my product, so long as it works."

"Alechka, *think*. Jørgen could use anyone to serve the machine. Of all the people at his disposal, why did he choose priests?"

While Michael spoke, the track came parallel to one of the gleaming pipelines. Mirror-bright and smooth as glass, it whizzed by scant centimeters from the verge. Rosencrantz extended a tentative hand toward it. His fingertips were almost in contact before Jørgen seized him bodily and hurled him to the far side of the track.

"Ow! Why did you do that?" the professor yelped.

"I saved your ungrateful skin," Jørgen snapped. "I might have let you touch it and relieved myself of your aggravating presence, but you've committed no crime worthy of losing your soul."

Chapter 8
Revelations

"Lose my soul? What does that mean?" demanded Professor Rosencrantz.

Jørgen's reply was patient but firm. "It means exactly that. You attempted to touch the primary pneuma bus. The homogenized industrial pneuma it carries is almost identical to the quintessential pneuma of your soul. Had you made contact, you would have been drained like a battery."

"Next you'll say I'd have become a zombie."

"I'm not joking. Pneuma is your volitional essence. Without it, your body can do nothing. It would live on for a while, until dehydration and malnutrition took it, or something else found a use for it."

Alexi tugged Michael's sleeve. He bent to hear her whisper. "Mishka, when you're right, you're right."

He whispered back. "I wish I wasn't."

The trackway came to an end, depositing the party gently on the smooth floor. The golden pyramid loomed over them. The pneuma bus plunged into the floor at the toe of its foundation plinth. This was surmounted by a blind niche that extended the breadth of the pyramid. Above the niche was a heavy lintel. Michael was not surprised when a constellation of black snail-eyes blossomed on it.

Jørgen called a halt. "We have arrived. This is the sanctum. Inside, the engines are filled and sealed."

"Excellent. Let us go and see," said Li. He took a step toward the pyramid.

Jørgen stopped him with a firm hand. "We may not. The sanctum will only open for whom it will."

Li regarded him with unkind eyes. "Just as I expected. We cannot enter. Here is another thing in which we must trust you completely. Mister Pangloss, you are very predictable."

Jørgen smirked. "I have been called many things, Mister Li, but never before has anyone accused me of predictability. Rest assured, when we cast aside our masks, you will find me anything but constant. But I do not lie. Only one has entered the sanctum and lived to tell the tale."

"You?"

"Aye. I once was an ignorant wanderer, a seeker without a goal. But I was not blind. For those with second sight, the foundry is a beacon that outshines a thousand stars. I was drawn from afar like a moth to a flame. When I realized what I had found, I claimed it for myself. Too late, I became aware of the Wrightmaster. His seat of power is within the sanctum. We contended for the mastery, but reached a stalemate. He had not the power to drive me out, but I could not slay him without destroying the foundry. In the end, we reached a compromise. In exchange for a continuous source of pneuma, the Wrightmaster agreed to fill engines."

Michael hazarded a question. "Where does the pneuma come from?"

"Do you recall the entombed Grig in the hall above? There are billions of them. This moon was their last redoubt. At the end of the War of Wrath, it was besieged. When it fell, the defenders were judged harshly. Locked tight in their time-prisons, the Grig are tormented for all eternity."

"That creature we saw...it's not dead!?" Alexi gasped.

"As we reckon death, it is. The body you saw will never breathe again. But a Grig soul is trapped inside, the better to suffer. This moon is not a space station. It is an antechamber of Hell. But with the aid of the church, the Grig souls can be harvested and put to good use."

Michael gulped. "The wrights aren't technicians; they're exorcists. The Grig souls they release become the pneuma."

"Yes. The wrights handle capture, homogenization, and transport. The Wrightmaster consumes it and excretes non-sentient aeonic ghosts capable of speaking the Words of Travel. These are put into the engine vessels. It's a most beneficial arrangement for all involved. The Wrightmaster is satiated, the Grig are released from torment, the church replenishes her treasury of merit, and we get Spooky engines."

The blood drained out of Michael's face. "Spooky engines, ghostrides—you weren't being ironic."

"Not at all."

"It's a fairy tale!" Rosencrantz said. "Ghosts, aliens, and monsters! You may choose to take this madman at his word, but I don't. Supposedly we make the rules of this game. It's my turn!" He grabbed Alexi and jammed the business end of a very familiar black cylinder against the side of her head: Mother Dumiel's forgotten neuron flail.

"*Gopnik!*" Alexi snarled.

"Be quiet." Rosencrantz growled, pulling her toward the sanctum. "I'm going to get to the bottom of this nonsense. You will be my witness and insurance policy."

"Alexi!" Michael yelled. Jørgen clamped down on his arm. The look on his face said *be quiet.*

Pushing Alexi before him, Rosencrantz climbed the plinth. He shouted at the congeries of baleful mollusk eyes on the lintel. "I know you're watching! Open up! I'm not afraid to use this!" He waved the neuron flail to punctuate his threat.

The back wall of the niche disengaged from the lintel and receded slowly into the plinth, revealing a dark gap. Rosencrantz shoved Alexi inside. When nothing happened, he followed. They were immediately lost in the thick shadows.

Michael glared at Jørgen. "Well? Are we just going to stand here?"

"Have patience, Michael Borisovich. The worm turns as we speak," the old devil replied, a vicious grin on his thin lips.

A piercing shriek burst from the sanctum.

It took every ounce of strength in Michael's body to break Jørgen's viselike grasp, but break it he did. He rushed for the doorway but stopped when Alexi emerged dragging Rosencrantz's bloody body. Her normally short fingernails had grown into shocking razor-sharp talons. When Alexi saw Michael's horrified expression they retracted into her fingertips with a meaty slurp. "I hope there's a surgery nearby," she said.

Chapter 9
Final Appeal

The food served in the dreary common building was every bit as uninspiring as the Abbess promised. Tired, enervated, and not the least bit hungry, Michael pushed the starchy mass to and fro on his plate. Across from him, Alexi was tucking it in like a thing possessed. She noticed his wide eyes. "Using the implants depletes my glycogen levels. It gives a girl a big appetite."

Jørgen slid a steaming tureen toward her. "Eat, *Lapooshka*. You must recover."

Li chuckled from his seat at the far end of the table. "I cannot imagine why that foolish professor didn't guess that you have an implanted weapons suite. That technology is your company's stock in trade, is it not?"

"It is," Alexi confirmed between bites. "I have our Mata Hari Ultimate Undercover Package. I like it because it can't be detected by security scans. I'd prefer the Minerva Full Spectrum Dominance System, but the eye lasers are too conspicuous. I don't want to scare shareholders at the quarterly meeting."

Li grinned. "I would rather enjoy doing that. But doesn't the Mata Hari include a stunner? Using it instead of your blades would have been less... inelegant."

Alexi paused, a flash of annoyance bunching her brows. Then she giggled. "I guess you're right. But where would be the fun in that?"

Jørgen and Li laughed. Michael joined them, to be polite. At heart, he felt naïve and foolish. He'd had no more inkling that Alexi was armed than had poor Rosencrantz.

The street door opened, and a familiar monk entered. Jørgen greeted him with traditional air kisses. "Fra Grimaldi!" he exclaimed. "What brings you here? I thought you were busy protecting His Holiness from imaginary assassins and sartorial emergencies?"

Grimaldi grimaced. "Normally, I would be doing just that. But with Mother Dumiel in labor, the Foundry post was vacant, and I..."

Jørgen cut him off, suddenly deadly serious. "In labor?! Is she well otherwise? What of her babies?"

The big monk nodded furiously. "She and the twins are fine. But her water broke while you were visiting the Rostrum. The doctors blame it on her shock. They chose to induce labor, just to be safe."

"That's a relief. How is the Professor?"

"Out of surgery and resting. He'll be in for a surprise when he wakes up. The canons are waiting for him. They have quite a list of charges–Kidnapping, Assault, Breaking the Ban–that's a bad one–and Malicious Use of a Hologram. How they'll prove the last one, I don't know. We can't find the emitter he used to project his explosion and black monster."

"It will turn up," Jørgen said brightly. "I'm glad that he caused no worse mischief than he did. Had the Reverend Mother or children been harmed he would have had me to deal with, not those fussy canons."

"That reminds me," said Fra Grimaldi. "Mother Dumiel sends Domina Petavia her deepest compliments on the superb use of her purloined neuron flail."

Everyone turned to Alexi. "I didn't realize that you used the flail on him," Michael said, even more aghast than before.

"I saw no weapon when you returned. Did you keep it?" Li asked.

Alexi blushed. "No, I didn't."

"What happened to it, then?"

She rolled her eyes heavenward. "If you must know, I shoved it up his ass," she said, reaching for her goblet.

"Bravo!" cried Jørgen, to peals of laughter all around.

Grimaldi turned to Jørgen. "Will your guests require meals tomorrow?"

"Only breakfast, and only for three. I must leave before dawn. I have urgent business elsewhere."

"Of course, but what of the contest? We are very interested in the outcome, especially after what happened last time..."

Jørgen coughed, loudly. "There is nothing to report yet. A little time remains. Perhaps we will know more in the morning, yes?"

"Indeed, I look forward to it. Good night to you, Dominie Pangloss," Grimaldi said, and left.

Li followed him. "Please pardon me," he called to Jørgen. "Today has been tiring. A walk in the fresh air will clear my head."

"Please, be my guest. I plan to relax a bit myself." Jørgen withdrew a small sheaf of yellowed paper wrapped in cloth from inside his jacket—Michael had heard of such things, they were called books—and began to read.

When Jørgen appeared sufficiently engrossed in his reading, Michael leaned close to Alexi. "We need to talk," he said quietly.

She eyed him over the dregs of her goblet. "Well?"

"Not here."

Alexi reluctantly pushed back her chair. "Let's walk, then. I'm curious about the safe room we're going to have for quarters. I can't imagine it's comfortable."

They bade Jørgen good night and left the common building. The harsh floodlamps of Wrightstown filled the alleys between the battered trailers and habitat modules with inky shadows. Li was nowhere in sight, but the safe room was easy to find: a stoutly armored pressure vessel with a massive airlock located directly across the street.

"How inviting," Alexi said.

"It'll do, come on."

The safe room was a standard model, identical to the units installed on space stations and large starships. There was a suit locker, a puncture-sealing patchgun, and twelve spartan sleep bays. Michael sat down in one of them. Alexi alighted opposite him, but was clearly impatient. "Okay, Mishka, talk."

"Alexi, you're still trying to win. Why?"

"Why not? Don't tell me you think I can be discouraged that easily!"

Michael shook his head vehemently. "It's not like that. I'm out. I don't want the foundry."

"You're afraid?"

"You saw and heard the same things I did. Aren't you at least bothered?"

She looked down at the gridwork deck. "Of course I am. The foundry is a nightmare. I've seen more than you did. I was inside the sanctum. The Wrightmaster was there."

"What was it like?"

"I only got a glance. It was a shadowy horror full of eyes. Don't ask me to think more of it! Jørgen is right. We are in hell."

"Then why, Alechka? Why fight for it? Let's return to Earth. We know where the Inscrutable is. Let's take it, and go home."

Alexi laughed out loud. "Where's your caution now? After all you've seen, you'd steal Jørgen's spaceship?"

"Alechka, we've known each other forever. The contest has changed you. This place eats the souls of the living along with the dead. If we stay we'll end up like Rosencrantz, or worse. I won't let that happen to me, and I won't stand and watch it happen to you. You're too good for this, Alechka!"

A squadron of strong emotions sailed behind Alexi's blue eyes, leaving them soft and thoughtful. She caressed Michael's cheeks with gentle fingertips. "My dear, sweet Mishka. You've always been my staunchest defender. I adore it, and I adore you, I really do."

Michael hardly dared to breathe. "Will you come with me, then?"

Alexi's lips curled into a strange, joyless smile. "In time, I may, if ever you can forgive me. Sleep, Mishka." A sizzling stun shock arced from her fingertips into Michael's brain, and he knew no more.

Chapter 10
The Huntress

Michael awoke cramped and stiff on the hard bunk in the safe room. By the faint light of the airlock telltales, he could see that the room was empty. The kinks in his back coaxed him upright. He cursed when his elbow encountered the sturdy cradle that held the patchgun, and again when he thought of Alexi. She had played him like a fiddle. Fuming, he checked his chrono, which still imagined him to be on Earth. It was 0400 back in Montevideo. A bit of woozy math revealed he'd been under for no more than an hour.

There was nothing to be gained by sulking. Michael cycled the lock and clambered down to the street. No one was in sight but there were familiar human noises in the still air. Somewhere nearby a couple was making love.

Light shone from a little window set in the door of the common building. Michael crept to it and peered inside. He saw a chaos of overturned chairs and scattered crockery around the dining table. Atop it, Jørgen was banging Alexi, and banging her hard. To Michael's dismay, she was enjoying it.

Her frenzied squeals of "*Yescho! Yescho!*" were as sincere as a heart attack.

Angry and ashamed, Michael beat a hasty retreat. He almost collided with Li, who stood in the shadows by the side of the safe room, a Buddha's grin on his pale face. "Excuse me," whispered Michael.

Li ignored his apology. "A fine night, is it not?"

"If you say so," Michael said glumly, and wondered what the wiry little president of Daiginga Corporation was getting at.

"It is. My enemy is making a mistake, and in accordance with Master Sun Tzu, I will not interrupt him."

"You count Jørgen as your enemy?"

"Don't you? Even as we speak, he is taking what is rightly yours."

"Alexi is not my property. If she wants Jørgen, that is her choice," Michael retorted angrily, though the muffled gasps of her pleasure stabbed him like knives.

"Her choice? None of us has any choice remaining. It is ours to play the parts assigned to us, to tick off the boxes of the test, pass or fail. Like trained monkeys we render ourselves up for his entertainment. Some for amusement, like your antics in the tree. Some for gratification, like *her*, and some to be ruined for sport, like that stupid professor. I am sure he has a dishonorable use for me as well, but I am not a dumb animal. Any test may be broken."

"What are you going to do?" Michael demanded. Li merely smiled.

The sounds coming from the common building stopped. In their place came the sound of a struggle. Michael rushed to the door and wrenched it open, but what he found stopped him cold in his tracks. Naked but for her jacket, Alexi knelt over Jørgen, squeezing his neck between her powerful thighs. The lean muscles of her legs stood out like hawsers. Jørgen struggled in vain against her nanotech-enhanced strength. "Alexi! What are you doing?" Michael shouted.

"She cannot answer you," Li said from somewhere outside. "Her implanted weapons are the best available, but even a perfect system is vulnerable. My agents long ago infiltrated Petavmash. They installed secret backdoors in their software to permit remote control of the implant recipient. It is crude, and unpleasant for her, but it will suffice for my purpose."

"Which is?"

"To eliminate obstacles, what else? Daiginga must have the foundry, or our spacecraft will go the way of automobiles and airplanes. I cannot allow that to happen. Miss Petavia, kill him."

After the faintest hesitation, Alexi grasped Jørgen's head in her hands and twisted it hard. His neck snapped with a crunch.

"No!" Michael screamed.

Alexi turned on Michael. Long talons slid from beneath her fingernails. They glinted like stilettos in the dim light. Li's voice came again from the darkness. "Kill him, too."

She took a menacing step towards Michael. He held his ground. "Alexi, it's me!"

She halted, advanced a few steps, and finally stopped less than a meter in front of Michael, quivering. "Alechka..." he whispered.

"For God's sake, Mishka, run!" she hissed through clenched teeth.

He needed no more encouragement but dashed outside. The narrow boulevard was empty. Li had vanished. Michael cast about for an escape path, but there was nothing but the gaping airlock of the safe room across the street. With only a single entrance, it was a terrible hiding place. Nevertheless, when he heard movement behind him, he catapulted into the safe room at a dead run.

Alexi followed, moving so fast that she hardly touched the ground. She shot through the airlock door and homed in on Michael like a guided missile, but he blasted her in the face with the patchgun he'd retrieved from its cradle by the door. Bright orange foam enveloped her head like a jellyfish. While Alexi frantically clawed the gunk from her nose and mouth, Michael darted out the door, stabbing the panic button as he left. The airlock snapped shut and an earsplitting barking horn announced that the safe room was locked and pressurized. With no plan but survival, he ran as fast as his feet would carry him into the featureless expanse of the Hall of Receiving.

Chapter 11
The Hunt

Michael ran. He ran to escape Alexi. He ran to escape Li. He ran to escape the foundry, the ghosts of the Grig, and the hundred eyes of the Wrightmaster. He ran until his sides hurt and his teeth ached. The soles of his shoes cracked, but he ran on. Once, he tripped and fell headlong on the translucent floor. He might have rested there, but the inhuman faces peering up from the depths below goaded him back to his feet.

Perhaps it was the spots before his eyes or an overlong glance over his shoulder, but for whatever reason Michael was taken completely by surprise when he came to the rim of the rostrum. He screamed the last of his wind as he flew into empty air. The invisible hand of the gravity lift caught him, and he sank slowly toward the rostrum far below.

Michael caught his breath. As his head cleared, he was clobbered by a tidal wave of guilt. Patchgun foam filled cavities instantly and hardened in seconds. If Alexi hadn't managed to clear her airways, she was dead. The thought made him sick to his stomach. Alexi had betrayed him. She was ambitious to a fault and always had been. But she was a friend, and once or twice more than a friend. The twist of fate that pitted them against each other wasn't fair. When the adrenaline wore off, Michael was going to hurt like he'd never hurt before.

There was a soft sound overhead. Michael blinked away his tears and looked up. A figure hung in midair high above him, naked and pale in the wan light.

Alexi.

Michael's heart caught in his mouth. "Alechka!!" he shouted. She didn't reply, and her hands and feet were black with blood. She'd shredded her feet chasing him across the empty kilometers. But why were her hands bloody? Who else had she killed? At least she hadn't died by Michael's hand. It was cold comfort.

She couldn't gain on him while they were both entrained in the lift. Michael took the opportunity to search for a hiding place below. There was none. The flotilla of massive cargo ships parked here earlier was gone, flown away to parts unknown. The conveyor lines were empty, and there wasn't a worker in sight. The only thing near the foot of the cliff was a cluster of antigravity sleds piled high with heavy equipment. A memory surfaced, and a desperate plan formed. Michael hated it and hated himself even more for making it, but it was his only chance.

The instant Michael's feet touched the floor he was off and running. He sprinted to the nearest antigravity sled, a brute of a machine bearing a massive tokamak auxiliary power unit. With his eyes on Alexi—descending like a destroying angel—Michael gave the floating sled a mighty shove toward the lift. It moved easily. Another hard push sent it fishtailing into the lift zone. The sled shot straight up like a rocket.

Alexi dropped the last ten meters like a rock. She managed to land on her feet, but her ankles shattered. She pitched forward onto her face and stopped moving. The shivering boom of the huge tokamak crashing to the floor nearby couldn't drown out Michael's wail of anguish. Throwing caution to the winds, he rushed to Alexi's side. Her blonde hair was matted with orange patch foam, and the back of her jacket was soaked with blood from a flechette wound in her shoulder. She'd been in a battle.

With trembling hands, Michael groped for her pulse. It was a foolish decision, for Alexi's swoon was feigned. Her razor-sharp talons came out in a flash. Michael squirmed away just in time to save his throat, but her slash raked his left hand, severing three of his fingers.

Alexi arose haltingly, like a marionette with too many broken strings. She squealed in pain when she put weight on her broken bones. "I'm sorry, Mishka, please forgive me," she sobbed. When she tried to advance, her smashed ankles gave way and she collapsed. But she kept coming, crawling on all fours.

Michael scooted away, leaving a slick trail of blood. "There's nothing to forgive," he gasped. "I don't blame you. This is Li's doing."

"No," she groaned, taking another swipe that missed his outstretched foot by centimeters. "Li didn't make me knock you out. I did that myself. It was wrong."

"Forget about that! Fight back!"

"I can't," she moaned. "I'm trapped in here."

"There must be a way. You could barely talk before," Michael insisted.

Her bruised face contorted in anguish. "Don't you understand? He's letting us talk!" she wailed. "He's getting even with us for daring to contend with him. He'll let me beg for forgiveness while I'm ripping out your heart! Get away, Mishka! Run while you still can—ulp!" Her mouth snapped shut. She'd said too much.

"I'm sorry, Alexi. I'll save you, somehow," Michael said. He dragged his body erect and ran for his life. Again.

Chapter 12
The Wrightmaster

Michael slumped against the plinth of the sanctum. He hadn't meant to come this far. His plan had been to work his way back to the edge of the rostrum and find a working spot on the lift system. But he'd blundered onto the antigravity trackway and been drawn inexorably to the foot of the pyramid. He hadn't the strength to try again, and the blazing pain in his mangled hand threatened his concentration.

He wriggled out of his jacket and shirt. The latter he tore into strips with his teeth, and used them to bind the oozing stumps of his fingers. When he was done, he was covered in blood and sick to his stomach, but the pain receded. He wanted to sleep. Sleep would bring forgetfulness, and he had plenty that he wanted to forget. But with Alexi on the loose, sleep meant death.

Nevertheless, he was roused from a dreamless slumber by a scraping sound. Forcing his eyes open, he got a terrible shock. Alexi was dragging herself toward him. Her shattered hands were worn to the bone, and her red, runny eyes were windows into Hell. Cut to his heart, Michael reached out to her.

"No, Mishka," she wheezed.

It was difficult, but he slid a little further away. "Is Li still in control?".

"Not for much longer. My implants have been powered up for too long. My body is consuming itself. I'm dying, Mishka."

"No, no, no," Michael protested. "Don't give up, Alechka. Please."

"Too late," she rasped. She thrust herself forward a few more centimeters and collapsed.

Michael's emotions overcame his survival instincts, and he rushed to embrace her. Her battered body was hot and clammy against his chest. He brushed the hair from her face with his good hand. She was still breathing in deep, ragged gulps. "I want you to know something," he said softly. "I love you. I've loved you since we were young, but I was never brave enough to tell you."

"I love you too, Mishka," she said faintly. "Always did. I was a proud fool. Forgive me."

"I do, Alechka. Has Li let go?"

He could barely make out her reply. "Yes. No use to him now. He's coming to kill you. He has a gun. Go."

"I won't leave you."

Michael rocked her gently. After a little while, she let out a shuddering moan and went limp in his arms. Michael wept like a child over her dead body. His tears washed the blood from her naked skin.

Eventually her last words bobbed to the top of his mind. *He's coming to kill you.* Michael looked up to see a tiny figure floating down in the gravity lift. It was Li, coming to finish his dirty work.

Reluctantly leaving Alexi's body behind, Michael searched for a place to hide. There was none to be seen. The primary pneuma bus was elevated on spindly supports, offering nothing but the barest of shadows for concealment. The niche of the sanctum was closed, and the lintel too high to climb.

It was then that Michael became aware that he was being watched. The lintel was alive with dozens of glistening black eyes. More surfaced all the time from the depths of the waxy stone. It could only be the Wrightmaster, studying the antics of the insignificant little creatures that swarmed over his dwelling place.

It enraged Michael beyond reason.

"Do you think I wanted this?" he shouted angrily. "Do you think I killed the only woman I've ever loved just to get your haunted engines? All I wanted to do was bring her home safe. I would have died to protect her if she'd let me!"

The eyes stared back at him.

Michael shook his bloody fist. "Why am I telling you this, as if you'd care? This must be fine sport for you. Did you make wagers with Jørgen on who will win or lose? Have you enjoyed watching us struggle and die? What do you know of us, anyway? We live for a moment and pass away, just smoke blowing in the wind. Whatever you are, you're immortal and powerful and perfectly safe inside your bloody sanctum. You're never in pain, never sad, never sick, never afraid! You can't possibly know the hopes and fears of people, or how we suffer for the little taste of life we get. Go away, and let me die in peace!"

The eyes blinked in unison. When they reopened, only two remained. They were changed. They were now the eyes of a man, with dark irises and pupils that glistened softly in the golden light.

The meaning was clear. "You... understand me?" Michael stammered.

A teardrop as big as an orange welled up from one of the eyes. It slid down the lintel and landed on the plinth with a splash. The sound dealt Michael's battered soul a hammer blow. He fell to his knees. "I'm sorry. I spoke rashly, without knowledge. What do you want with me?"

Michael didn't expect a spoken answer, and the Wrightmaster did not surprise him with one. But off to his right, the pneuma bus flashed brightly. Michael focused on it just in time to see it flare again, this time even brighter.

Like a bolt from the blue, he realized what the Wrightmaster was trying to tell

him. *This is for you, Alexi*, he thought, and hastily drew up his battle plan.

Chapter 13
The Price of the Stars

Li soon appeared with a heavy gauss rifle at the ready. His suit was fresh, and not a hair on his head was out of place. Alexi had done all of his fighting. He passed her broken body without so much as a glance. He immediately noticed Michael crouched in the shadows beneath the pneuma bus. "There you are," he sneered. "Is that all the better you can do?"

"Where'd you get the gun?"

"I picked it up from the ground. Its owner no longer had a use for it. The soldiers the church sent were no match for your supercharged girlfriend. If those lazy priests hadn't left their equipment lying around unsecured this would be over. That was quick thinking on your part. I didn't imagine you had the nerve to try something like that."

"At least I don't use innocent people to do my fighting," Michael snapped.

"I would not call anyone innocent, least of all her. But she is gone, and I have a job to do. Will you come out and take it like a man or die in your hole like a rat?"

"Screw you."

Li chuckled. "No, thank you." He knelt to get a clear shot. But when he shouldered the rifle, a gigantic figure made of ropy shadow reared up beside him. He sprang away from it, right into the side of the gleaming pneuma bus. For a second, he hung transfixed, surrounded by a nimbus of grey light. Then a seizure overtook him and he fell to the floor.

Michael scuttled out of his hiding place, pointedly ignoring the silent monster. He went to examine Li. The dapper little man lay rigid with his hands clenched at his sides. His breath came in long, slow swells, like a sleeper's. A sharp poke elicited no response. Michael shuddered. Jørgen's warning had not been for nothing. Li's body was still alive, but his soul was gone.

Michael stooped to retrieve a small crystal disk lying at the feet of the looming monster. He touched a stud on the side, and the hideous creature vanished. "Thanks, Professor. I couldn't have done it without you," he said and tossed the holoemitter away.

Michael returned to Alexi's corpse. He caressed her once-beautiful cheek. "Please forgive me, Alechka. I was too late. I failed you, I failed myself, I failed..." he trailed off, choked by tears.

Someone laid a hand on his shoulder.

Michael whipped around and discovered Jørgen Pangloss standing over him, very much alive and wearing a satisfied smile all out of keeping with the situation. "On the contrary, Michael Borisovich. You have not failed," he said.

"I watched you die!" Michael stammered.

Jørgen's silver eyes sparkled with amusement. "Were I so easy to kill, I should be dead a thousand times over. But this moment is yours, not mine. From the first, you have not failed to impress me. I marked you as a man of quality, but by itself that would hardly suffice. Yet to quality you have added humility, and to humility resilience, and finally resourcefulness. There remains but a final test."

Michael glared at him. "I don't want your compliments and I don't want to take your test."

"What do you want, then?"

"I want Alexi!" Michael shouted. "I want to see her smile, to hear her laugh! I want to dream big dreams with her. I want to play with the children we would have had together. Since you ask, that is what I would have. Because you can't give it to me, you can keep your flattery, and this evil factory, and let me take her body home."

Jørgen rubbed his sharp chin thoughtfully. "An excellent answer, but your assumptions are faulty. Is Alexi your price?"

"My what?"

"Allow me to put it another way. If Alexi is returned to life, will you agree to become my servant and take possession of the foundry?"

Michael was thunderstruck, his anguish drowned by a numinous wave of hope and fear. "Are we negotiating her resurrection?" he hissed.

"We are. Say quickly. Flesh is a forgiving medium, and there is a convenient source of living essence nearby, but without a body, her soul must soon fly. I cannot compel it to stay."

"So, this is the price," Michael said wonderingly.

"The price of the stars? Aye, it is."

"No. The price of my soul." Michael cast his eyes down to the dead woman in his arms. "But I will gladly pay it for you, Alechka," he whispered.

An immense grin blossomed on Jørgen's face. "To your enviable portfolio, you add self-sacrifice! The last test is complete. Congratulations, Michael Borisovich! I look forward to doing business with you."

"Enough of business! What of Alexi?"

"She'll soon want these," Jørgen replied, tossing him a bundle of fabric. Michael caught it with his good hand. It was Alexi's clothes and boots.

Jørgen glanced down at his ancient timepiece and frowned. "I have important business elsewhere that can no longer be put off. Fra Grimaldi will show you to your office. Once you've settled in, he will release the Inscrutable to you. Good luck in your new position. I'm sure you'll do just fine." He bowed politely and turned to leave.

"Wait, wait!" implored Michael. "Who are you?"

"I am your liege lord and master, forever. Good day, Michael Borisovich," Jørgen replied, and disappeared into thin air like a ghost.

Michael gaped at the spot where he'd stood, astounded. Then his eyes fell on the body of Li. It was dead, parchment-dry, and crumbling. Jørgen's words were fresh in his mind. *"There is a convenient source of living essence nearby…"*

Alexi stirred in his lap. She sucked in a deep breath and shook herself awake. No injuries marred her naked skin, and her eyes were blue and clear. "Ah, Mishka! What a terrible dream I've had," she exclaimed.

Chapter 14
Only the Beginning

Nine years later.

The midday sun kissed the cloudy limb of the gas giant Tiber and false dusk fell across Sacra Cor. The filtered light painted the patio of Michael's Palatine Hills residence in soft royal and salmon hues. He dismissed a hologram of the quarterly reports and sat back to enjoy the scene. He could survey the entire park from his lounge chair, and quickly spied where his little Natasha and Pyotr were playing hide and seek with their friends. There were few places for them to hide. The largest tree in the park was only shoulder high. When he purchased the property, it had been nothing but gritty Sacran highland. The duck pond next to the patio was an impact crater. Sacra Cor was, after all, just a terraformed moon.

A ruddy disk shone forth in the darkling sky. The foundry moon was a beautiful sight, but Michael quickly looked away. He did not visit the foundry except at uttermost need. He desired no reminders of his personal Hell, but it was hard to ignore the three cybernetic fingers on his left hand.

An unexpected tread announced that Michael had company. When he looked, panic flared in the pit of his stomach, for his caller was none other than Jørgen Pangloss, dressed just as he had been on that long-ago day in Montevideo, right down to a straw fedora. Michael saw his master rarely, and liked to keep it that way. Ever the responsible host, he swallowed his anxiety and greeted his fearsome guest. "Good afternoon, *Gospodin* Pangloss. To what do I owe this pleasure?"

"The pleasure is all mine, Michael Borisovich. I'm roaming about and going here and there as is my habit. I thought I'd check up on you. How is your family?"

"They are fine. Natasha has entered school, and Pyotr has taken up holosculpture. Even at age five, he's a natural."

Jørgen saw the children playing in the distance and smiled. "They are remarkable, just like their parents. How is dear Alexi?"

"She still runs circles around me, even after two kids. I freely admit that she has a better head for business than I do. She's back on Earth overseeing the takeover of Daiginga Corporation. It hasn't been amicable. I managed to talk her into retaining Tuan Li's son as a vice-president. She wanted to sack him, but I refuse to hold him responsible for what his father did to us."

Jørgen smiled. "Such delicious irony! It is as I hoped. Your grace and Alexi's decisiveness make an unbeatable combination."

"You meant for both of us to win the contest?"

"Not at all. I wished for her to win. I marked her early, because I fancy strong women. But as the game played out, I realized that she was relentlessly single-minded. On the other hand, you were admirably judicious but cautious to a fault. I reasoned that together you would offset each other's weaknesses."

"I'm grateful, but you took a huge risk. Before the contest, Alexi and I had never had a lasting relationship. There was no guarantee that we'd succeed."

"It was a gamble, but I relish games of chance. This one will pay handsome dividends, both now and in the future. I foresee that the foundry will always be controlled by a couple. Let us hope that they always balance one another as well as you have balanced the exquisite Alexi."

Michael nodded agreeably, but this turn of conversation displeased him. He disliked being reminded that, in addition to the other things that he might name, Jørgen relished his wife. Alexi never spoke of him, and her affections for Michael were all that he could wish for, but he wondered if it was entirely coincidental that she'd decorated her boudoir with an oil of Jupiter ravishing Europa.

To his relief, Jørgen changed the subject. "Rosencrantz has returned and taken up his old chair at Tycho University. Was that your doing?"

"Yes. The Canon Court recommended a penal mindwipe, but I spoke on his behalf and obtained a lesser sentence."

"Which was?"

"Seven years of indenture. The Court agreed, and he spent his time serving Mother Dumiel in a peculiarly demanding capacity. I've heard that it improved his demeanor tremendously. Among other things, I am told that he is prone to silence unless commanded to speak."

Jørgen chuckled. "Aye, that would be a welcome improvement! He probably barks like a dog on cue, too! Justice has been served. I think this calls for a toast, don't you?"

Michael called the roving bar. It promptly appeared on the patio, but in addition to a bottle of his cellar's finest, it bore five bowls of ice cream.

"Please forgive me for meddling, but I would love to meet my little friends again," Jørgen said apologetically. He stood and waved, and the children came running.

"Dyadya Jørgen!" Natasha shrieked, but Pyotr got there first and enfolded his legs in a bear hug. Mother Dumiel's sturdy twins Andre and Bleriot came next, and bowed politely. Shy little Capucine was last, her beautiful golden locks flying behind her. Jørgen hefted her onto his shoulder, where she happily remained. Michael grinned at the sight of the old monster contentedly sipping port while a little girl played with his hat and spilled ice cream onto his immaculate black jacket.

Michael raised his glass. "All's well that ends well."

"It is only beginning, my friend," Jørgen replied, and they toasted.

The sun blazed out from behind the limb of Tiber, and false dusk gave way to high sunrise. The children finished their treat and scampered back to their games. Relaxed again at last, Michael yawned and wondered if Jørgen would mind if he finished reviewing the quarterlies.

"Don't you have something better to do?" Jørgen asked.

Michael shot him a quizzical look.

"A few years ago, a certain man told me he wished to play with the children that cruel fate had denied him. This day, his wish is fulfilled. Go."

Understanding dawned on Michael, and his heart leapt for joy. Work forgotten, he ran as fast as his feet would carry him to join his children. He only looked back once.

The patio was empty.

Jeff Stoner was born on April 6, 1968 in Westminster, Maryland. His earliest memories are of the Apollo moon landings, and these left an indelible mark on his spirit. When new frontiers to explore proved elusive, he created one for himself. He sold the first Reversed Black Maria short story in 2016. His novel, Made In His Image, is available now on Amazon.com.

Dead Planet Drifter

By J.D. COWAN

Galactic Enforcer Ronan Renfield finds himself prisoner of a death-worshiping cult! Can the whispers from his past aid him in his battle against the cannibals?!

The universe exploded at the same moment the shuttle went up in flames. Shards of metal stuck through the Ronan Renfield's skin as he rolled across the grass at the same moment the fiery wreck of his ship went off in the sky. Death nipped at his fading consciousness. Was this how it would end?

But then the dying man woke up.

The remaining scraps of the universe broke away as he sat up in the fields of his village. Warm winds from the days of his youth wrapped him like the blankets he usually wore sitting before the fireplace during winter. Children chattered, and horses clopped at the bottom of his position on the hill. Rows of grey sycamores and redwoods sat along the unpaved country roads. They went on forever, as far as kids knew. He took a deep breath and found that the dream had ended. He was home again.

"Bad dream?" she asked.

It took a moment for him to recognize the girl, the same one he had known since he was six years old, but slowly the memories returned as he scanned her over. Curly dark hair ran down over the freckles on her pale face. Something about her reminded him of another life—a long-lost one. Of course, such a thing was silly. They were both nine years old. What other life was there?

"I don't dream," he said. He overlooked the village from his position on the hill. The distant laughter of children reminded him that the local schoolhouse had just let out. "Just waiting for Dad so we can go to the spaceport. The ships come in today. They found some Jindosaurs in Sector 72. We might be able to ride them."

"Nah, forget about that." She waved at him to follow. "Come on, I'm going to the river. The elves are playing there again."

"Stop it. Teacher says we're all baptized, God's children. We shouldn't play with those kinds of things. The other kids already make fun of you for talking to mice at the well that one time. You're so weird."

"Forget you, then. I'm going on my own."

"My parents say it's dangerous to play alone in the forest. We don't know everything about this planet."

"I'll be fine. Mama says if you catch a junosparrow you get three wishes. I almost got one last week. Once I get one of those, we're gonna be so rich you'll wish you listened to me."

"Fat chance."

"You'll see. One day you won't be so dumb. You'll get it then."

Though the boy did get older, he never felt like he got smarter. Instead, like everyone else, he found focus with his life and moved on from childhood games. But whatever happened to her? He couldn't quite remember anything beyond her name or her face. It was another life, somewhere far away.

"*Catalina*," he mumbled.

The world came back into view again as a swirl of black haze and the muffled pounding of horse hoofs settled his headache to a dull roar. He awoke on his back staring up into the rattling wood ceiling of what he could only determine was a wagon. His entire skeletal structure flared with jagged aches.

Two men pressed his arms down against the floor. He could barely see them through the darkness of the wagon, but he could smell their stink. Was that embalming fluid? The pair of aggressors held blank expressions in their empty eyes. They weren't even looking at him!

Their empty, unfocused gaze locked on his general position, but it was as if they were asleep or unconscious. Neither budged at his repeated movements to break free—they merely held him down as if that was the natural course of action.

These hooligans wore shabby grey cloth over leather jerkins and torn pants, but on their backs, some sort of metal pack wrapped around their shoulders and waist in tight wires. These cables pushed through their mangled clothes and into their sickly green skin, allowing a low metallic hum to break the silence of the wagon. These men had been modified.

The prisoner glanced out towards the back to see two more of these guards sitting near the rear entrance. Past their looming figures, the purple-capped sky bore down on the world, and white lightning crackled through the mauve swirl. This world had gone mad. Rumbles of thunder masked the injured man's breaths as he tried to think of a way out of this.

"How much longer until we are permitted to reach the next plane?" someone asked.

Two men sat at the front of the wagon, directing the horses. They wore purple cloaks and square-shaped matching hoods over their heads. Neither appeared to notice their prisoner was awake.

"It is not soon enough," the companion said. "Meniscus has broken the threshold. Once we return to the Temple, and dispose of this wanderer to the bog, we can reclaim our place in the ritual."

"Steel yourself. Meniscus sent us because we always complete our tasks. With this anomaly out of the way, we will be rewarded greatly."

"I shall claim the seat at his left-hand side."

While the two robed men prattled on, the prisoner scanned the artificial men around him. Were these men part of this Temple? No, there was something off about them. They had an aura that felt somewhat *ancient*. Aside from stiff breathing, they gave no impression of life. Perhaps the answer lay with the packs on their backs.

His flight jacket had been taken by one of the guards at the rear of the wagon, wrapped in the corded muscles of their stiff arms. Certainly, they had his weapon and communicator, too. But since they didn't know who their prisoner really was, they probably didn't take his tools.

Instead of fighting against his captors, the prisoner twisted his right leg. He bent his knee towards his right hand. Sure enough, neither of the men holding him down acknowledged him. They kept their empty stares forward. This left the injured man to struggle for his boot.

He slipped open the small panel on his heel. There, the Enforcer removed the small lighter-sized black rectangle. The hum inside the EMP flasher remained low as ever, but the vibration shook fiercely as he slid it out from the safe casing of his boot. He had one shot before the flasher turned to scrap.

Neither captor reacted as their prisoner took the tool in hand and pressed the jutting button on top. He flicked it forward with a wrist flick. The hum rumbled into a growl as it went off. He closed his eyes in time for the squeal to erupt into a scream. The flasher had burst.

An EMP explosion shot across the wagon. It tore into the ceiling, ripping into the fabric. The men beside him flinched as the packs on their backs shorted, leaving them in seizures as they hit the wood. The men at the horse bellowed in confusion. The prisoner wasted no time charging toward the two guards at the back.

Seizures rocking the pair allowed him to crash into them. He sent the duo tumbling out of the wagon.

The injured man hit the dirt in a roll, with every inch of his attention on grabbing at the man with his flight jacket. His momentum carried him sideways with the oncoming road slamming at his shoulders and hips, leaving his prey just out of grasp.

Behind him, the wagon slowed to a crawl just as he steadied himself on his chest with his elbows. He shook the dizziness away and leaped forward.

A heavy weight tackled the Enforcer. His assailant fell to the dirt with him, kicking up clouds of dust. Fists crashed against the former prisoner's face, and the two rolled across the ground. His robed opponent landed underneath him. He punched down—once, twice, and three times, until his attacker's face twisted into a bloody mess. The Enforcer seized him by the throat and held the enemy in a choke, wishing he had cuffs.

"He is free!" the seized enemy shouted to the wagon. It had only stopped twenty yards away. "Aid me!"

The Enforcer swore and scanned the dirt. Behind the right wheel, he found a downed guard still clutching his jacket, in full seizure. The darkened eyes stared blankly at the two fighters. The lawman slipped the torn-up flight jacket free from the guard and put it on. He found his revolver and communicator, removing the gun as he held his attacker in an arm hold.

The wagon driver stepped around the left side of their transport. He stopped when he glimpsed their former prisoner holding his injured ally with a firearm against his neck. "What red magic did you cast on the wagon, cur?"

"I am a Galactic Enforcer!" Ronan said. "You're both under arrest for conspiracy against the natural order. Hands to the sky, deviant!"

"Enforcer?" the man in his grip muttered. "Are you a knight come from the Upper Sanctum?"

The wagon driver pointed a shiny flat object at the pair twenty yards from him. It looked like some sort of handheld mirror. An orange hue glinted across its tiny frame. Its sinister glow held a force deep inside.

The Enforcer nodded to the enemy. "Arms up, or I'll plant you in the ground."

"You are fortunate, Datringalis," the wagon driver said.

The man in the Enforcer's grip suddenly stiffened and whispered. "It is time!"

Datringalis bit the Enforcer on the arm. The ex-prisoner flinched at the sensation, taking his eyes from the second cultist. The sound of glass shattering brought his attention back up in time to see the white beam of light, around three inches tall and wide, shooting towards him like a rifle shot. The Enforcer reacted by instinct, leaping backwards and losing his grip on his captive.

The beam speared through the robed man's body like tissue paper. The Enforcer leaned back, the stink of singed flesh and blood piercing his sinuses as the bright flash blasted past him. He landed in the dirt on his arm at the same moment the corpse of his enemy rag-dolled over.

The Enforcer aimed past the falling corpse and pulled the revolver trigger. The first bullet whizzed past the robed man's shoulder, and the enemy clutched at the shattered mirror in his palm as if it were a baby. The Enforcer fired again.

The second shot struck center of mass, burrowing a hole in the robed man's abdomen. The mirror man spun with the impact, landing against the wagon. He slid down to the dirt and did not rise again.

With a hard breath, the Enforcer kept his weapon trained on the fallen criminal as he allowed his shaking nerves to settle. When it was clear the robed man wasn't getting back up, he finally stood up from his prone position. He slowly slunk towards the wagon, wiping his dirty brow of sweat.

"*As impulsive as ever.*"

On the corpse of Datringalis, the Enforcer spied the open wound sizzling. This was the man hit with the beam of light through his chest, and he was certainly dead. So whose voice was that? Come to think of it—that wasn't even a male speaking.

The gaping hole leaked a strange greenish blood from the gnarled flesh into a small pool inside the wound. It bubbled like a cauldron as the Enforcer peered into the living liquid.

"*He isn't dead,*" the voice said. "*Not yet. His flesh has transcended his mortal binding.*"

The Enforcer snarled. "And how would you know that?"

"*Have you forgotten everything, Ronan?*"

In the haze of dark green blood, the visage of a young woman's face appeared floating in the murky liquid, just slightly out of focus and in heavy shadow. He stared at the thin face and familiar dark locks falling across her familiar pale skin.

"I don't even know who you are, lady." He aimed at the reflection. "Are you with them, or not?"

"*You said my name earlier. You should know.*"

His grip tightened on the revolver. "That makes it worse. I don't know anyone named Catalina."

"*I have a limited time to talk, Ronan. Take the wagon to the Crypt of the Living up north along the trail. It is where their master awaits.*"

You will have your answers there."

Before he could say anything, the image of the woman faded from the black blood. The pool of dark liquid in the corpse's wound seeped out into the dirt.

In an instant, there was a rustling of leaves. None of the bushes or trees so much as blew in the non-existent breeze, however. The Enforcer listened hard, trying to process what the source could be, then realized it came from the corpse itself.

Underneath the broken body, thin wire-like vines pushed out of the dirt to grasp at the arms and legs. The larger ropes wrapping around the corpse's chest told the Enforcer that they weren't actually vines at all. It was worse: they were decrepit limbs and fingers. It was difficult to tell underneath the rot, dirt, and moss, but these were definitely old bones sticking out of the ground.

The eyes on the dead man, however, were not dead. As the bones pulled the body deeper into the dirt, the pupils swept back and forth, growing larger as if an unexpected sight had come into view. How could a dead man be conscious? Nonetheless, this one was. The remains sunk down through the earth, slipping out of sight as if this man had never been there to begin with.

The Enforcer choked down a breath and wiped the growing sweat from the back of his neck. He barely remembered how he had received the coordinates to this planet, and now he wasn't even sure that he hadn't died in entry. The mission log said nothing about this. But then, that was part of the job. You never quite knew what you'd find in the furthest corners of the universe. He

pushed forward on shaking legs, his revolver still at the ready.

The second robed man gripped the bullet hole in his gut as he leaned against the wagon wheel. His breaths arrived hard, his sheet-white face scrunched in agony. When he saw the Enforcer approach, a blood-smeared grin slid onto his pained visage.

"Datringalis has been chosen," the robed man said. "A new lord of the Under-Dwelling. We should all be as fortunate as he. But there is no guarantee, even with loyalty to the Pit. I would beg you to spare me the chance, Mage, but I know those with your level of conviction can never be persuaded to the Truth. It is a sad state of affairs when the sky is mistaken for the mud."

"Get up." The Enforcer took hold of the downed enemy's elbow and forced him to his feet. He pushed his new captive towards the wagon. "You're taking me to the Crypt."

"You would do me the honor of allowing me death on the Ascended Grounds with the Master Seer? Perhaps you are actually a messenger sent from the Pit!"

The two boarded the wagon with the robed man at the horses and the Enforcer behind him with his revolver drawn and loaded. Better to be certain this freak wasn't playing games. He would take the lawman wherever he needed to go, no matter how long it took. And the Enforcer wasn't even certain where that was.

The robed man peeked over his shoulder. "How does one such as you know of the Crypt of the Living?"

"Concentrate on the horses."

"Should you know about the Crypt, then

you know that only those of the Temple can approach the site lest the mud itself devour their souls. The Under-Dwelling is protected by the Master Seer. The pact has already been made."

"Eyes on the road."

The loon laughed. "As you wish."

As the hoofbeats plodded on mercilessly, so too did the growing migraine in the Enforcer's skull. It didn't help that he hadn't had the chance to bury the bodies of the fried men in the back of the wagon. Their unmoving corpses couldn't help but unsettle him, especially after what he had seen happened to Datringalis. This planet was cursed, lost in a haze of missing time and unreality, a place where the dead didn't rest. What even was death in a place like this? He half-expected the corpses to seize him from behind. What would prevent them?

Despite that irrational fear, he kept his weapon trained on the bleeding man. Now, of all times, was not the time to fall to superstition.

The lawman attempted to use the communicator in his pocket. Though it turned on, he received nothing but dead air from the other end. This accursed storm had to have been blocking it. No backup would be coming. He choked off a swear as he put the device back in his shabby jacket.

"Your breathing is ragged, Mage. Does death frighten you so?"

"For a man with a hole in his gut, you sure like to prattle. Be thankful you're even breathing at all."

The driver laughed. "Very well!"

But nothing was well. The longer they rode, the more the smell of the horses began to irritate the Enforcer. It reminded him of home, a place he never thought he'd see again.

Most planets in this system were abandoned, reminding him very much of where he came from: backwater worlds where life went on detached from the larger tapestry of kingdoms and republics far from these alienated sites of shacks, frontier towns, and seasonal festivals. He had been just another one of their residents—a boy dreaming of a crusade against all sorts of the worst beasts hiding in the shadows. Never did he imagine such an unremarkable drive would lead him so far from home. And yet here he was, investigating an uncharted world not too dissimilar from his own.

Then there was that woman. He had never met her before, and yet she knew his name. Who was she really?

"What did you uncover in the Crypt of the Living?" he asked his new prisoner. "Does it have to do with the storm?"

"It matters not. Over a dozen moons have passed since we last saw the Emerald Temple and the Still Waters. Your arrival was foretold, as we were sent to seek the interloper from the Sky Kingdom, and now I will get my reward for accomplishing our task. I am content, even in this life."

"This is why I'm here, I suppose. You've broken something, and now everything is going to the dogs."

"The dogs are where they belong, Mage—underfoot. Soon, however, they will serve in the Under-Dwelling where they belong. Baptize yourself in the Fires of Uncreation and be saved."

"I'm already baptized, thank you. One God is plenty."

"You only have one god here."

A queasy feeling caused the Enforcer to wretch. His sixth sense was normally quite reliable, but now it was going off like fireworks at the autumn harvest festival. Death hung in the air.

Sure enough, as they travelled onward through the woods and out into the countryside, they passed an abandoned village. At least, he thought it was abandoned until he noticed the bodies lying unmoving in the fields and in the doorways to their homes. They wore simple rags and tunics wrapped in a purple mist that wafted like smoke from their bodies. As the wagon rode by, he could swear their watery eyes watched him pass.

A hard breath exhaled behind him. His hair stood on end. It took everything the Enforcer had to avoid turning around, and yet he did so regardless. The dead men behind him remained as such. But still the breathing persisted from somewhere close by.

The wagon soon arrived upon a wide-open gully. Piles of bodies were left strewn about the grounds, embedded like railway spikes. These purple-robed men and women looked somewhat different from the civilians seen along the way. Green patches of moss and bone grew out of their bodies, not unlike Datringalis before he disappeared underground. As the wagon rolled by, their glaring red eyes and drool on their chins nearly brought his breakfast up.

None of that compared to the temple in the center of this mess, a green cylinder that travelled up about a hundred feet. This has to be the Emerald Temple. The burning torches by the large ajar door were the only hints that anyone might still be inside these grounds. The stench of sewage blew out of the opening. Was this where their Master Seer lived?

"It is time!" the driver suddenly said. "Do you hear it?"

The Enforcer grimaced. From behind him he thought he heard the sound of groaning in the wagon. His nerves begged him to look, but he couldn't risk it this time. Just like the breathing—it had to be a trick. He was too close to lose his only lead now.

Another low growl from behind brought achill down the Enforcer's spine. What was happening on this world? Still, he steeled his resolve. The lawman kept his weapon trained on the ranting loon before him.

"I don't hear anything," he said, sweat trickling down his arms.

"Liar. No one escapes the Master Seer's vision."

The groaning grew louder, and perspiration dripped down the center of his back. The stench of ash and gravedirt flooded his nostrils over the temple's stink. He felt a harsh breeze through the tears in his beat-up clothes. One thing was certain: he shouldn't have come to this place.

"You can sense it!" the robed man shouted. "Now it is done."

A clammy grip seized the Enforcer's neck. His heart jumped in his throat, and he whimpered in a spasm of fear. Who was behind him? He choked back his cowardice and pivoted around, his revolver ready.

Nothing. There was no one there. All the bodies remained where they were, motionless and dead.

The prisoner leaped off the horses as he

was distracted. The robed man dashed past the wagon towards the alien temple. He shouted unintelligible gibberish in his full tilt run across the grounds.

The lawman followed after his prey. Regardless of the bad premonition in the back of his mind, he would have to keep moving. His former prisoner had already made it into the temple, and he wouldn't let him get much farther than that.

None of the stiffened corpses planted in the earth budged at the Enforcer's approach. Nonetheless, their pupils appeared to follow him despite the dead expressions on their faces. Were they actually alive? He could swear that he saw exposed bone under their purple robes . . .

"*Keep moving, Ronan,*" a voice whispered in his ear like a passing breeze.

"Who are you, woman?"

"*Inside, hurry! Seal the fissure!*"

Not that the lawman needed to be told to do his job, but he still didn't know what he was facing on this dead planet. The woman's voice disappeared, leaving him alone without any hint again. The splashing of water broke the silence ahead of him. The temple of abominations was not as barren as he'd hoped.

The interior structure betrayed the rather mundane exterior. A circular forty-yard space with torches hanging on the dank walls and no roof awaited him. A closer inspection revealed that the "sky" beamed a darker crimson-and-mauve light than the outside world did. He was looking up at a sight that shouldn't exist. The false sky drizzled upon this unholy place.

More concerning remained the carved three-foot indentation in the floor, filled with murky, stagnant water. The stink of swamp and sewer clogged his sinuses. In the center of this abomination, he spotted a lone figure sitting cross-legged on a small platform with arms outstretched. The black-robed man sat just above the water, a purple-tinted light shining down from the false sky as if he were in a one-man stage show. This silent stranger didn't flinch or move at the Enforcer calling out to him. It was impossible to tell if this person was even alive, or just like the earth-embedded corpses outside.

The makeshift swamp gave the Enforcer pause. Though the water was stilled, his nerves told him that something had to be in that murkiness. Besides, what had happened to the man who brought him here? He was nowhere to be seen in this bog. There were no other clues or options remaining. All that remained was the statue-like man before him.

The Enforcer swallowed his nerves and stepped down into the bog, his gun above the filth. The warm water pulled at his ripped pant legs with every push he made forward through the heavy liquid. Each step gave the impression of a weight chained to his very bones. At least the water only went up to his waist. Being tall had its advantages.

However, every step he made tugged at his legs harder and harder, causing sweat to pour down his bruised and battered frame. He still could not see anything aside from his own reflection in the murky mire below him. Muscles ached, but still he forced each foot in front of the other.

A face appeared on the water's surface before fading into the bog in an instant.

Had his exhausted mind imagined that? As he tried to press on, the splash of swamp water caused his jaw to tighten. He wasn't alone.

The Enforcer scanned the flooded temple with his revolver, finding nothing. A light weight tapped against his right knee. His face paled, and his stomach nearly flipped inside out. The corpse of the wagon driver bobbed up in front of him. The robed man was nothing but a skeleton, only the skin on his face remaining. The body floated harmlessly past the jittery lawman before sinking back down into the goop.

Despite his quivering nerves, the Enforcer rushed towards the center platform. Something was alive in this place, and he had jumped into this mess like a novice. All he could do was rush forward, praying whatever was below him had a full stomach. It was far too late to turn back now.

The panicked man reached the center platform and aimed his weapon at the unmoving man sitting upon it. The head obscured by the ashen robes, no reaction arrived from this potential corpse.

"I am Detective Ronan Renfield, Galactic Enforcer," the lawman said. "Raise your hands and come in silence, or face Justice where you sit."

A brief pause followed. The hooded man took a deep breath, remaining still on his platform. "How are you able to cross Ruinous Mire without being devoured? Are you a Mage as my compatriot insisted?"

"Comply, or face Justice. Murderers do not get a second warning."

"Murderer?" the hooded man asked. His hood fell from his head as he glanced up. "An ancient concept that has no bearing on this world anymore."

The Enforcer looked upon the face of this man and felt his breakfast rise to his lips. A monster? Though Renfield involuntarily shivered, he kept his revolver trained on the monstrosity before him.

"What is wrong, Mage? Are you frightened of seeing our true form? I am Meniscus, the man who defeated death and rules the Kingdom of the Midnight Sun."

Meniscus was not human, or rather, he was no longer human. His bloodshot eyes were red saucers with dark pupils. His teeth were a black, jagged maw of sharpened shards. His nose was a beet-rouge scrunch of a pig nostril. Even his cheeks contained two perpendicular grooves that could be mistaken as scars from giant claws. His ashen skin and matching grey hair also prevented any humanity from showing through. Whatever Meniscus once was, he had long since sold it away.

The Enforcer's nerves got the better of him, causing him to shoot. The bullet cut through the silence of the sunken temple, echoing across still water. The shot planted itself in Meniscus's mouth, causing his neck to bend back awkwardly. But he didn't fall.

"How?" Renfield asked.

The monster straightened his neck forward with a jerk. "I just told you how."

"*He has already lost,*" the woman said. "*Do not be afraid. He cannot consume you.*"

"You're insane," Renfield said, not knowing who he was talking to. He was a sitting duck, and about to suffer a fate like the wagon driver. He growled, "What have you done to yourself?"

"I am willing to make you an offer, Mage." Meniscus rubbed the back of his formerly crooked neck. "It isn't every day I find one that frightens the stalker of the bog. So here is what I will gift you: a chance at true eternal life. Become like me, or become like the villagers. Life or death. The choice is yours, stranger."

Ronan Renfield had always decided that should he have the choice, he would always fight until his last breath. Warriors fought with all they had. This was his chance to die as he had always wished. Somehow that didn't comfort him. He couldn't run away, and his opponent was beyond his capabilities as a lawman. Despite how every part of him shook, he was happy for the chance to die in battle.

But that wasn't a Galactic Enforcer's mission. The job wasn't just about him. Not to mention that the mysterious woman's words stuck to him like crazy glue. She had spoken to him multiple times ever since he arrived on this world, even invading his dreams and memories. She was clearly no friend of Meniscus, but Renfield still didn't understand her. How did she know his full name? If he was going to die anyway, should he risk trusting her? Would dying like a dog in a backwater world be worth the embarrassment?

The Enforcer remembered those suffering townsfolk. Unlike the members of this temple, they didn't look like they were yet dead—their flesh was still on their bones. They lived in Undeath. Unless he acted here, they would be trapped forever. Dying now was not an option.

"You win." Renfield put his arms up. Trusting that woman was his only recourse. "Now what?"

Meniscus grasped at the Enforcer's right arm. "Now you are mine, another servant of the Midnight Sun."

The inhuman freak sank his razor-sharp teeth into Ronan Renfield's forearm. A jagged rush of sheer agony flared in the detective's bones. He couldn't help but shout in pain as blood gushed out the new opening. Meniscus greedily lapped as Renfield tilted over, his very essence fading. The woman had lied to him.

Moving shapes slipped across the water's surface—reflections of people. Their image danced madly on the surface, their forms obscured by the shadows of reality itself. Hundreds of these shades encircled the pair of living men, bounding and prancing like children at a Christmas festival. They slowly closed in when a cry suddenly broke the silence.

Meniscus screamed louder than anything Renfield had ever heard. The inhuman spat out the Enforcer's arm and tripped backwards into the swamp. His skin smoked and burned as he fell into the thick bog. The monster man gripped his platform, blood pushing its way out of every orifice and pore on his alien body. Breaths arrived hard and stiff as he stared at Renfield with trembling rouge saucer eyes.

"Poison!" he screamed. "No one can have a pact made with one higher than blood itself. Who are you?"

Renfield stared blankly at the alien's boiling flesh when the whisper returned to his ear. Catalina congratulated him. But for what?

"Our schoolteacher would be proud," she said. *"Your soul already has a Master. You know this."*

"Catalina," Renfield whispered. "How do

I know your name?"

"End him now!"

Meniscus charged the Enforcer, his claw-like hands swiping. The first slash gashed Renfield's chest, slicing upon his tattered jacket and sending him twisting into the bog. Blood gushed from his cut. Meniscus continued to swing wildly, aiming for a swift kill. Renfield kept his revolver tight in his left arm as he looked for an opening.

"I won't eat you, then! I'll just cut you open like a pig."

Renfield pivoted under a wide swing and backhanded the inhuman with his revolver. Blood jetted from his pig-nose. The Enforcer used the opening to aim, his muscles trembling. The sizzling enemy leaped towards him, but it was too late now.

The Enforcer fired his revolver twice through the burning chest of the inhuman. The monster flopped back as though a cannon had shot through his body, chunks of flesh breaking up into the mire. His very flesh melted even as he pushed against the steaming swamp towards Renfield. Meniscus's face fell apart like bad makeup in the sink as he flopped towards his enemy, claws out and ready to take the lawman's head off.

Slashes cut nicks into the detective's skin, making retreat difficult. Renfield's vision blurred as he backed up, the dying demon shouting in triumph with every push. The Enforcer nearly fell over as he leaped backwards from his opponent. He only had one shot left. If he risked reaching for a speedloader, he would be dead. This final bullet was his last chance.

"Now, you are mine!" Meniscus roared.

The monster took a step forward and stopped. His body locked up as if he were flash frozen. He keeled over and vomited a mucus-like stream of blood and bile from his sizzling maw. Hunks of skin and flesh from his arms broke apart. Screams escaped boiling lips as he fought towards the Enforcer. All four limbs snapped apart, leaving the smoking torso floating in the swamp.

The head barely bobbed above the putrid waters, eyes twitching and staring at the Enforcer. The remains continued to cook like beef on a grill. Renfield placed his revolver on his enemy's pulsating and steaming forehead.

"Nothing is yours," the Enforcer said, "except my last shot."

"You basta—"

Renfield pulled the trigger, and the inhuman's head exploded like a mucous watermelon. The detective took hard breaths as he watched the rest of the enemy's corpse break apart into the mire.

A vicious howl of wind pitched through the flat space of the temple. The planet itself appeared to quake as the bog bubbled and shook. Renfield wobbled with the resulting fissure. He turned back towards the entrance in time to see the swamp water recede down into the sunken floor. The bog quickly drained into the ground as if a floodgate had been released.

Within ten seconds, the tremors had stopped, and the water had disappeared. The Enforcer stood alone in the middle of the emptied swamp, a sticky warmth clinging to his throbbing bruises and cuts under his mangled clothing. The false sky had also disappeared, leaving the black cap of a ceiling again.

At the edge of the lowered section of the floor, a steaming lump remained unmoving. A naked man? No, the bones were slightly curved at wrong angles, and the corpse was a bit too wide without the proper matching bulk to be a human being. It had the same pale skin as the robed men did, except its face was missing. It might have already burned away, but there was no way to tell. The shape of the jaw reminded him of a mutant piranha. He guessed it to be that bog monster. Regardless, this creature was dead, its remains melting away before the Enforcer's very eyes.

"*You haven't changed,*" the woman said.

Renfield scanned the area for the one whose voice had helped him, finding no one. However, in the rapidly evaporating puddles on the temple floor, the shadows from earlier whirled about in silent dance. One of the shapes looked like it was staring at him.

"Are you Catalina?" he asked.

There was a slight pause. "*You remember now? I was told I would be forgotten until death.*"

"Remember? You mean those are real memories?" The fogged vision of younger days played in his mind. The more Renfield thought, the more her face slipped in there, as if she had always been a part of his life before and had simply been airbrushed out of the past. He remembered a young girl always going off on her own despite protests from parents, the schoolteacher, their priest, and even the sheriff. Years passed as she only grew more and more curious of the woods, and the townspeople grew more and more cautious. One day she never returned. And no one noticed. "Who are you, Catalina?"

"Perhaps your experience in the Between jostled something awake. I found *them*, Ronan. I crossed the bridge, and now I cannot return. Part of the deal was to abandon my old life and memories—not from me, but from all those I left behind, as if I had never existed to begin with. I am no longer one of you. Now I am part of the Forest, far from home."

The mists of Renfield's mind cleared more the longer he heard her voice and stared at her ephemeral shadow. Perhaps his presence in this hellscape had jostled something inside of him loose. Catalina was warned to stay out of the woods and to stop wandering off on her own, but she wanted to know what lay out there in the unknown. It looked as if she had discovered it.

"How do I bring you back?" he asked.

"That is not up to you. I made my decision, and now I live with it. But before I leave, I wanted to congratulate you. An Enforcer! I never would have thought it possible. It looks as if we're both drifters now, of different sorts. By the way, you can try your communicator again. The storm has passed."

"All it took was for me to nearly lose my arm and head."

She giggled, her voice echoing around the dead temple. "Like I said, you never change. It has been a treat, Ronan, but I must go. I do not think we'll meet again. At least, not in this world."

Renfield wanted to reply, but his tongue dried out as the last patches of swamp evaporated. He stood still in the torchlight for a while, letting the quiet overwhelm him before finally trying his communicator. He sent out his message of a completed mission, and it clicked through. Now to wait for a reply.

The Enforcer shuffled out of the temple on sore legs. The purple hue of the sky had cleared to reveal a bright blue tint, reminding him of his far-off home. The mangled corpses on the grounds had all vanished, leaving those familiar purple robes blowing away across the grounds into the nearby woods. Crowds of villagers approached him. They carefully scanned the empty area, their farming tools in hand like weapons. Renfield leaned against the door-frame as an old man stepped forward from the pack. The wounded man nodded to the elder.

"You have slain the vile ones?" he asked the Enforcer.

"They are all dead, yes." Renfield flinched at his cuts and bruises. He would definitely need a vacation after this one. But still he couldn't help but remember the girl who had thrown away everything to chase ghosts. Just like Meniscus, the world wasn't enough for her—neither was the universe itself. "It was never going to end any other way."

"Thank you, stranger. We will raze this abomination to ashes."

Renfield smiled. "And keep doing it. No matter how many times it takes."

The sun covered the world in bright, white blankets, stifling the aches inside the detective's bones. The dead planet was no more. Soon enough, he would leave this place behind for good, for new frontiers. He thought of Catalina as the light smothered the ache in the back of his brain.

"You never know if the next sunrise will be your last," Renfield said. "It's our job to keep them coming."

The old man cocked an eyebrow. "Who are you, anyway?"

Ronan Renfield stepped past the old man into the warm embrace of the sun. There were other missions ahead. Silently, he hoped Catalina was watching him and would realize the mistake she had made. It was never too late to turn it around. How many sunrises like this one had she thrown away? He wouldn't make that mistake. There would always be another one; Enforcers would always make sure of that.

The Enforcer glanced over his shoulder at the confused elder. "Me? I'm just a drifter."

J.D. Cowan is the writer of the Grey Cat Blues, Brutal Dreams, & The Pulp Mindset. He is also a contributor to both StoryHack and Cirsova magazines, as well as the Planetary Anthology series. His musings can be found at wastelandandsky.blogspot.ca.

People of the Stone God

By HAROLD R. THOMPSON

Bookish explorer Anchor Brown is sent on a seemingly simple task: smuggle an artifact to the Hargurs! But is the Molletur really the soul of their sleeping God?!

Excerpt from *Travels in the Eastern Extremities*, by Captain Anchor Brown, OAE, Corps of Exploration.

No sooner had the old Corps of Exploration dissolved, with me finding myself on half-pay with no regiment to call home and no orders, than I was summoned to the War Division, to the vast marble office of the Sub-Minister of Defence, where I sat in a plush chair and wondered what I had done to deserve this honour.

"Here's the thing, Brown," said the Sub-Minister. "This new Corps of Exploration will consist of exactly one member. You."

The Sub-Minister was a small man, round of belly, dressed in a suit of fine tweed, much like my own, and wearing a scarlet cravat where mine was white. His smile seemed genuine and not the mask one so often sees on the faces of these Government types.

"This is a special assignment," I stated, understanding the situation.

"Indeed, should you accept it."

This was entirely to my satisfaction, and a sense of well-being returned. I was saved from once again having to seek the role of a combat soldier, which I had spurned to become an explorer. I had circled the globe more than once in the past ten years, with a small team of other like-minded types, members of the Corps of Exploration, to learn as much about the world and its places and peoples as we could. The fact that this intelligence was for the glory and expansion of the Artorian Empire had not diminished our sense of curiosity and discovery, nor our confidence that we had acted for the advancement of all of humanity.

"You understand that this is not to be confused with the Corps of Geographers," added the Sub-Minister, "whose job it is to make maps and get the lay of the land, though there may be some overlap. Your job will be to take on very specific tasks. Some will have a military function, and some will be somewhat broader in scope."

"I see," I said.

The Sub-Minister opened a drawer and took out a small object, which he placed in the middle of his enormous oak desk. It was a perfect half-sphere of what looked like polished stone, greenish-gray in colour.

"I know this," I said. "A half-dome, the Hargur symbol of life, or of the soul."

"Yes, very good, Captain. They call it a Molletur."

"I seem to recall they are rare and sacred. How does this come to be here?"

The Sub-Minister rubbed his small hands

together.

"That is the crux of this situation. You know the ancestral country of the Hargur has for some time now been under the heel of the Valgurnian Empire."

I nodded. The Valgurnians had long been our chief political rivals and could be cruel masters in the many lands they had conquered.

"This object," the Sub-Minister went on, "was liberated from a Valgurnian museum, and the Hargur thieves delivered it into the safe-keeping of one of our agents. That agent smuggled it back to us, but not before tangling with the Valgurnians. The original thieves are dead, and our agent has also since succumbed to wounds."

I reached for the Molletur and took it, holding it in my hand and feeling its surprising weight. It seemed to vibrate with a pulsing rhythm, as if alive.

"The Hargurs believe this stone," said the Sub-Minister, "will wake one of their so-called stone gods, who will then help them drive off the Valgurnians."

"Magic, then," I said, skeptical as ever, despite all the many wonders and horrors I had encountered on my travels. "I am to assist them waking their imaginary god? Or is it imaginary?"

The Sub-Minister laughed.

"That isn't for us to decide, Captain. Simply return the Molletur to the interested parties. That's the mission. Our interests in these people do not extend very far, but we expect those interests may increase in the future."

I quoted, "My adversary's adversary is my ally," from Dornicus.

"Indeed," said the Sub-Minister. "Bring this to them as a gesture of our sympathy, and whatever disruptions it causes the Valgurnians will be to our advantage."

I was elated as I left the halls of the War Division. Here was a renewal of sorts, although now I was alone. That suited, for after ten years I was ready for some independence. This mission was something new, something more specific and with a degree of inherent danger. That was an exciting prospect, but also alarming, and I felt a sudden pang of fear that I should fail. I had been a fighting soldier and a traveller, but never one for intrigue of this sort.

There was nothing to do but begin. I was reminded of a line from one of my favourite old texts, Bamflout's *Terribus the Mariner*: "We set out, with plans well laid, and cast our fates to the winds."

I have said that I was alone, but that was not truly the case. I had the help of a growing web of Artorian agents that had been established largely as a result of our work in the old Corps. I was well-supplied and well-informed along my long and event-filled journey to Hargur, a thousand miles to the south and east. I had many an adventure along the way, by pneumatic rail, by steamer, by camel caravan, on horseback, and on my own feet. After many weeks, I found myself on the frontier between Gonwall and the border of the ancient land of the Hargur people, now part of the eastern portion of the Valgurnian Empire.

Crossing the border proved a simple affair. Hargur was by no means an advanced or modern country, more an outpost where time has stood still, save for the presence of Valgurnian troops, who seemed out of place with their crisp gray tunics and gas rifles. I entered as part of a merchant caravan, dressed as a local in a wool hat and a long sleeveless tunic over a thick woolen shirt. I carried a pack, water bottle, and weapons in hidden pockets within my tunic. These last consisted of my gas pistol and a sabre with a blade that folded in half for concealment. When drawn, the blade swung open and locked in place where it hinged in the centre.

The Valgurnian border guards spoke to the leader of the caravan, some coins exchanged hands, and we continued on our way. Typical frontier corruption, but it was a relief to have a major hurdle passed with so little fuss. The road took us through a cleft in a massive rock formation that was covered in ancient and wind-eroded carvings of human and animal figures. Beyond this natural gate lay a landscape of rolling grasslands dotted with herds of sheep and goats and numerous pillars of rock and massive erratic boulders. Most of the rock formation bore sculptures of some kind, for the Hargurs have long been great stone workers. Many of the carvings were of oversized human faces and flowing abstract designs that made me think of the wind.

My destination was a village built into one of these massive stone outcrops. It lay about five miles north of the border, and the caravan stopped there for a single night. The next morning, leaving the caravan, I entered the village through a short tunnel that ended in a natural courtyard. The dwellings were carved into the rock itself, in five tiers. I thought the place would have made a fine fortress, although it would not have fared well against Valgurnian

pneumatic cannons.

Thanks to our web of agents, I had a contact within the village, and a code word to find her. I spoke the code word to a group of old women who were chatting at what must have been the main village well, and the chatter ceased at once. One of the old women led me to a wooden stairway, then up a level to one of the cave-like dwellings, and there I waited, sitting on a low cushioned stool, my pack at my feet. Soon two people entered, a young woman and a man of about my age. The woman was small with enormous eyes and straight black hair, quite beautiful in the manner of her people, but stern. The man wore a sheepskin robe with coloured pebbles stitched into the seams. It must have been quite heavy.

"I am Karella," said the young woman, speaking Artorian, "and this Nemok... uh, what you say... priest?"

I bowed my head.

"I am honoured to meet you," I said.

Karella's sense of urgency was palpable.

"You have stone? Molletur?"

The stone was in another hidden pocket within my tunic, and I tore the seams and brought it out, letting it vibrate in the palm of my hand with whatever strange power it contained. My companions gazed upon it with awe, and I offered the stone to the priest. He took it, holding it with his fingertips. My mission, I realized with some disappointment, was complete. This was all I had been tasked to accomplish, and it had been all rather simple, without the danger and hardship I had anticipated.

"Tell me about the stone," I said to Karella, not prepared simply to take my leave.

"Stone is key to life of stone god," she said, not taking her eyes from the Molletur. "We Hargur are people of this land, people of stone. For five thousand years. We are here. Stone Gods, they protect us, but new people come, we fight. Great battle. Stone Gods… er, wear out? Go to sleep. Souls are in Molletur. Valgurnians come and take Molletur, lock away."

I nodded.

"I'm happy to have returned this one to you."

Nemok said something in his own tongue, seeming both angry and excited.

"We go tomorrow to wake Stone God," Karella said. She looked at me. "Stone God will drive away Valgurnians. We go to… grave? Resting place? You come?"

I had not expected this, that they would put the stone to use so soon, or invite me to bear witness. What would happen to me, I wondered, when the magic failed to work? Or would it actually produce some result? Whatever the case, I knew that both duty and personal curiosity dictated only one course of action, and that was to agree and so extend my mission.

"Yes," I told Karella. "I would be honoured to go with you to your god's resting place."

I slept in a chamber on the top tier that night, the wind making a strange music through the hollowed rocks. In the morning, I was astonished to see what must have been almost the entire village turned out and prepared for this journey, save for a few elderly folks who would remain with the children. There was something of a carnival atmosphere, with singing and laughter, and a group of six young women, adorned with dresses covered in coloured pebbles, performed an endless circular dance as the rest of us walked. Everyone was joyful that their liberation must soon come, but I worried that we would draw rather too much attention. And what of the other Hargur settlements? Had they been informed? I wondered where this particular group fit into their hierarchy.

I walked with Karella and Nemok, following a rutted track across the grassland.

"Is it a long journey?" I asked.

"We arrive before sun is high," Karella said, pointing at the sky.

I nodded and gazed around at our surroundings. To our left I spied a goatherd and his charges taking shelter in the shadow of a large outcrop. The imposing stone edifice had been carved into the shapes of men with spears and clubs engaged in a desperate struggle.

"That is Great Battle," Karella explained when I asked. "When people try to take this land, but we prevail, thanks to Stone God."

I remembered this story from when I had been here before, with the old Corps of Exploration. It seemed a central defining tale or myth, and I thought of how proud these people were of their ancient lineage and connection to this strange country.

After about two hours, the country grew even stranger. For some time, I had been hearing what sounded like distant thunder, and then noticed the rocky peaks around us were becoming more conical in shape, like miniature volcanoes. As we passed one of these formations, an explosion of steam erupted from its peak, making the thundering sound I had heard. A moment later, we were showered by huge drops of warm water and dozens of small fat golden fish which flopped and twitched in the grass. As I bent to pick one up, Karella stopped me.

"Can eat," she said, "but must dry first. Get out... what word? Acid? Cook in oil."

From this explanation, I presumed there was something harmful in the water, though only mildly harmful. I noted that the drops, where they had landed on my skin, felt viscous, and where they touched rocks on the ground, they steamed and left a small depression. The little volcanoes, or chimneys as I thought of them, apparently spewed a substance that reacted with minerals, but not flesh or hair.

The sun was growing hotter, and we rested in the shadow of one of the chimneys. The dancers continued to dance, as if they could not stop, while everyone else ate cold rations in the form of dried goat meat. I ate a biscuit and took one of my books, a volume of Artorian romantic poetry, from my pack.

"Why you carry books?" Karella asked me. "One should carry food, carry weapons. Books?"

"This is like food for me," I said, and did not add that many a lonely night in my travels were only made bearable by the presence of the few volumes I had brought. I read another line, a poem from Lyman about strength and resistance to adversity, and it made me think of the Molleturs and what they represented.

"Tell me," I said, "why have you waited until now to try and wake the Stone God? Has no one tried since the Great Battle?"

"Stone Gods only return," Karella said, "when need is greatest. Priests decide."

"Nemok and his fellows assemble and vote on it?"

"Every year, for five thousand years."

That struck me as unlikely, but I reminded myself that some rituals can last a very long time.

"And there is price," Karella added. "Big price. What is word? Sacrifice."

I felt a sudden chill.

"What sort of sacrifice?"

She looked away.

"You see soon."

Over her shoulder, near the flat western horizon, something flashed, like the sun on metal. Bright metal was not something I associated with the Hargur, so I reached into my pack and took out my little spyglass. Extending the brass tubes, I twisted the eyepiece and scanned the area where I had seen the reflection. Heat shimmer distorted the image, but I made out six men on horseback, Valgurnian mounted troops in grey tunics with shiny brass buttons. Was this just a patrol, I wondered, imperial troops making the rounds of the local villages, or were they following us? If the latter, how much force was I willing to use to defend my unarmed companions?

I had not decided on an answer when Karella rose to her feet and said, "Come. We will be there soon."

We walked for another ten minutes, and a cluster of chimneys that I had been observing for some time proved to be our destination. The cluster may have been a single volcano with four craters, or four chimneys that had melded together. The tallest crater looked to be about eighty feet high, with a narrow footpath winding to its summit.

Arrival at this geological feature brought exclamations of joy from the people, and they rushed toward the chimneys just as one of the craters blasted steam. The people laughed as the shower of water and fish landed amongst them, but I felt a mounting sense of unease. I was concerned about Karella's mention of a sacrifice, but also worried about the Valgurnians, and kept glancing to the west. Each time I looked, the horsemen were closer.

Reaching into my tunic, I removed my gas pistol from its secret pocket.

"Come," Karella called. She and Nemok were at the base of the volcanoes, and I noticed an entrance, a masonry archway half-hidden in shadow. I started toward it, but at that moment a spurt of dust erupted from the rock face just to Karella's left. I knew a bullet strike when I saw one and looked back to see the Valgurnians spurring toward us, firing their gas rifles and shouting.

I ran for the shelter of a large boulder just as the Hargurs seemed to realize the danger. With screams and shouts of alarm, they rushed for the archway. Meanwhile, I steadied my arm on the boulder and fired three quick shots, the pistol jumping in my hand. The enemy were over seventy yards away, and I thought I had little chance of hitting anything at that distance, but luck was with me, and I saw two saddles empty.

"Come, Brown!" Karella called again from the archway. Everyone else was inside the tomb, so I leapt up from my hiding place and joined them. I did not know whether we would be trapped or if the tomb would provide adequate sanctuary, but I could see no alternative course. Bullets ric-ocheted around me as several Hargurs pushed closed a pair of stone doors, which swung on silent and well-maintained hinges.

"Valgurns cannot open these doors," Karella said beside me.

The air was hot and close, and we were in complete darkness until I saw a spark, then a torch made from bundled grass sprang to life. The dancing orange light of the flames revealed an arched ceiling and a tunnel lined with statues of human figures standing with joined hands.

More lit torches appeared. Karella took my sleeve and pulled me through to the head of the crowd, where Nemok waited with the dancing women, who somehow had the strength to continue their gyrations. Nemok said something and turned and led us down the passage, which ended at a large domed chamber, its circular walls and ceiling covered in more carvings of human figures, all holding hands, the fine details untouched by the erosion of wind and rain. It should have been beautiful, but I found the place oppressive and lonely, even sinister.

At the far end of the chamber stood seven statues in a semicircle. At first I took them to be just piles of rough stone, but then I discerned they were human figures like those on the walls, albeit rendered in a cruder fashion. The central figure was about eight feet tall, a man shape of piled stones, while the other figures were shorter at about five feet. At the base of the central figure was a carved stone bowl, with a stone cup at its centre.

Nemok walked toward the bowl and cup and knelt. Karella still held my sleeve, and

I felt her grip my arm with tight fingers, which increased my disquiet. Behind us, the people were murmuring and whispering, filling the chamber with sibilant echoes. Nemok had taken the Molletur out of his tunic and held it in both hands, chanting a series of Hargur words over and over. The hairs on my neck stood on end. The air seemed charged, the oppressiveness building. I felt no sense of hope in what was about to happen, whatever it would be, and looked at Karella, saw her smile for the first time, but was shocked to see the glint of madness in her eyes.

Behind me, the dancers still danced, sweat pouring from their bodies.

Nemok placed the Molletur, flat side down, on the little cup, and I saw it made a perfect fit.

The priest's body suddenly lurched upright, and he extended both arms to either side. His fingers twitched, then broke off and fell to the floor. His hands then crumbled, turning to dust, then his forearms, and finally his entire body, clothes and all, falling to dust. I took a step back in astonishment, not believing my eyes, but where Nemok had knelt was nothing but a pile of grey powder.

A great wailing went up from the assembled people, loud in the chamber, but I could not tell if it was a shout of joy or horror. My heart was pounding and sudden cold sweat soaked my clothing. Karella released my sleeve and went down on one knee, spreading her hands as she gazed at the crude stone figure. Again I wondered if my eyes were playing tricks in the firelight, for I saw the figure move its stone arms, then turn its boulder head side to side be-fore taking a step forward.

Gripping my gas pistol, I edged back, fearing that something was wrong. Karella stared at the stone figure, which must have been a Stone God, or a being these people took to be a god. It seemed to be glaring down at her, though it had no eyes or facial features.

"Why have you come?" a voice spoke in my head. "Why have you come here?"

I cannot describe the voice, for it had no true features and spoke in no language. I simply understood the meaning and understood that it came from the Stone God.

Karella answered in her own tongue, and I only understood a few words, "praise" and "awake."

"You are not my people," the Stone God said. "You are the usurpers, the destroyers!"

Karella seemed to falter, and I saw confusion in her eyes. She began to speak again, but only managed a few words before the Stone God struck her a blow on the side of the head with its blunt stone right arm. I saw a spray of blood, and Karella fell lifeless to the floor.

A few shouts of shock and surprise came from the people closest to the front of the gathering, but most did not see what had happened and were slow to react. I admit I was also struck dumb, frozen in place. This Stone God was meant to be the savior of its people, but instead it lumbered forward and struck down one of the dancers, then another and another. It swung its club-like arms from side to side with more speed than I would have thought possible. Meanwhile, the smaller sculptures were also advancing.

"Fools!" said the voice of the Stone God.

"Have you forgotten? Your people came in conquest and destroyed mine and imprisoned me in this place! Now you wake me to your peril."

A dozen bodies lay on the floor. I raised my gas pistol and fired twice, knowing my effort was wasted. The bullets struck with puffs of silica dust against the Stone God's head, but the creature ignored me and continued to wade into the crowd, its smaller minions joining it, striking left and right. At last, the Hargurs realized things had not gone as planned and started to flee back into the tunnel. I saw a bright shaft of sunlight as someone pulled open the doors.

The Stone God went after them, leaving me alone in the domed chamber with the dead. The creature seemed to have discounted me on purpose as it pursued the Hargurs. I knew I had to try to stop it and remembered the Molletur. Leaping back to the bowl and cup, I grabbed the little stone half-dome, thinking that removing it would put the creatures back to sleep.

Screams still echoed from the tunnel.

I did not know what else to do, so I followed the chaos, the Molletur vibrating in my left hand, my useless gas pistol in my right. Outside in the sunlight, a scene of death and destruction met me. Bodies covered the ground, lying with heads and limbs crushed. The screams and shouts had ceased, for no one was left, not even the Valgurnians, who lay amongst the dead. I saw two of their horses, cropping grass about fifty yards away.

The Stone God and its smaller companions stood amongst their victims. The boulder that passed for the Stone God's head at last swiveled to look at me.

"You are not one of the conquerors," the voice said, "but you too will die."

I could not fight these things, so I ran, taking the footpath that led to the top of the largest chimney. Just as I started to climb, two of the chimneys erupted, showering me with water and little fish. I put my hands up in a feeble attempt to shield my face from the warm droplets, and the Molletur started to burn. I came close to dropping it but managed to wrap it in one of my wool shirt sleeves, noticing that it was pitted where the water from the chimney had touched it.

In my head, I sensed a deep groan of anguish.

"You will die," the voice repeated.

Any hopes that the Stone God would be unable to climb were dashed as it began to follow me up the footpath, its minions in tow. I went as fast as I was able, but the path was steep, the day was hot, and my breath was loud in my ears. I had an inkling of a plan, but it was desperate.

Reaching the summit, I saw there was nowhere else to go. I stood on a natural platform, and to my right was the crater of the tallest chimney. Inside lay a circular pool, and I saw the fish swimming in the water.

The Stone God continued to advance, and I turned to face it. My situation was close to hopeless, yet I took a moment to ponder the nature of these beings and their relationship to the Hargurs. It was obvious that the Hargurs were mistaken in their legends, that this was not their god, but the god of a people they had conquered, most likely in the Great Battle. Perhaps they had created the Molleturs and somehow imprisoned the Stone God or gods, or perhaps the earlier people had done so as a means of preserving their deity to be awakened later. Over time the Hargurs had incorporated the stories of the conquered and thought them their own.

The Stone God reached the top of the path.

"I will take vengeance for my lost people," the voice said.

I decided to gamble on my plan, although I was by no means certain it would work. I had remembered that the Molleturs were symbols of life, of the soul, so I cast the little half-dome into the acidic water of the nearby crater.

The Stone God halted its advance, and I sensed the cry of anguish again. Steam or smoke billowed from the creature's surface, as if it burned from within, and cracks began to appear.

My gamble had been correct. The Molletur gave the Stone Gods life.

The voice in my head was trying to speak, and I knew its continued wrath, its desire to slay me.

The folding sabre was in my tunic. I took it out, drew it from its short scabbard, and extended the blade with a flick of my wrist. The blade locked into place. Dropping into the guard, I performed a single lunge, striking the Stone God's crumbling chest with the point of my blade. The force of my thrust was enough to cause the creature to topple backwards onto the path, where it shattered into countless fragments.

I shouted in victory. The smaller stone creatures were also crumbling to dust just as the unfortunate Nemok had only a short time ago.

I had survived, defeated my strange adversaries, but needed a moment to gather my wits. Eventually, I made my way to the bottom of the path, where I sat on the boulder I had used for cover earlier. I stared at the bodies of the people I had come to help and felt a deep horror and sorrow at their fates, wondering if I could gather the corpses and set them alight. There were too many to bury. I also wondered about the Stone God's lost people, who they had been, and whether the Hargur had destroyed them.

One thing was clear: my first independent mission was a complete failure.

Movement caught my eye, and I heard a groan. A man in a gray tunic was struggling to rise. Blood stained his temple, and he clutched his left arm.

Taking my water bottle from my pack, I went to the man's assistance.

"You must do something for me," I said in Valgurnian as the wounded man drank. "Return to your commanding officer and deliver your report. Tell him that the Hargur people will unleash the full wrath of the Stone Gods, as you saw it here, and that only I know the secret to stopping that wrath. This will happen unless the emperor begins negotiations and offers these people some semblance of independence."

The man was too dazed and in pain to question me or argue. I helped him onto one of the horses and watched him ride away to the west, toward where the local garrison must lie. I considered my plan to gather the bodies, but realized I had no fuel to make a pyre, so I left the fallen where they lay and hoped what I had done would be enough. I decided I owed these people nothing, that they had been deluded about their history, but I knew enough to understand that all peoples are so deluded, in some fashion. The Hargurs did not deserve to live under the heel of the Valgurnians, so perhaps, with my warning to the horseman, I had salvaged something of my mission.

I took another of the stray horses for my own use. "'Travel light,'" I quoted out loud, my favourite line from *Burwell's Journey*. "'Leave behind your selfishness and fear.'"

Turning to the south, I headed for the border and the long journey home.

Harold R. Thompson writes short science fiction and fantasy, and is also the author of the bestselling historical adventure novels Dudley's Fusiliers, Guns of Sevastopol, *and* Sword of the Mogul.

The Last Khazar

By REV. JOE KELLY

Two men, one a Polish Jew, the other a Prussian Nazi, are bound by dreams and bound by destiny to confront one another, both in the present and in the past!

I have always been possessed of a withdrawn, misanthropic temperament. He's a rare Polish Jew who came of age in this accursed century, in this world gone mad with hate and murderlust, who lacks a certain gloomy streak. After all, we're hemmed in by a pair of madmen, each obsessed with conquering the world, each nursing a savage hatred of us, a mad conviction that we are the driving force behind his hated enemy.

But even among those dark and brooding young men, I was unique. There was always an alien and atavistic streak in my soul, a barbaric ferocity that constantly struggled to break through the façade of the stoic young son of a wealthy and respected Warsaw merchant. It manifested itself in an obsession with repudiating the effete lifestyle of a gentleman. Much to my father's frustration, I refused to learn the family business as I should have, as his eldest son. Instead, I worked long hours in the warehouse, while the floor men stared in baffled wonder at the dark-eyed, powerfully-built boss's boy who toiled silently in back-breaking labor.

But this alone was inadequate to sate the unaccountable simmering of my blood. So I threw myself into street boxing and wrestling as well, with a mad, violent fervor.

Time and again, I sneaked out to bloody my fists in a snarling, savage bare-knuckles match. Time and again, my father shouted to the heavens, demanding to know, why? Why would a young man like myself, who would never want of anything, who had all the promise of wealth, wits and good looks, why I would throw it all away, beating my brains out in some vicious back-alley match?

I never had an answer for him. And as he raged on all the louder because I could not answer him, I too smoldered, nursed swollen knuckles as I brooded, and I asked myself, why?

And the only answer I could find, as ridiculous as it might seem, lay in my dreams.

As long as I can remember, I was haunted by inexplicable visions in my sleep. I might have put them down to the pulp adventures I devoured—but it was the dreams that inspired the reading, and not the other way around. For a long time, I could remember but vague, fleeting images of storms of arrows that blackened the sky, of the flicker of steel and the cries of men stricken, of the thunder of hooves and the smell of horse sweat—a smell that, when I first encountered it in real life, I was shocked to find was precisely that which

143

haunted my dreams. And there was a certain sensation, as well: of flight and freedom, completely unlike any I had known in my waking life.

But it was only when that devil Friedrich von Hoffman forced his way into my life that the dreams abruptly sharpened into lucid clarity.

He was a colonel in the Heer, an attaché to the occupying government, a tall, thin, perfectly blond, perfectly dressed, immaculately groomed, hatchet-faced Prussian son of a bitch with a savage streak a mile wide that his calm blue eyes and his polite smile and manners utterly belied. I could see it, though, that day he walked into my father's office and politely demanded a requisition of all the cloth he had on hand. To assist with the mobilization of the Wehrmacht, he explained—but what in the hell did the Wehrmacht need with all our ladies' silks? That schmuck—beneath his polished knee-high boots, his immaculate shoulder boards, beneath the shining metal he plastered his chest with, he was a grinning, greedy gangster, a thug, a street hood. I clenched my scarred fists and glared him down. I was the only one in the room to do it. All the other Jews, they averted smoldering eyes and nodded with forced politeness. Even my father bowed his head before von Hoffman. But not I. And he saw it, and he matched my hate with a cruel smile that said, I'm coming for you, yid, you and your whole fucking family, and there isn't a thing you can do about it.

I just glared back at him, and for my father's sake, for my family's, I fought down the overwhelming urge to lay him out, jump on top of him, and beat his smirking Teuton face into hamburger meat.

I went to bed that night angry and more than a little drunk. And it was out of the blackness of that wine-soaked sleep that the lucid dream welled up, as vivid as life.

"Bek Joseph is dead. Svętoslavŭ beheaded him on the field of his defeat. The steppe belongs to us now."

My retainers and I glared at the smirking gold-slathered Friðuric, but we said nothing. We could say nothing, for he spoke the truth. Khazaria was broken. By the savagery of the pagans of the North and the East, by the guile of the slinking Christians of Constantinople who fought with honeyed words and gold rather than the steel of honest men, the great Khaganate that had brought peace and prosperity to the steppe for three centuries had been shattered. And now, squatting before us, this Saxon hound licked his chops, eager to feast on the remains.

Friðuric slurped his mead noisily, considered the jeweled rhyton idly a moment. "I hear tell that, even now, the Pechenegs seek to devour those Khazar bands who still ride free. Bands like yours, Aaron." Again he turned his smug, greed-tinged smirk to me. "You would do well to ally yourself with a stronger man. One who can bring you under the fold and protection of King Svętoslavŭ. Elsewise, you are likely to find yourself at the mercy of the steppe hounds."

I growled, "And we would do so much better to trust to your tender Varangian mercies? I know well how you damned Northmen treat the women and the children of your captives. Never—NEVER!—will I give you my wife and daughters!

Your filthy Pagan hands shall not touch them!"

Friðuric's smile slipped into a snarl. He threw the jeweled rhyton aside, splashed his sickly sweet mead all over the side of my yurt. "You can give yourselves to me, or you can see your women ravished by the Pechenegs!" His lips twisted in a mocking sneer. "You do me injustice, Aaron; I am an honorable man. Your family will be treated well."

My knuckles whitened with clenched fury. "I will treat you to the edge of my saber, you heathen son of a bitch!"

Friðuric leaped to his feet, fuming. "I will not be so talked to by a whipped dog of the steppe! Your people are broken, Aaron—you have no choice! You WILL submit to me!"

I shook my head stiffly. "As long as my steel rests by my side, as long as my mare rides beneath my legs, I have a choice. If you come for us, Friðuric, you will find not groveling slaves but fearless warriors. We will fight you to the last man. We will never surrender."

"Then you will all die!" Friðuric's face turned beet red with rage. "I will crush your pitiful band, and I will slaughter your women and children! You will watch as I ravage your daughters and slake the steppe with their blood!"

I rose to my feet, answered his flaming blue eyes with the cold steel of my stare. "Come and try, you Saxon dog. Face us, and meet your doom."

We glared each other down for a moment. I, Aaron, last free leader of the Khazars; he, Friðuric, the sneering lapdog of a mighty conqueror—

Abruptly we stared at each other in shock—for he knew me for Aaron Frydman; and I recognized his face as the same as Friedrich von Hoffman!

The dream dissolved. I awoke abruptly, feeling like a triphammer was going to work on my skull. I stumbled out of bed, went to splash some water on my face.

Staring into the mirror, the dream returned to me. I examined my face closely; in particular, I peered into my own eyes. Like many of the men in my family, they were strangely narrow, the lids rather smooth. I had always assumed a Russian strain in our blood. But just then, with the memories of the yurt and the feel of the steppe saber in my hand so fresh, I wondered. Was there some stranger blood in our distant past, of which I was unaware?

The name returned to me: Khazaria. The Khazar Khaganate. I had heard it before, and always, when it surfaced in the historical romances, it had triggered a feeling of dark attraction. Some strange fascination with the antique past of this mysterious steppe khanate that no other steppe people, not even the mighty Mongols with all their glory and intrigue, had inspired in me.

I would have to find out more about them. Perhaps I would find some answer to my dreams...

And, perhaps, I would find an answer as to why von Hoffman had so abruptly appeared in my dream. And had his face replaced that of the Saxon? It seemed to me, perhaps, that they had always been one and the same face... and if that were so, what would a mirror reveal, were I to hold it up to the Khazar Aaron?

I found an answer the next day, at a quiet bookstore run by a small, kindly old man with piercing eyes and the sort of mysterious smile that can be a welcome or a warning. Everything on the shelves was pre-approved by the Nazis and their bootlicks, but as soon as I asked about the Khazars, the old man put a finger to his lips, led me to a dim back room, and pulled out a half-dozen well-worn periodicals.

"My favorite stuff on the Khazars," he explained. "Used to be a popular subject with the intellectual crowd. Not much they talk about nowadays except how to keep their heads down." He gave me that funny smile again. "It's good to see young men finding out about their past. We aren't all the sons of wandering merchants and rabbis, you know."

I'd never gone in much with the college crowd. Brandy snifter bullshit never held any interest for me. But just then I wished like hell I'd paid a little attention, because right under my nose was an answer to the inexplicable, furious drive that burned unquenchably in my blood: a theory that a strong strain of the European Jewry was descended from the refugees of the fall of the Khazar Khaganate in the mid-tenth century.

Well, God damn it. There it was. The strange aspect that recurred in the men of my family. My barbarous temperament that infuriated my father and drove me to the brink of madness. Somewhere along the line, the ancient blood of those steppe folk had resurfaced itself in me.

I smiled to myself just then. Real Jungian bullshit, that. Perhaps it was my lack of interest in higher education, but I had always dismissed the concept of racialism that all the intelligentsia seemed to be so enamored over, the concept that we could trace all the bloodlines of the Earth, and through them determine the temperaments of different peoples. Take a look at a family photo, and you'd never accuse my mother of infidelity; and yet, of all those boys, so clearly of the same heritage, only I was a wild one. Only I felt the call of some antique people in my blood.

Racialism? The idea of temperament stemming from bloodline? Crap, as far as I was concerned. But what if there was something to all of Jung's weirdness, after all? What if there was something in the blood, in the genes, that could resurface, leaping generations, the space of centuries, to reincarnate a personality...

I smiled to myself again, shook my head. I was letting my fancy get away from me. They were dreams, that was all. I was an irritable soul with an overactive imagination. They couldn't possibly be any more. I thanked the old man, stepped outside—

And came face to face with Friedrich von Hoffman himself.

Instantly my blood rose to his very presence. My hands clenched into fists. And Friedrich answered with his dapper Prussian smirk.

He nodded. "I knew I would find you here. I told myself that it was simply too improbable, and yet somehow I knew I would find you here."

I growled, "Whaddya want?"

"I was looking for the same answers you were. This bookstore..." He waved lazily at the unassuming storefront. "It is strongly suspected as a gathering point for subversives. What better place to find propaganda supporting a more noble and lofty origin for the Jewish people?"

He paused and took a step closer, uncomfortably close for me. I had to fight the urge to slug him, with his hatchet face hovering insultingly close to mine. He muttered, "But, of course... you, and I, we know that there is more to it than that."

I gritted my teeth. "Where's this going, von Hoffman? You taken a special interest in my reading?"

"I am interested, herr Frydman, in your dreams."

Despite myself, I paled a little.

He nodded carefully. "You, and I... we had the same dream last night, did we not? A meeting of rivals upon the ancient steppe. You, a vagabond refugee of a fallen khanate. Me, your conqueror, declaring an ultimatum: bow, or be destroyed. And we recognized each other, in that dream."

The aggression in my blood was totally drained out by the shock. I shook my head, my fists suddenly shaking a little. "No. No, we can't have had the same dream. It's impossible..."

Von Hoffman chuckled. "Impossible? I think not, my boy. Jung has written much of the collective unconscious. Of inherited memories. Genetic resurrection.

"Do you believe in fate, herr Frydman? I do. I believe that certain conflicts are destined to be fought, perhaps over and over. The hero, and the villain: these archetypes are very real things. We fight out their battles, here, on Earth, as they struggle on some metaphysical plane."

I managed a snarl. "This is bullshit, von Hoffman. Jung's nonsense, all your meta-physical babble—it's all crap. We live here and now, and that's all that's real."

Von Hoffman sneered—that damn sneer... the same as in my dreams. "And yet, was not the past real, at one time? Was it not, too, the here and now, as you so eloquently put it? I, for one, believe that the past is destined to be replayed at critical times in history. And is this not the most momentous of times? The Aryan peoples are reuniting, for the first time since their great drift so long ago; they are poised to retake their place as the rightful rulers of the earth. And standing in their way?" Very delicately, with one slender finger, he touched my chest. "You. The Jew."

My blood flared up again, that furious barbarism that knew no other way of dealing with an enemy than with my fists. I bared my teeth. "You touch me again, and so help me, you swine, I'll lay you out flat. They'll have to make it a closed-casket funeral before I'm done with you."

There was an answering blaze in Friedrich's eyes. A barbarous crack in the suave, sophisticated gentleman's veneer. He snarled, "Go ahead, yid. Raise your hand against me. See what happens when you strike a German—an officer in the Heer, no less. See what happens to you, to your family."

I shook with rage, but I said nothing, did nothing. The son of a bitch was right. This was no fair fight. I had easily fifty pounds of solid muscle on him, but what he had over me was the arrogant, smirking superiority of a conquering people. For all my strength, I was a plaything in his hands, an insect that a small child tortures as he laughs.

Von Hoffman sneered; the façade re-sealed itself. "That's right. Keep silent. Know your place. Anyway… it does not matter. I will destroy you, tonight."

I frowned. "Tonight? What are you talking about?"

"In our dreams! Do you not feel it coming, tonight? I have, long before I met you—indeed, for all my life. For years, I have reveled in the glory of my ancestor, Friðuric the Saxon. For years, ever since a hypnotist unlocked the mental door to my past, I have conquered, pillaged, made love to a hundred slave women… but always, the crowning moment of my glory, my greatest victory, has eluded me. I never understood it, that blank moment in my ancestor's past. But now, I do. We must face each other, you and I."

I shook my head. "You're crazy, von Hoffman."

"Crazy? Then why do we both share the same vivid dreams? Why do we both feel the call of the ancient past in our blood? You feel it as well—don't try to deny it. I saw it in your eyes, yesterday, in your father's office. All the other kikes, they cringed and fawned and smiled. But in your eyes, I saw the fury and the pride of your Turkic ancestors.

"Well, mister Frydman… Aaron… you will have your chance. Tonight, we do battle. And tonight, history repeats itself. Tonight, my ancestor slays yours—tonight, I slay you. And afterwards, I promise you, I will ensure that you and your family are slaughtered once more." His lips twisted with cruelty. "It will be my crowning pleasure to kill my greatest enemy twice over."

He turned on his heel and left at a smart military clip. Left me shaking with fury, impotent.

That night, I prayed to God. I have never been a religious man. I barely go through the motions at the sabbath and the High Holidays. But, somehow, I had a sense, a premonition, that von Hoffman was praying. And not to the hollow God of the churches. No, I had an image, of a tall, wiry-muscled Prussian, his perfectly trimmed blond haircut all ruined as he sweated with fury and fervor. He was stripped to the waist, and the civilized, imperial Prussian veneer was stripped away to lay bare the blond, bloodthirsty savage beneath, the rapist of nations, the darkness of barbarism incarnate. And before him was his secret shrine to the gods of that darkness. Wotan, Donar, the blood-ravening lords of slaughter and destruction—and it seemed to me that those idols were not entirely silent.

And so I prayed to Adonai, because I knew I would need all the help I could get.

There came, at first, only a confused succession of fleeting images. A morning sky, splashed violent and sanguine. The rabbi-shamans, glowering at the ill omen as they muttered darkly that Tsevaot had abandoned us. The fervent singing of the camp imam, leading the Mohammedans at the morning prayer they knew would be their last. By day's end, they would stand before the god Allah, just as I would stand before Tsevaot.

Tsevaot, who had abandoned us.

Impotent fury washed over me, a fury born of the betrayal of fate and the Gods, a red madness that dissolved the images into a blur of fearsome struggle, the chaos of battle.

And then the blur coalesced, even as I swung my saber and cleaved the arm of a terrified Slav who fell to the ground, screaming his death throes, as I snarled my rage and hacked on through the mass of cringing levies before me.

It was the very height of the battle. The last stand of Aaron of Khazaria. I was aware of it for but a moment, aware of myself, slinging my blood-dripping saber ceaselessly, the spittle flecking from my lips, in the midst of a sanguine battle-fury which was at once alien and starkly familiar. I had felt but a shadow of it, in the basements with their blood-slicked floors as the crowd hollered and whooped and shook fists stuffed with money as two men snarled and pummeled each other until their faces and bodies were swollen and bloody, like two gore-streaked snarling ogres.

It was nothing compared to the tide of raw rage, of terrible slaughter. All about were howls of bloodlust, screams of the stricken, the reek of body odor and horse sweat and raw blood and ruptured innards. All about the ground was a churning mass of blood and meat and entrails and spattered bits of brain and bone that men trudged through and slipped in and fell stricken, thrashing and clutching at mortal wounds, as the boots of the others blindly stomped them to death.

It was a single, palpable thing. Battle. It surrounded me, sucked me down; and no longer was I Aaron Frydman. I was Aaron the Khazar; here I stood, and here I would win my freedom, or die trying.

Our camp was at our backs. There was nowhere left to turn. The women and children had taken up spear and shield and joined the fray. Better to die quickly in battle, after all, than live long enough to be captive to the horde of Friðuric. Before us swarmed that horde now, snarling and biting with steel fang and claw; and a more contemptible and motley pack of pirates, rogues, and slayers, I never saw. In the center struggled a mass of unarmored Slavic conscripts in ragged lines, human meat to choke us on. On the flanks swarmed Friðuric's steppe mercenaries, Cumans and Bulgars, honorless vermin of the steppe who sold their bows to the highest bidder. They darted in and out of the fray, loosing their arrows when they could, shying from the flights of our own that bore them screaming to the earth. They shied from charging home, even as Friðuric had us cornered and outnumbered, for they were no fighters. These were looters, brigands, men who preferred to slit the throats of dying men, and they knew they had merely to wait long enough for the battle to be over to sate their greed and lust. It was all that kept them from scattering and fleeing.

Such miserable excuses for warriors, we might have scattered them before our fury and the sure flights of our arrows, even as they outnumbered us so. But there was one thing that held the rabble tied together, an armored beast whose sides even our sharp blades could not pierce: the druzhina. Friðuric's retainers, a pack of vagabond raiders from the north who had attached themselves to the petty tyrant's cause, welded into an armored core of bow and sword-wielding cavalry that wreaked havoc among their softer foes. They rode rapidly from end to end of the battle, charging home wherever we made progress against the Slavs, wherever we threatened to scatter the steppe bandits. They were a terrible maul in his hands, one that smashed our ranks again and again. And my own armored retainers were helpless to stop it: he outnumbered us three to one, and all the while, we were whittled down amid the tangled melee, while Friðuric's men seemed untouched as they plunged into our ranks time after time.

The fury of impotence welled up in me once more. It was as though all the Gods of the earth, as though fate and the sky itself, were turned against me. As though existence itself mocked me, laughed at me, dared me to do anything other than die. And my blood boiled in response. I wanted to live! I wanted to ride free across the steppe, to feel the wind in my hair, to go where I pleased, with a strong mare beneath me, and a sharp sword by my side. I wanted life—but Tsevaot—all the Gods—they mocked me!

It was at that moment, as my retainers and I stood about, panting with our horses, seething with fury at our impending defeat, that he appeared.

The druzhina rode to a halt across the battlefield from us. From their ranks emerged Friðuric, the grinning blond ogre. He howled wordless mockery to us as his men laughed. With clenched fist, he shook his bloodstained blade in the air and dared us to meet him.

My blood leaped to the challenge, to the insult to my courage. Around me, my men snarled, gripped their reins, waited for me to howl the charge. If I could but kill Friðuric, it would all be over. His horde would scatter—and even if it did not, my honor would be avenged. All would be made right when his blood ran down my saber.

I twisted my reins, made to call the charge—

And it was as though a thunderbolt from heaven illuminated my skull. I was Aaron of Khazaria—and I was Aaron Frydman! And at once I knew the trap. I knew what fate awaited Aaron of Khazaria if he charged Friðuric just then. The damned Saxon would fall back amid his men, draw me and my followers further in, until his druzhina and his Slavic rabble had surrounded us, and they would grind us to pieces. It would happen—indeed, it had happened, a thousand years ago.

But it did not have to happen!

Within me, Aaron of Khazaria rebelled, fought as a wild beast against my restraint. I grappled with him, struggled with him, desperate to make him see reason, even as his men watched in confusion. Little by little, I wrenched his head about, to see the right flank. There the men, the camp women, struggled valiantly on, but they were failing. Sooner or later, they would break, and when they did, they would be slaughtered, the women violated, the men mutilated by the grinning steppe bandits and the vengeful Slavs. And if I threw my life away, I would be the cause of it all.

Like a man wrestling primal forces of the dawn, I fought Aaron of Khazaria.

I fought the red tide of fury that washed away all human reason.

I fought against the tides of fate itself—

And something snapped—I had won!

With a monumental effort, I, Aaron of Khazaria, fought down the berserk rage that threatened to grab hold of me and hurl me to my doom. With a deep breath, my mind cleared of the red mists; and as it did, I saw about me a far clearer picture of the battle.

It was not hopeless as I had thought. Friðuric's men were not untouched, not tireless; their numbers had been whittled worse than our own, for Friðuric had been overconfident and careless with his men. His horses were exhausted. He needed me to come to grips, for only by slaying me could he hope to break my men. If not, his own men would lose heart. They were cowards, conscripts and pirates of the steppe. They were no warriors.

But we—we were warriors!

My blood flushed with the scent of victory. I could see a path to freedom, and I took it. I swung my saber to the right flank. "Never mind the druzhina! The right fails. We continue as we have: we charge the right, we keep our brothers and our sisters in the fight. We will win!"

I grabbed a man next to me. "Fetch us fresh mounts. We should have changed horses long ago. Have them waiting when we disengage."

As he hurried back to the camp, a young warrior cantered before me. Despite their exhaustion, he and his mount remained feisty, their blood inflamed by battle. "Do I hear true? Does Aaron flinch before his enemy?"

My eyes turned to hot steel. The young warrior quailed a little, but he kept his head high. He threw his saber back. "Friðuric taunts us—and you do nothing!"

I growled, "I do not charge because I know he will not meet us. He will run and hide behind his men until he knows he has us surrounded. We cannot face the druzhina yet, not with their curs still swarming all around us. They will bite our heels so that their masters can slay us without honor. We scatter his lesser warriors—they quail even now, they will run soon, and when they do, we fall as one upon Friðuric, and we kill him and all his men!"

Hearty ayes met my words, but the young warrior's eyes still burned. He waved helplessly at Friðuric. "But the druzhina—!"

"DAMN THE DRUZHINA!" I bellowed. "Are you so unmanly as to be stung by the impotent insults of a fearful heathen?! The lives of your brothers—the lives of your families—all will be lost if the line breaks! You will throw your sisters, your wives, your mothers, to the very cur who mocks you!"

I kicked my mare's flanks savagely. She leaped into a full gallop, and as I rode I shouted: "Ride, you sons of bitches! Ride—ride to your brothers' side!"

The sound of my words, the sight of my charge, galvanized the ragged remains of my company. As one, they fell alongside me, bellowing and howling like demons of the winds, and in a full gallop we raced across the battlefield. As I rode, I glimpsed Friðuric, cursing and spitting as he whipped his tiring men, his staggering horses, to follow us once more. I grinned to myself as I rode. Where Friðuric had glimpsed victory and plunder, now disaster loomed; and behind it rode grinning death.

Into the fray we plowed once more, sabers slinging, horse hooves pounding. Once more the bare-chested Slav spearmen cringed before the bite of the armored cavalry that fell upon them, slicing their flesh and felling their brothers as wheat before the mower. Their numbers remained overwhelming—but they were whittled down one by one, and with them went the best and bravest of that lot of rabble. And even as we disengaged, and Friðuric's druzhina struggled to counter-charge, to shore up his line, we were racing, amid the cheers of desperate warriors, to receive a batch of fresh horses.

And it was at that moment, when we changed mounts, that the winds of fate shifted in our favor.

In my blind fury, I had forgotten the most basic lessons that every warrior of the steppe must know: to be fleeter than your enemy, yet to race only with purpose; to ensure that your sword stroke swings not only swift, but true as well. To use your fury, your bloodlust, and not to be used by it: not to be blown about blindly by it, but to ride it as the hawk rides the wind, hunting and seizing his prey as he wills.

And like the hawk, we now pounced upon the Slavs, charged the furtive Cumans and Bulgars, with terrible speed, a speed that Friðuric, with his mounts now exhausted and staggering, could no longer match. Like a snarling lion, we burst among the Slavs again and again, our sabers reaping a crimson harvest, and before Friðuric could match us, we were gone and charging into another part of the line. Again and again we dove, we seized our prey; and even as the mighty maul of Friðuric's druzhina dragged in his fist, our nimble sabers

danced among his men, and the flicker of the steel, the ceaseless pelting rain of our black arrows, were terrible death and doom to the Slavs and the steppe dogs.

The end was inevitable. They had been promised easy victory and ripe pickings. Where, then, was the easy victory? Where were the fearful, broken dregs who would quail before them? Even the women, whose soft bodies they had dreamed of the night before, stood fast with spear and shield and fought with a strength and ferocity that overmatched their own.

At last, one of the companies of Slavs broke. And like a thread pulled, the whole pack unraveled at once. The conscripts threw their arms aside and ran screaming before the women who howled bloodlust and ran them down to slaughter them with daggers even as they begged mercy. The Bulgars and Cumans scattered as hyenas before the lion, and they vanished into the steppe as mist before the rising sun. Only the druzhina were left—and, with their horses driven to exhaustion, barely able to reach a canter, they could do nothing to avoid the light cavalry that surrounded them at once, snarling, with bloody vengeance in their eyes. We reached them even as the lighter cavalry had shattered their exhausted ranks, even as the footmen dove through the kicking legs of the horses to drag the Varangians screaming from their mounts and butcher them like pigs. The armored beast howled now: its sides were broken, and we devoured its soft flesh beneath.

My armored brethren and I cut through that crumbling mass effortlessly; and at its center we found Friðuric. His heavy sword remained in his hand, and even as he saw us, the terror in his eyes turned to black vengeance. With a howl of fury, he swung for my head. I dodged, stabbed my saber up beneath his faltered guard, and pierced the mail over his heart—

And I awoke, panting, my sheets soaked with sweat.

I shook my head. Hell of a thing. That had been no dream. I was unhurt, but my body ached with phantom pains. I stumbled to my washbasin, took a deep drink of water, and a deep breath.

I grinned and chuckled at a sudden thought. If I felt this bad, how did that son of a bitch von Hoffman feel just now, after waking up to the feel of a saber stabbing his heart?

I got my answer the next day.

A clerk sent me up to the office as soon as I arrived. "Good news!" he whispered with an excited smile.

I went up, frowning, to find my father smiling as well, and shaking hands with a man in the uniform of an officer of the Heer. He was a tall, dapper, blond Prussian; but where there had been a coldness and cruelty about von Hoffman, there was a warmth in the man's smile as he turned and politely nodded to me.

I nodded back, still baffled, and my confusion only increased as my father introduced me to the man, who extended a friendly hand.

"Colonel Teller, my oldest son, Aaron." A warning flashed in my father's eye: be polite. I was polite, all right; I was too baffled to do anything else. My father, making chummy with a Nazi? I didn't get it.

I shook my head as soon as the guy left. "Dad... what's going on?"

My father fixed me with an earnest seriousness. "That man's just canceled von Hoffman's requisition order, that's what's going on."

I laughed my surprise. "Von Hoffman can't be too pleased about that."

"Von Hoffman ain't gonna be pleased about anything anymore. That bastard dropped dead in his sleep last night." My father spat on the floor. "Good riddance."

Once more, shock rooted me to the floor. "He... von Hoffman's dead...?"

My father nodded. "Colonel Teller's his replacement." He took a step closer to me. "And you mark my words... we're gonna be thankful Teller's in the position he is. He might be a German, he might call himself a Nazi, but I got a good feeling about him."

I nodded. I trusted my father. He had an uncanny ability to read men. And he had read no falsehood in Colonel Teller's warmth.

There was a moment, as I looked at my father, nodding and smiling, that I saw a different man. A rabbinic shaman of a steppe tribe, a thousand years gone, smiling because he alone of all his fellows had not lost faith in Tsevaot, and because his son, whatever he had growled, had not either; and for that, they had triumphed when they should have perished.

I saw something else, as well: a glimpse of a possible future. A cramped boat ride to England. A safe passage, in the hands of a certain Colonel of the Heer with a disarmingly warm smile. A passage that we would take, along with dozens of others—maybe hundreds, if only he could keep from getting caught.

I know what you're thinking: I was proud to have saved all those people. But, as I said at the start of my tale, I've always been a strange man. And what I was glad of at that moment was not all the others who would be saved, now that von Hoffman had so mysteriously dropped dead in his sleep. All I cared about was that me and my family would be free and alive a little longer; that I would be able to walk this Earth without fear, a little longer.

And, that a thousand years away, another man rode the steppe, free; that he would be spared the final abyssal sleep of death, for just a little while longer.

And that's about all a man can ask for in this short life of ours.

Rev. Joe Kelly has also been published in Heroic Fantasy Quarterly and Wyldblood Magazine. He can be contacted on twitter at @reverendjoefake when he bothers to check it.

Melkart and the Crocodile God

By MARK MELLON

An evil and sorcerous monster plagues the land of Kush! Can Melkart stop the crocodile-headed man-beast Sosostris from enslaving the people of Meroë!?

Thus it came to pass that Melkart undertook the long and perilous journey to Meroë in Kush, a semi-mythical land deep to the south of Aegyptus, the source of cotton textiles, ivory, jewelry, and most valuable of all, fine worked iron, the best in the world. Melkart traveled by sea from Tyre to Aegyptus, to Inbu-Hedj at the delta's base where he traded imperial red mantles and tunics for goods the Kushites prized, faience jewelry, palm wine, and white linen kilts and cloaks. He sailed with his cargo along the black river Ar to Asyut where he bought donkeys and hired drovers and a guide, Psammetichus, a wiry, lively man.

Small donkeys laden with goods and supplies, water most important of all, they took the harrowing Way of Forty Days, a narrow trail through the arid, hot desert that bypassed the Ar's uncrossable cataracts. After a brief rest at the great oasis of Kharga, they went on into the desert. Psammetichus proved as good a guide as he bragged. He led the caravan by careful stages to stone built caravansaries where men and animals could rest during the day's hottest part. They feasted in the shade on a white antelope Melkart shot with his bow.

"So Meroë prospers?"

"Aye, friend Melkart. For three centuries, the Kushites languished like Aegyptus under a drought. They shrank to a shadow of their numbers. Yet now the gods' favor is restored, the Ar's waters run freely, and the Kushites are returned to their former glory. Meroë is as great a city as Inbu-Hedj. They have a Pharaoh who sits in great state, Tantamani. He rules with the Queen Mother's aid, Tabiry the Kandake."

Psammetichus draped his linen head cloth over his face. "Sleep now. We still have twenty suns' journey."

They traveled mostly by night in the relative cool. Drawn by the donkeys' bleats, bandits mounted on half wild onagers rode out from the hills one night, sure of easy prey, but were driven off after Melkart's arrows killed three. Psammetichus and the drovers cheered. Yet the grim, wearying, endless trek still continued, donkeys and men weighed down by their burdens, grit in their teeth as they sweated, thin sandal leather worn down by endless leagues over rocky ground.

With no little relief, the exhausted travelers came to the savannah at the Way's End, Ta-Seti, the land of the Kushites, inside the Ar's enormous eastward curve. Desert gave way to grasslands that teemed with game, lions, elephants, leopards, antelope, oryxes, and zebras. Herdsmen clad in brightly dyed cotton smocks tended flocks of cattle and goats. Smiling, handsome, ebon-skinned, they greeted the caravan with upraised crooks, glad to relieve their loneliness, offering fresh milk from calabashes the travelers gratefully drank.

After fifty days' journey from the First Cataract, the caravan reached the city of Meroë on the Ar's right bank, between the Fourth and Fifth Cataracts. Clustered along the river like Inbu-Hedj, buildings rose two and three stories high, made of palm wood interwoven with baked bricks, much like those in Aegyptus. Temples to the most prominent gods were built from gleaming white limestone, the one to Amun the grandest of all. Three clusters of pyramids flanked the city, Meroë's most impressive feature. The necropoleis for Kushite royalty stretched back a thousand years, hundreds of distinctively steep, narrow, cut-stone pyramids, many fronted by fine marble temples, grander even than those of Inbu-Hedj in sheer number and extravagance of detail.

Psammetichus dickered in Kushite with a ferryman who agreed to carry men and donkeys across the Ar for a bronze talent. The crossing took several trips and most of the day as donkeys balked and the heat grew. Twilight approached as Psammetichus led them to the caravansary and the journey's end. Meroë's prosperity was evident. The whole city seemed one vast market, squares full of merchants' booths with animal pelts, finely woven, brightly embroidered cotton mantles and tunics, red gold ingots, bright carnelians, white elephant tusks, and ironware from stout pots to long swords far sharper and sturdier than any brazen blade.

Graceful and tall, many adorned with heavy gold jewelry, Kushites smiled and greeted the caravan, happy for their trade and with a long tradition of hospitality. Women mingled freely among the men, uncovered and unescorted, yet still treated with respect. The caravansary was fly-ridden and dusty, but had water, shade, and straw pallets to sleep on. After a brief rest, Melkart went to the courtyard where Psammetichus sat eating goat stew with flatbread. Melkart joined him and ate heartily also.

"I want to go to the market early. I'll need you to translate."

"We must first see Shubba, the Pharaoh's chamberlain, to pay duties and receive his seal on a tablet. Then we can go to the market."

"When does he see merchants?"

"Early or late in the day when it's cool."

"Then we'll rise at the night's tenth hour and await outside his chambers."

Psammetichus sighed. "So be it, friend Melkart. We'd best sleep."

On the morrow, well before Ra-Horakhy's golden falcon had begun his journey across the firmament, Melkart stood with Psammetichus in the darkness before the chamberlain's quarters, clad in his imperial red tunic, a lion skin cloak draped over his shoulders to keep off the cool, early morning air. Other merchants awaited as well, mostly from Aegyptus, but also jet black tribesmen from beyond the swamps of Sudd, dignified in red woolen tunics and hide mantles.

When the false dawn tinted the courtyard in gray shades, slaves drew back wooden screens and admitted the merchants to an anteroom. They were given three-legged stools and served hot tea. Merchants sipped tea in companionable silence.

"How much longer now?" Melkart whispered.

"Until Shubba decides we're sufficiently impressed by his importance. It may take time, so be patient."

Slaves pulled back the inner screens only when the sun god's celestial barge rode high over the palms that fringed the Ar's banks. Shubba sat in state in a gilded chair on a high dais, striped headdress held in place by a golden band, tunic of the whitest cotton, a heavy gold chain around his neck and a fly-whisk in one hand, identical to any high-ranking official of Aegyptus. At his feet, six scribes knelt by their desks in a single rank, blank wax tablets stacked beside them, ready to keep records of the day's transactions.

Once Shubba heard the merchants, business moved quickly. Melkart soon stood before him with Psammetichus translating. Psammetichus handed a bill of lading written in black ink on a strip of papyrus to the chief scribe. He spoke briefly to Shubba, who gave a lordly wave of his fly-whisk. The scribe named a figure to Psammetichus.

"Two silver mina in duties, friend Melkart."

The big Tyrian smiled. "Very reasonable. I expected to be skinned."

"Kushites are sensible. They want to encourage commerce, not strangle it."

Melkart took his leather purse full of shekels and handed it to the scribe. He filled out a receipt on a wax tablet. When he finished, the tablet was handed to Shubba, who pressed his carnelian signet ring into the bottom left corner. He smiled, baring large white teeth, and briefly spoke.

"The chamberlain welcomes you to Meroë for he knows you are new here. You're under the protection of the Pharoah Tantamani and may do business here without fear of being cheated or robbed," Psammetichus said.

Melkart smiled. Hand to his heart, he bowed low, and was about to speak.

GGGRRRAAAWWWNN

An appalling roar drowned out all other sound. The very earth shook beneath their feet.

"Earthquake. Get outside, Psammetichus."

Along with everyone else, Melkart and Psammetichus ran to the courtyard only to find reality inverted, the once welcoming, great city of Meroë transformed into a nightmare. Buildings stood shrouded in darkness, birdsong and animal cries stilled into deathly silence by the sun's absence, eclipsed from view by a black disc that appeared from nowhere. Psammetichus pointed in horror.

"By the gods, Melkart. Behold. The Ar parts in twain!"

And indeed the Ar's waters did seethe and surge before Meroë like a pot brought to a roiling boil. In the strange half light, curling waves pushed a wide space open to reveal the river's bed. A sepulcher lay there, granite stones covered by foul ooze.

GGGRRRAAAWWWNN

The earth shook again, the sepulcher with it. Stones fell. Clawed, scaly, powerful hands ripped them away.

"Isis save me, what horror is this?"

"Stay calm, Psammetichus. Wait to see what we face."

The sepulcher destroyed, a figure stood revealed, at least five cubits high, on two legs like a man, but with a long, sinuous tail and a reptilian snout for a face. Yellow eyes raged with burning pitch's intensity as he strode toward Meroë, pale pink tongue revealed by open jaws lined with razor-sharp, yellow teeth.

Melkart could only watch motionless like the rest, horror-stricken by the bizarre, incomprehensible monster before them. The monster walked to the city's edge. He raised muscular, squamous arms and declaimed in a voice heard throughout Meroë that even Melkart strangely understood, more a reptilian hiss than true human speech.

"People of Kush. I am Sosostris, your true Pharoah. After long exile, I have returned to rule my land. Any usurper must flee or face my wrath. You're all my slaves, bound to obey my will. Behold my power."

He held an open palm behind him. The Ar resumed its flow, covering the sepulcher's scattered stones. The black disc disappeared as well. Ra-Horakhy's golden falcon once again flew unimpeded through the sky. Sosostris walked into the city with lordly confidence. All those who even glimpsed his black irises' narrow ovals knelt before him and bowed like the slaves they were.

There was turmoil throughout the royal compound as officials scurried back and forth, in an absolute panic with no idea what to do. Word went forth from Tantamani. His guard formed up, armored in steel cuirasses and helms, equipped with long spears and swords.

"We should run to the caravansary, gather up our goods, and flee."

"There's no time, Psammetichus. It's not my way to run anyway. God or sorceror, this Sosostris is evil and must be put down. I'll fight with the guard."

"You're mad, Melkart!"

"So be it. Let the gods decide."

In an armory, Melkart found a spear, shield, and a helm that fitted him and joined the guard. Rather than grow angry or show surprise, the Kushites welcomed him, glad to have such a mighty warrior in their ranks. They marched out of the compound to attack Sosostris. He stood in a market square, everyone abased in the dust before him, from rich merchants to naked slaves.

The captain gave an order. The guard raised their shields and lifted their spears. Melkart followed their lead, ready to throw his spear into the monster's heart. Sosostris only raised his snout and hissed laughter. He pointed to the guard captain.

"You. Come here."

Helpless to disobey, in thrall to the malarial eyes, the captain sleepwalked toward Sosostris. The monster opened his enormous jaws and in one savage bite severed the captain's neck. Blood gushed as the headless torso fell to the ground. The head lay in the dust.

Sosostris pointed to the guard. *"Cast down your arms and bow before me."*

They meekly did as he commanded, even the mighty Melkart, proud of never submitting before anyone in servitude. He lay with his face in the dust, hands held out in supplication.

And from that moment on, like every other man, woman, and child in Meroë, Melkart was the abject slave of Sosostris, the crocodile god.

Stripped of his fine tunic and lion skin cloak, clad only in a loincloth, Melkart labored in the hot sun along with the Meroëites. Mud bricks in enormous quantities were fired in kilns and carried on hods to the open space where Sosostris had decreed his palace should be built. Eyes empty, bent to their tasks, they worked like bees in a hive as the walls steadily ascended, heedless even of those who fell to their deaths from the walls' tops. Fed on gruel served from huge iron vats in the morning and evening, they grew steadily more malnourished and haggard.

Sosostris lived outdoors in bizarre splendor in Tantamani's grand courtyard. For most of the day, he lolled in a pool of tepid water constructed by his slaves, half-asleep, one eye slit open, no one even daring to approach. When he roused from his slumbers, Sosostris had courtiers attire him in a Pharaoh's full regalia, complete to a blue and white striped headdress held in place by a golden band adorned by an uraeus, a stylized falcon, the royal emblem. He sat upon a gilded chair specially joined to hold his enormous frame, knotty tail protruding from behind, a crook and fly-whisk held in his crossed arms. Incense burned while shaven-headed priests chanted prayers to Sosostris as the living incarnation of Sebek-Re, the sun god personified as a crocodile.

Enormous banquets followed where Sosostris ate grotesque quantities of food, roast haunches of hippopotamus, speared to death in shallow waters by hunters indifferent to their own casualties, an entire roast antelope Sosostris swallowed bones and all, and his favorite dish, human meat, usually some poor courtier he grabbed and shoved head-first down his throat, devoured without warning. Gut stuffed full to bursting, twice its usual size, Sosostris sidled off his throne, back to his pool to sleep again while the remaining courtiers returned listlessly to their tasks.

One evening Melkart sat with his fellows, spooning gruel into his mouth. Thousands squatted in the open, docile, obedient without being bidden, a slave empire with no need for overseers or taskmasters. Melkart ate the last of his gruel and was left still hungry, vaguely dissatisfied.

"Here, friend. You look thirsty. Drink this."

Melkart mindlessly took the flask held before him. He drank deeply of the water infused with bitter tana leaves. A sudden, violent spasm passed through Melkart. He convulsed like a man plagued with the ague.

"By Ishtar, Marduk, and Ba'al Hammon!"

Restored to his right mind, Melkart looked around him. People lay asleep around him, huddled on the bare, hard ground, extinguished like oil lamps' wicks. He was dirty, almost naked, and much thinner. Psammetichus sat beside him, grimy and shaggy, but still recognizable as his trusty guide.

Melkart almost spoke, but Psammetichus put a finger to his lips. He motioned for Melkart to follow. They stole away from the open square. Nearby, exhausted priests cried out Sebek-Re's praises in hoarse voices to lull Sosostris to sleep yet again. Psammetichus led Melkart down streets to the South Necropolis where almost two hundred pyramids stood, a cut stone forest providing ready cover against Sosostris's penetrating eyes.

They entered an unlit temple before a pyramid, shrouded in darkness. Figures huddled in the portico, spears ready to attack. Psammetichus whispered a password, and the guards relaxed somewhat. He took Melkart to a small, old woman who sat cross-legged by herself on a leopard pelt, back rigidly upright, plainly highborn despite her hide mantle.

"You stand before Tabiry the Kandake, the Queen Mother, guide to the Pharoah Tantamani and the Kushite people."

Psammetichus bowed low before her and spoke in Kushite. Melkart followed his example and bowed also. Tabiry gestured for them to sit before her on rush mats. She gently clapped her hands. Attendants served Melkart flatbread and meat that he eagerly ate along with watered wine in a wooden bowl.

"Careful not to eat too much, friend Melkart. Your stomach can't take it."

Melkart reluctantly pushed the food aside. Tabiry held out her fly-whisk and spoke at length. Psammetichus translated.

"The Queen Mother says she still remembers the famine when Ta-Seti withered without water from the Ar and her people scavenged like jackals in the brush. Before she died from hunger, her grandmother warned of an ancient legend about a sorcerer named Sosostris, the unholy byproduct of a man who mated with a crocodile. Sosostris had himself entombed alive when the drought first came, to sleep and wait until the Ar flowed once again."

"So he's simply an intriguer, a blasphemer against the gods' divine will."

"Aye, Melkart. From his crocodile dam, Sosostris learned the power to subdue his prey with his gaze alone while his cursed sorcerer father steeped him in the magic of Aegyptus, Ta-Seti, and the ancient Chaldees. He holds her son Tantamani captive like the rest of Meroë and plans to slit his throat like a sacrificial bull at the Feast of Sebek-Re."

"By the gods. What villainy. How do we stop him?"

"That's what the Queen Mother wants to know. She asks if you're brave enough to try to kill Sosostris, to strike him down in his sleep."

Refreshed and invigorated by food and wine, Melkart rose to his feet and thumped his chest with his right hand. "I am Melkart, not some skulker. I'll strike that ugly reptile down while he sits on his throne."

Psammetichus translated. Tabiry spoke at length in response. She gestured with her fly-whisk for Melkart to sit down again. He bowed and resumed his place.

"The Queen Mother says you're brave but not sensible. The only reason Sosostris didn't subdue the Queen Mother and her retinue is because they took refuge in the necropolis when he arrived, hidden from view. The Queen Mother remembered her grandmother's warning."

"Tell the Queen Mother she's wise. What would she have me do?"

"Anyone caught in Sosostris's gaze must obey his will. He's at his most vulnerable asleep. Even then he keeps one eye half-open. Someone must approach him backwards, using only a brightly burnished mirror to guide him by the moon's light, until he can strike him down in his basking pool."

"Gladly. Give me some more of that meat and flatbread, a sharp knife, and that mirror you spoke of. I'll cut him to ribbons."

Psammetichus translated. Tabiry laughed behind her fly-whisk and clapped her hands again. Her attendants fetched more food while Tabiry spoke.

"The Queen Mother says she wishes she'd met you when she was younger."

Melkart laughed heartily.

By a half moon's light, Melkart crept through Meroë, armed only with a dagger and an obsidian mirror with a handle in the shape of the goddess Isis. Secure in his sorcerous power, Sosostris slumbered among his comatose subjects with no guard posted. Melkart threaded his way past men, women, and children, sprawled like the dead in streets and squares, the only sound a kite's disturbing cry.

Exhausted after repeated ministrations, shaven-headed priests slept in the royal courtyard, granted a brief rest by their rep-tilian master. Sosostris lay on his side in the pool, a huge, scaly bulk, claws a half cubit long. His chest gently heaved as he faintly snored.

Melkart forced himself by sheer will alone to turn his back to Sosostris. He slowly moved in reverse, guided by the mirror's dark sphere, amplified by the moon. He carefully passed prone figures, every step as agonizingly slow as the one before. After what seemed an eternity, Melkart stood beside the crocodile god, dagger raised high.

Everything was frozen, immobile on the verge of bloody violence under the stark moonlight. Melkart turned to stab his dagger deep into Sosotris's throat. The crocodile god rolled over, yellow eyes phosphorescent in the darkness.

He grinned at Melkart. *"Come to me, my rose-scented bride."*

Sosostris reached out his arms, snout wide to bite off Melkart's head. Yet swift as fleet Akhilleous, Melkart was already upon him. Aware of his eyes' hypnotic effect, Melkart had snapped his own shut the moment Sosostris turned.

They thrashed and writhed in the shallow pool. Melkart's attempt to kill the crocodile god with one blow had become the battle of his life. Sosostris wildly snapped his tail to and fro, each thrash a certain, man-killing blow. He flailed his claws, raked them across Melkart's back. Smashed against the pool's hard stones, handicapped by his closed eyes, Melkart clung tight with his legs and free hand.

He kept his head tucked against Sosostris's torso so the snapping snout couldn't reach him. The long dagger stabbed again and again into the soft, white underbelly.

Agonized, Sosostris dug his claws into Melkart's broad back, but the big Tyrian doggedly held on. He drove the dagger in deeper.

"*Jackal,*" the monster gasped. "*You transgress Sebek-Re's will. You sssssssin by ssssstabbing me.*"

Drenched in blood and offal, Melkart hacked away, bent upon killing Sosostris despite his threats. Sosostris snapped his massive snout shut, but only grabbed air. Eyes scrunched shut, Melkart aimed by feel alone.

He stabbed his dagger deep into the crocodile god's throat.

Sosostris gasped. Blood blossomed from the open rent in his throat. He reached up to pull out the dagger, but Melkart blindly batted his arm away. Melkart pulled the blade in a straight line across Sosostris's throat.

"*Nay. I cannot die. I'm immortal. A god.*"

"You're no god. Die, sorcerer, tyrant!"

Sosostris emitted one last, awful, strangled scream. His terrible yellow eyes rolled into the back of his head. The monstrous crocodile god expired with a last, horrible death rattle that shook the very stones of Meroë.

Melkart stood over Sosostris in the shallow, red water, covered in gore, back torn to ribbons, chest heaving as he sucked in air, about to collapse from his ordeal. Around him, the people of Meroë stirred and awoke, drowsy and disoriented like someone recovering from a long, opium-induced delirium. Emboldened by the carnage's end, Tabiry entered with her entourage. Her warriors stuck their spears deep into Sosostris, but Tabiry drove them off

with blows from her fly-whisk.

In the Aegyptian manner, Tabiry knelt and bowed low before Melkart in gratitude. Her retinue followed suit. Despite his pain and blood, Melkart bowed in turn, as always determined to follow the rules of hospitality. Handmaidens staunched the blood with cotton towels, gave him a soothing potion of wine infused with opium and hemp, and stitched his wounds shut with a sharp copper needle and waxed cotton thread.

Tantamani was led in, a mere stripling just now freed from captivity, a Pharoah's double crown stuck on his head, a crook and fly-whisk hastily thrust into his hands. White teeth ablaze in his dark face, he bent low in gratitude before Melkart, as did Tabiry, the rest of their extended family, their retinues, and the people of Meroë, humbly and honestly grateful to their benefactor.

Psammetichus smiled. "You're the most beloved man in Meroë. Name your price. Tantamani will fulfill it, anything. Even your own weight in golden shekels."

"A good meal would be enough for now. After that, some sleep and then we can talk about doing business."

Rich beyond measure and duly grateful, at Tabiry's urging, Tantamani recognized Melkart as a favorite of his court and endowed him with five golden talents and other riches, ivory tusks, iron swords and shields, a fortune in goods to return with back to Tyre. His lionskin cloak was restored to him. As a special mark of favor, he was presented with a kilt made from Sosostris's flayed hide, a trophy the big Tyrian proudly wore until the end of his days.

And peace and justice prevailed once again in Ta-Seti, the brief reign of Sosostris the crocodile god no more than a soon-forgotten nightmare, as the black Ar flowed peacefully northward and Melkart embarked on the arduous trek back to Aegyptus with his faithful companion Psammetichus, his drovers, and donkeys laden with treasure and valuable goods.

Mark Mellon is a novelist who supports his family by working as an attorney. He writes two-fisted, hardboiled, blood and guts pulp fiction and has four novels and over eighty short stories published in the USA, UK, Ireland, and Denmark.

Website: www.mellonwritesagain.com.

My Name is John Carter (Part 12)

By JAMES HUTCHINGS

Though the ship may be blown on a course not its
    own,
and the maps drawn by guesswork or blank,
though the sails may be rent and the sailor's
    strength spent,
and what rations remain have turned rank,

though the storm has no lull, and the waves lash
    the hull,
and the lifeboats are leaky as sieves,
human nature dictates Man cold-shoulders the
    Fates,
and he fights on as long as he lives.

So I always assumed—for who speaks to the
    doomed
and enquires of how they behaved?
And I reckon that few look too hard at their view
when the world calls them noble and brave.

And I seemed to recall, from the day I could crawl
I was praised for these virtues and more,
no one seeming to need any statement or deed,
all assuming I welcomed the war.

It seemed now I was sent to that bloody event
under cheering, admiring duress,
that Cain's brand burnt my skin ere I echoed his
    sin
as an envelope bears an address.

Are we fashioned so hollow that many will follow
a man, hailing traits they invented,
and the one they enthrone makes their folly his
    own?
Are we willingly blind, or demented?

And I thought of the field where our regiment
    wheeled
and we virgins of war were deflowered
and the men I had rallied with barrack-room sal-
    lies.
"The gals don't give nothing to cowards!"

I would rather have lain with the dead on that
    plain
than have people I knew call me yellow.
Did I charge at those guns, or in truth did I run
from the thought of the scorn of my fellows?

For the death I had faced in this very same waste
had not spurred me to rage and defy it.
I'd been silent, and soon I'd have lain on a dune
and passed out of this life still and quiet.

It is said he is wise who has learned to despise
his own knowledge and draws no conclusion.
I was wise by that guide, for my thoughts seemed
    to slide
past each other, to naught but confusion.

It may be I had wrought all these phantoms of
    thought
to fill up the great desert around me.
Though Barsoom was all strange, it appeared I had
    ranged
past some vital, invisible boundary,

for the landscape had harshened till human and
    Martian

alike would recoil in disgust,
and the sand, red and fine, seemed no natural design
but some mammoth machine gone to rust,

and the wind was so cold—and it shrieked, as foretold,
as if joyful to see how I shivered,
and I felt still more vile with each terrible mile,
like a slave who is sold down the river.

But the *thoat* was unshaken, with never a break in
its stride, as if finely-tuned motors
and not flesh were its goad, though I knew that I
rode
the way demagogues ride on their voters:

ever dreading the day it would cease to obey,
almost feeling it stumble or balk,
nearly certain that hour would see me devoured,
unable to get off and walk.

But, as always, in this my beliefs were amiss,
for my mount served me loyally and well.
Wish I'd known in advance. I'd have welcomed the
chance
not to fear or despair for a spell.

But that place was not meant for the calm and
content,
but the frenzied, the damned, and the lost,
for who else would abide such a wind? Who would
ride
till his hair was all stiffened with frost?

And who else would persist through a thick, chok-
ing mist
that turned day to a virginal canvas
and the night to a void with the stars all destroyed?
Could a man sane and sensible stand this?

Would that nothingness cheer him—not seeing,
not hearing
not sure that he even existed?
Would a man of that class find those great walls of
brass
that were right where the legends insisted?

My admittance was barred by a handful of guards
who observed me with seeming alarm
till one struck on a gong that rang out loud and
long,
and it summoned their comrades in arms.

Every sword had a hilt incandescently gilt.
Shields and breastplates all glimmered with gold.
Golden greaves clothed their shanks, and they
formed up in ranks
with a discipline fine to behold.

In mere minutes, a few gilded guardians grew
to a horde that could readily best me,
though I fought like a god in the days when they
trod
among mortals. The captain addressed me.

WILD STARS V:
The Artomique Paradigm
Collected Edition Out This Summer
From Cirsova Publishing!
www.thewildstars.com

The man's tongue was unknown, yet the adamant
   tone
and belligerent gestures made clear
I could quit their domain and return whence I
   came
or fight one to a multitude here.

It may be they presumed I would see I was
   doomed—
I who laugh when the cannonball crashes
and the blades leap at play in their fatal ballet
and my six-shooter bellows and flashes.

Show an opium fiend who has sworn to be weaned
from his habit the pipes and the couches.
Let the smoke be but smelt, and that vapor can
   melt
all the firm resolution he vouches.

And another may break for his mistress's sake
or the dice as they tumble and rattle,
and self-loathing and sorrow are things for tomorrow.
So, too, with John Carter and battle.

Thus I rode to the fray with no greater dismay,
though my odds of survival were slim
than as if that vast swarm were a lake, calm and
warm,
and myself heading in for a swim.

How my brave, foolish men would have cheered for
   me then
as my *thoat* reared and raked with her claws,
and the blades of my foes slashed in vain, and my
   blows
sundered flesh without mercy or pause.

How I laughed and I roared as I bloodied my
   sword,
but delight turned too soon to dismay,
for I severed a head, and the body fell dead,
but the head up and slithered away.

I suppose I was shocked, and my guard must have
   dropped,
for a sword pierced my guts, and I swore,
and my body went slack, and the world became
   black,
and I felt, and I knew, nothing more.

James Hutchings lives in Melbourne, Australia. The nostalgia of things unknown, of lands forgotten or unfound, is upon him at times.

Reviews

By J. COMER

The Cuckoo of Space: A Review of *The Deep Man* by Michael Mersault

When Edward ("Doc") Smith published *The Skylark of Space* in 1928, science fiction was still a novelty. Smith began the work as an edisonade, a fictional tale of invention named for Thomas Edison. When the novel and its sequels were finished, it was clear that something new was in the hands of readers. Travel between planets and stars; encounters with weird unhuman space creatures, war between worlds and solar systems, gonzo-nutcake science to beat the band—Smith had struck a new chord in the world of fantastic fiction, and created space opera. Smith followed *Skylark* with the much grander *Lensman* series, and space opera continued to thrive until the 1960s, when much of science fiction turned to themes of sociology, sex and so on.

Michael Mersault is a fan of the grand old classics as well as sea adventure tales.[1] In his first novel, *The Deep Man*, Mersault combines themes from *Dune*, *Hornblower*, and the Aubrey/Maturin books by the late Patrick O' Brian, to create a space adventure tale.

Saef is a young warrior, always described as "scowling," whose best friend is a foolish fop coded as gay. Saef meets Inga, a distant relative whom Mersault introduced in a short story called "Flops."[2] They collect a crew and set off in a starship with a quirky AI obsessed with pubic lice (yuck) to fight battles, take prizes, and win glory. They go through numerous simulations (one wonders whether the *Star Trek* term "Kobiyashi Maru" was the source of Saef and Inga's family name, Sinclair-Maru), then fight a battle, and return with a rich prize: a ship and a hoard of alien treasure. Saef is tried and found innocent amidst theatrics worthy of Lord Ramage. He buys his ship and its lice-liking AI, who now knows alien secrets. The ending more or less signals that there will be a sequel.

Homage (*The Eternity Brigade*, *Saturn's Children*, *Rite of Passage*) and parody (*Star Smashers of the Galaxy Rangers*, *Bill the Galactic Hero*) both have a place in SF, but *The Deep Man* seems to fall afoul of Samuel Delany's dichotomy: take your heritage knowingly and be its silent master, or take it unknowingly and be its loud slave. Emphasis on Saef's family being ruined, the need for rich prizes, and on noble status made me think of the British Empire. This book feels more like an homage to the Ramage, Aubrey-Maturin, and Hornblower series wrapped in space-opera coloration (an astronautical phasmid?) than a military

---

[1] An interview is here: https://paulsemel.com/exclusive-interview-the-deep-man-author-michael-mersault/

2 https://www.baen.com/flops

SF series on its own. A crossover or fantasy series (*The Two-Space War, The Morgaine Saga*) might be an option for this writer. Mersault has real potential, and I'd gladly read more of his work. Recommended with reservations to fans of Honor Harrington, Eric Flint, and Patrick O'Brian.

The Gods Grown Wacko: a review of *This Broken World* and "The Rot's Last Laugh" by Charles Gannon

In 1969, war gamers in Minnesota were playing a Napoleonic game set in Braunstein, a German town.[3] Suddenly two players announced that their characters in the game were dueling and asked the game master (Dave Wesely) to adjudicate by rolling dice. Of course, this eventually led to the rules for role-playing characters on adventures known as *Dungeons and Dragons*. More than fifty years later, RPGs live on and have influenced both literature and society.

Charles Gannon is an author of stories for the *Man-Kzin Wars* series and Eric Flint's *1632* books, as well as work for the *Traveller* RPG and other military SF. He is a gamer, author, and one-time college professor (and Hugo nominee in the "puppies" era). In his fantasy novel *This Broken World*, a scholar explores a world with its secrets, but many readers will be lost.

We begin with Druadaen, who lives in Arrdanc, a cod-medieval fantasy world. He grows up wanting to be a soldier but instead ends up an archivist. An old lady scholar becomes his patron, and he treks

across the frontier researching orcs, who are becoming a 'horde' a la *Magic Realm*.[4] The author deploys a large vocabulary to describe all of this.

Druadaen meets new friends, and a wolfhound, who go on the dungeon-crawl adventure earlier referenced in the story "The Rot's Last Laugh."[5] Huge fossils abound in the dungeon. There is something about the Red and the Rot.[6] Then the 'fellowship' goes on a sea voyage, talks a lot, and finds a library bearing strange knowledge. They find out that the doings of the "gods" make no sense. The government punishes Druadaen, and we're set up for a sequel.

So what can we make of all this? Well, one influence is the gaming world, which was as much a start for Gannon as for Charlie Stross.[7] Some RPG clichés such as "luminous lichen" and caves with flat, sandy floors will chafe for readers who know real lichen or real caves. As with Gannon's other works, there is well-drawn action. The main character, Druadaen, spends a long time growing up; the novel could've easily begun with the dungeon-crawl with backstory kuttnered in. Much conversation could have been condensed as well. This novel didn't need to be 750 pages long.

One point in Gannon's favor is that his world is well fleshed out, and his attention to material factors is another: how do the orcs feed and bear children? Where do they

---

[3] Tresca, Michael. *The Evolution of Fantasy Role-Playing Games.* New York, McFarland, 2010.

[4] A boardgame from 1979. https://boardgamegeek.com/boardgame/22/magic-realm
[5] Available here: https://www.baen.com/rots-last-laugh
[6] Reference to *Animal Man*?
[7] A good interview is here. https://www.dragoncon.org/dailydragon/interviews/engage-an-interview-with-charles-e-gannon/

come from? Readers may well enjoy this.

What's next for Druadaen? We'll see. There will be more novels, perhaps unfolding the mysteries of the gods. The series may end up being more than the sum of its parts. Gannon might consider writing up the World of Arrdanc for an RPG system.

Recommended to military-SF and dungeon-fantasy fans.

J. Comer is a writer and a teacher. He lives in Texas.

Notes From the Nest

So, this is it. The end of another exciting issue of Cirsova Magazine!

As you may have noticed, we've now got a regular reviews department: Baen sent us a ton of eBooks, and we've passed them along to J. Comer, so this will be a feature at least for the rest of 2022.

We're half-way through the new latest Wild Stars novel, which we hope you're enjoying. By the end of the year, Michael will be half-way through his plans for the series. I hope we're able to stick around long enough to publish it all! The Artomique Paradigm should be out soon enough in a collected edition, so please pick it up if you haven't had a chance to yet. It'll be on Amazon and probably Lulu.

We're also entering the final arc of Mongoose and Meerkat. It's been a wild and exciting ride, and we hope you've been loving it so far. We're putting out a collection of the second year [in universe, from the fall of Alness] of Jim Breyfogle's adventurous duo of rogues. I'm sure you've already ordered a copy via the Kickstarter, but we'll keep it in print for you.

All of the Julian Hawthorne books are out and available in print and eBook through Amazon. We can't really control whether Amazon sends out a first printing of The Cosmic Courtship or a version with the corrected text [sorry, we didn't have another 5 ISBNs to burn, we just fixed the files on the KDP version]. If you want to be sure you get a version with the corrected text, Lulu gives you a 100% chance.

There's not a lot else to say, at the moment. I'm still trying to get a handle on things so we'll be ready to accept 2023 submissions.

P. Alexander, Ed.